PRAISE FOR JEANETTE MURRAY'S SANTA FE BOBCATS SERIES

LOVING HIM OFF THE FIELD

"Engaging . . . Jeanette Murray writes a believable story that drew me in from the first page." —*Cocktails and Books*

"I was pleasantly surprised at this modern romance because along with the obvious love story the author developed the characters enough that the story shone through the chemistry and subsequent steamy 'sex scenes' between them."
—*Open Book Society*

"Well-written." —*Bookpushers*

"The ending of *Loving Him off the Field* was everything that I hoped for." —*The Reader's Den*

ONE NIGHT WITH A QUARTERBACK

"The heat between them is *hot* . . . This one delivers fast and long and yummy . . . For the romance and sports lovers out there." —*Stuck in Books*

"A real hit . . . It was a fresh idea with a tried and true genre, and I loved that. I can't wait to see what she has in store for us next." —*Bookpushers*

D0377540

AGAINST THE ROPES

JEANNETTE MURRAY

BERKLEY SENSATION, NEW YORK

BERKLEY

An imprint of Penguin Random House LLC
375 Hudson Street, New York, New York 10014

AGAINST THE ROPES

A Berkley Sensation Book / published by arrangement with the author

Copyright © 2015 by Jeannette Murray.
Excerpt from *Fight to Finish* by Jeannette Murray copyright © by Jeannette Murray.
Penguin supports copyright. Copyright fuels creativity, encourages diverse voices,
promotes free speech, and creates a vibrant culture. Thank you for buying an authorized
edition of this book and for complying with copyright laws by not reproducing, scanning, or
distributing any part of it in any form without permission. You are supporting writers and
allowing Penguin to continue to publish books for every reader.

BERKLEY SENSATION® and the "B" design are registered trademarks of
Penguin Random House LLC.
For more information, visit penguin.com.

ISBN: 978-0-425-27927-4

PUBLISHING HISTORY
Berkley Sensation mass-market edition / October 2015

PRINTED IN THE UNITED STATES OF AMERICA

10 9 8 7 6 5 4 3 2 1

Cover art copyright © Shutterstock/159790454/Alessandro Guerriero
Cover design by Rita Frangie.
Interior text design by Kelly Lipovich.

This is a work of fiction. Names, characters, places, and incidents either are the product of
the author's imagination or are used fictitiously, and any resemblance to actual persons,
living or dead, business establishments, events, or locales is entirely coincidental.

If you purchased this book without a cover, you should be aware that this book is stolen
property. It was reported as "unsold and destroyed" to the publisher, and neither the author
nor the publisher has received any payment for this "stripped book."

Penguin
Random
House

*To those teachers who not only lectured, but explained;
who showed, as well as told; who forced me to think, see,
hear and experience in new ways, and who opened
my eyes and my heart to new paths.*

Thank you.

CHAPTER

1

A nd now, he was officially one of the team.
Gregory Higgs turned from the list on the door of Coach Ace's office and scrubbed a hand over his face. That was that. He was officially on the Marine Corps boxing team.

Oo-rah and all that.

"Hey, is it up yet?" Graham Sweeney jogged over, beating the crowd. "The list, it's up?"

"Yeah." Greg stepped aside to let Graham by. "I forgot to check for your name. Sorry."

"No problem. You were checking for your crew. I totally get it." His friend's finger slowly scanned down the list, pausing every so often as he noted a member of his own unit. "Damn, Monticino didn't make it."

Greg wasn't sure who that was, exactly, so he said nothing.

"And . . . there." He breathed deeply. "There we go. I'm in."

Because he knew it mattered greatly to his friend, Greg slapped his shoulder. "Well, look at it this way, even if you'd have been cut, the commute home would have been simple."

"Back gate, five minutes into Hubert." Graham grinned and punched Greg's shoulder. "Congrats, man. We did it."

"No shocker you two managed to pull through." Walking carefully, Brad Costa ambled toward them. From one hand, a black knee brace dangled.

Just to mess with his roommate, Greg stepped in front of the list. "Pull through what?"

Brad made a face and stopped in front of him. "Move."

"Why?" He glanced at Graham. "What's he want?"

"*He*," Brad said sarcastically, "wants to see the list. Move."

"It's like he cares," Greg added, eyes wide. "Grandpa, are you ready for your nap yet?"

Brad bent over as if he were ready to charge and Greg sidestepped, laughing. "You're too easy, man. You've really got to tone it down or I'm going to have way too much fun poking at you while we're traveling."

"So . . ." Suddenly serious, Brad stepped up and scanned down the list. Much like Graham, he sighed when he caught his name, then went back to find the rest of his team. "Damn."

"Missing one?"

"Two. Or maybe one and a half."

Greg glanced at Graham. "Half?"

"Chalfent's listed as an alternate." Brad turned, face grim. "What the hell does that mean?"

"I think it means they send them home, but ask them to keep training while they're there. If someone on the team gets hurt or can't compete, they'll bring them back."

Brad gave a tight nod, then headed toward the mats the team used to warm up. A few younger Marines walked in to the gym and jogged toward Coach Ace's door.

"Who else did you lose?" Greg asked, catching up.

"Tibbs. But I already knew that. There was no way they'd keep him after that debacle with the motorcycle last weekend." Sitting down carefully, Brad began to stretch out his legs. The brace lay next to his hip, unused.

"Forgive me for my lack of a medical degree, but aren't

you supposed to be, I dunno, wearing that?" Graham pointed to the brace. Brad kicked it at him. Graham kicked it back.

"You're kidding me, right?"

At the sound of their pint-sized drill sergeant of an athletic trainer, all three men froze. The sounds of groans and cheers from across the gym—Marines who were checking the list— echoed. As one, the three Marines turned to see Marianne Cook standing just off the mat, looking surprisingly adorable in an oversized T-shirt he could easily guess was from Brad's collection, and some sweatpants that bunched at the ankles and were clearly about five inches too long. The toe of one running shoe tapped, and her arms were crossed. The scowl she sent Brad could have frozen the nuts off a bull.

And all at once, Greg was very glad Brad had been the one to catch the cute AT's eye early in training camp, and not him.

"Bradley Costa, you put that brace on right now."

Graham snickered and bent over his knees, hiding his grin.

She turned on him in a snap. "Don't feel superior, Marine. You're on my shit list, too. You didn't come in so I could look at those two fingers yesterday like I asked."

He held his left hand high, keeping his chin tucked to his chest. His voice was muffled as he said, "Here they are. Still attached."

"Everyone's a tough guy," she muttered as she marched over to look at the fingers on display. "Put it on," she demanded of Brad without even sparing him a glance. Gingerly, she probed Graham's hand. It was only because Greg sat next to him that he heard his friend's sharp intake of breath.

"Falling apart, both of you," Greg said cheerfully as he pulled his heels in toward his crotch and bent over.

"Figures the guy who wasn't even sure he wanted to make the team remains suspiciously healthy," Brad muttered as he struggled to get the brace on over his shoe. After a minute, he gave up and took the shoe off before slipping the brace on.

More Marines joined them, spacing themselves out across the mat. Greg's unit—teammates now—came over as they filed in to tell him they'd made the team, except the one who had been cut. He stood to shake the man's hand, wish him luck and a reminder to add him on Facebook so they could keep in touch.

Brad gave him a baffled look as he sat back down. "You just make friends everywhere, don't you?"

"Him?"

The loud, booming shout stopped conversation cold as every Marine turned his head to look toward the door. Two men stood at the coach's door, one clearly attempting to calm the other down. The enraged one shook his friend's restraining hand off his shoulder and pointed toward the group stretching.

"Him? They kept the old guy with a jacked-up knee and let me go? Is this some kind of joke?"

"Uh-oh," Graham muttered under his breath. Brad groaned and got to his feet. Greg stood beside him. His fists instinctively curled; his heart raced in anticipation of a fight. He forced his hands to relax, shaking them a bit. *Calm down. Calm down.* After a moment, Graham stood as well, forming a three-strong wall.

The pissed-off Marine stormed toward them, and Greg had a momentary vision of a bull charging a red cape. Right before he would have slammed into Brad, Greg dove for him. Catching the man by surprise at a diagonal, he sent the two of them sprawling over the mat. He first went for restraint, but anger lent the dude too much strength.

The other man's anger fueled his own, and despite his earlier attempt to remain calm, Greg felt his own temper snapping at the leash.

Oh, well. Practice came a bit early today.

Dodging several clumsy, if strong, blows, Greg ducked and shouldered the man back a few steps. The other Marine had strength, but if memory served, the guy was never fast enough to keep up. His jabs were like swinging tree trunks. Potentially dangerous when he could land one, but inaccurate as hell. And Greg was too fast to get hit.

Another swing and Greg tossed the man to the ground. Arms wrapped around his waist, keeping him from going back for seconds. Graham sat on the downed man's chest, *tsking* his tongue.

"That was pathetic. No wonder you got cut instead of the old guy."

"Shut up," Brad said easily.

The man squirmed, but Graham found a pressure point in his shoulder that had the man moaning and subsiding quickly.

"Ease it down, Higgs," Brad said quietly as Greg fisted his hands again, breathing heavily, and not from exertion. "That was my fight, anyway."

"I needed the exercise. Not that he gave me much." Greg forced his fingers to relax, mentally willing the adrenaline to die down. Knowing the way his body and mind worked together, he could do too much damage in two minutes with an amped-up system. He had to calm down.

"Oh, lovely."

They all turned as a clicking sound echoed over the hardwood floor. And the business-suit-hottie they'd all seen lurking around the gym the last week or so headed toward them on curvy legs, hips swaying in her dark skirt.

"Testosterone for breakfast. Move over, Wheaties." The woman paused by Marianne, who had a disgusted look on her face. "Are they done now or will there be another round?"

"They're done," Marianne said with finality.

"Since today was an informal practice anyway, Coach Ace said I could use his office." She pointed at Greg, or more specifically, at his still-heaving chest. "You, come with me."

Greg—and probably every other Marine—watched as she spun on pinprick heels and sashayed across the floor toward the office.

"Anytime," he breathed, shaking Brad's grip off before following.

REAGAN sat down in Coach Ace's chair, grateful to be alone for a moment while her hands were still shaking a little. "Stop that," she ordered, but they didn't quite hear the order. There was no way she'd be able to take notes like this, let alone type on a computer in the borrowed office. And let's not even mention appearing to be a professional in front of a bunch of hardened warriors.

Because nothing said *I'm a professional who has it all under control* like limbs quaking like a tree branch in a wind storm.

A quick rap on the door made her jolt. She glanced over to see the dark blond with moves like lightning looking in. "You rang?"

"I did, yes. Please come in." She motioned toward the only other chair in the small, cramped office that smelled like six-day-old sweat socks and must. Lovely. To hide her trembling hands, she smoothed her skirt down, then folded them in her lap. "Your name, please?"

"Higgs. Gregory Higgs." He settled his body down into the chair and smiled easily. "Yours?"

"Reagan—sorry, Ms. Robilard," she corrected quickly. *Keep it together, Reagan.* "I'm the athlete liaison for the team, and will be handling all PR, travel, and outreach efforts for you gentlemen."

He relaxed back a bit, as if knowing her name made the entire thing less formal. One ankle crossed over his knee, and his hands rested comfortably in his lap. No tremble, she noticed with a little resentment. "That sounds like a fun job."

No, not really. "It's fascinating, I assure you." Putting on her best I'm-an-adult voice, she added, "You know fighting outside the ring isn't a wise decision, right?"

"A fighter's a fighter. And anywhere can be a ring." He

grinned. "Back alley, barroom, living room . . . gym. All it takes is two sets of fists and a reason."

"That right there will be our second problem to tackle with this team."

"What's the first?"

She grimaced. "These acts of vandalism. The last one was threatening. It's a concern, especially as we don't know the motive."

"I'd say motive isn't really the problem when the message is 'Eat shit and die' written on the walls of our practice area." Greg leaned forward a little, as if imparting a secret. "But it wasn't really the most creative threat, nor was it the most violent. Probably kids."

"Maybe, but nonetheless, Mr. Higgs, I—"

"Greg."

She blinked. "No, I really—"

"Normally I'd say Lieutenant Higgs, no mister about it. But we're not really playing the rank card here. So Greg's good enough."

She had to admit calling him *mister*, or by his rank, didn't seem to fit the situation. "Fine. Gregory, first I would like to—"

"Greg."

Her ears flushed with annoyance and she puffed out an exasperated breath. The man was impossibly stubborn. But bonus, her hands had stopped shaking enough to grab her notes and leaf through them. "Greg," she bit off. "I'm compiling a list of the current roster along with any potentially interesting snippets I can give to media outlets that might come calling or could be used in the future. Any experience you have with boxing outside of the Marines, for example. Anyone famous you trained with, any little personal anecdote you might have to add to the more factual bio I have. Any fun stories about why you joined the Marines. The media loves a human interest piece."

He snorted at that. "Nobody gives a crap about the Marine boxing team but Marines . . . and maybe the other branches' boxing teams. We're not exactly professional athletes here, Mrs. Robilard."

"It's miss," she corrected absently, glancing through the biography the program director had given her. Like the others, it was mostly details. Important dates, FITREPs, any awards given, and a list of the numerous deployments and TDYs. Unlike the other bios, though, where he'd had the option to fill in personal information himself—hometown, family, interests outside of boxing—he'd left it blank.

"I'll need you to fill this out all the way." She slid the paper toward him, doing her best to avoid touching him at all. "You left the bottom blank."

He glanced at it, then passed it back. "I filled out all the necessary stuff. Nothing more to say."

"There's always something more to say. If you could just—"

"Look, Miss Robilard," he said, standing abruptly, "I didn't sign on to be a talking figurehead. I came here to box and have some fun with my new teammates. That's all. If that's not enough for the Corps, then I can just as easily head back to my home base and be done with it. It's no skin off mine." With that, he slipped out of the office like smoke.

"Well," she muttered, noticing her hand had begun trembling again. "That just about sucked."

AN hour later, Reagan's heart rate had returned to normal and her hands had calmed down enough to sort through all the Marines who had been cut and the ones who had made the team. Those Marines who had stayed for the impromptu, off-the-books workout had been called in one by one to evaluate potential PR gold mines, and there was a list of the few she hadn't seen yet. She was in control. A force of organizing nature. A professional, competent, capable woman. She was a cool cucumber who—

"Hey."

"Oh my Jesus!" Rocking back in the springy chair, Reagan grabbed the edge of the desk, praying it would keep her from being thrown to the floor. A few seconds of bronco-riding later and she was right side up. When she heard a snickering from the doorway, she shot a glare at Marianne Cook. "Why is that so funny?"

"You'd have to see it from my angle to understand the humor." Marianne grinned and shut the door behind her, flopping into the seat across the desk. Normally, the short, spritely athletic trainer wore a Marine Corps boxing team polo and khaki bottoms of some kind, combining the practicality of being able to move with the professionalism expected of her. Today, however, she wore simple sweatpants and a large man's T-shirt.

Feeling testy, Reagan gathered the piles she'd scattered and started stacking them back together. "Where's the work uniform?"

"My day off equals my day to slop it up. No point in getting all dressy to watch them go at quarter speed. They're barely breaking a sweat out there." She tilted her head to indicate the gym beyond the office door. "Most of them are so thankful they made the team their legs are still like jelly."

Reagan could relate. She finished stacking and slapped the last pile down a little harder than necessary. "I spoke with Brad."

"Hmm." Marianne picked up one of Coach Ace's pens and started twirling it.

"We talked a bit about you and the situation with your relationship."

"Uh-huh." She doodled a bit on the edge of a piece of paper. Reagan shifted it slightly to the left, out of range. Marianne just settled back and watched her. Then, with a sigh, she added, "Am I supposed to be defensive about it? Reagan, you knew we were dating. He made the team on his own merit. I'm still here on *my* own merit. That's really all."

"He said as much. And you don't have to feel defensive. I'm

not the one in charge of hiring or firing anyone." Reagan blew at the hair that threatened to fall over her eyes. Why didn't her hair stay in its nice, professional chignon like it was supposed to? The women in the *Harvard Business Review* made their hair look effortlessly professional and grown-up. "But I still had to ask. I can't just stop doing my job. If there's a PR disaster or treasure trove, it's my job to find it and use it."

"Well, there's neither. No treasure troves or disasters. We just want to date in peace." Marianne propped one running shoe–clad foot on the corner of the coach's desk. "As long as that's clear."

"It is." Reagan debated it a moment, but then decided to try. "Wanna get drinks later?"

Marianne blinked in surprise. "I just gave you a snotty warning and you invite me to drinks? You have very weird responses."

"I'm desperate," Reagan said honestly.

"Well, in that case, sign me up!" Marianne said with a laugh.

Reagan's mouth dropped open when she realized what she'd said. "No! Oh, God no. That's not what I meant." She let her forehead drop to the desk, lifted it and dropped it once more. "I'm awful at this."

"If you're asking me out on a date, then I have to tell you, it's not going very well."

Reagan tilted her head so she could look up with one eye. Marianne's amused face told her the trainer was kidding. "You're not my type."

"Shame. Now why are you desperate?"

"I'm desperate for female company. Legit, intelligent female company. I still don't know my way around this town, I get lost on base anytime I have to go somewhere besides here, and I'm about eight states away from anyone I know." She sighed and settled back, smoothing down her jacket. "Desperate."

"Sounds like it." With a gentle smile, Marianne stood and held out a hand. "Phone."

Reagan handed it over without protest, knowing what the other woman was up to. "Call yourself or text yourself or something so you have my number, too."

A few seconds later, a pocket low on Marianne's thigh began to sing. She pressed a button through the fabric of the sweats and shut the music off. "Got it. I already promised I'd go out with my friend Kara tonight—"

"Oh. Right, of course. Plans. You've got plans." And here she was, horning in like a lost puppy, desperate for a belly scratch and a single word of praise. Would she ever get it right?

"But," Marianne added, "we'd love to have you join us. Normally it's just us chilling at her place because she's got a son, but she sprung for a babysitter tonight. We're painting the town red."

"Isn't it already red and gold everywhere around here?" Reagan asked, looking around Coach Ace's office. The predominant pair of colors were splashed all over. The Marine Corps colors were deeply embedded everywhere.

"Good point. Nevertheless, I officially invite you to join us out. I know what it's like being the new kid, and it's not always easy. So it's time to join the in crowd."

"The in crowd, huh?" Reagan took her phone back from Marianne, feeling like she was being handed a lifeline. "That's you and your friend?"

Marianne *pffft*ed. "Who the hell knows? I'll text you the location, but be ready for questions. Kara and I are going to demand to know your life story from beginning to end."

"Right. Life story. So that will take up five minutes. What will we do with the rest of the night?" She laughed when Marianne did, feeling more relaxed since the trainer had come into the room. "Thank you."

"No prob. I'll see you later on tonight." With a wave, the short woman disappeared into the gym. Not five seconds later, Reagan could hear her voice shouting, "No, Carmichael! You're going to blow out your elbow like that! I gave you a pamphlet on that last week!"

CHAPTER

2

Greg settled into what he officially referred to as his spot on Sweeney's couch. He'd just about broken in the end cushion to his liking. Lifting his beer, he saluted his two teammates. "Well done, men."

Sweeney lifted his own bottle in return. Costa acknowledged it with a small tip of the water bottle.

"One beer, for crying out loud. Just one." Greg took a sip of his own and gestured toward the kitchen. "Go get one. I'm begging you."

Brad simply shook his head and capped his bottle. "I have my reasons."

"If you reach for your phone to check it again, I'll sit on you and let Higgs toss it out in the front yard," Sweeney warned as Costa reached into his pocket.

Costa's hand froze. "You know, I'm not sure why I agreed to be dragged out here tonight. We've got practice in the morning, our first *official* practice as a team. One might think you two would want to be rested up. We're the old ones out there. We have to keep up with the infants."

"Speak for yourself. Everyone else has to keep up with *him*," Sweeney said with a mock sneer for Greg. "Greased lightning asshole."

"Jealous," was all Greg said. "Don't reach for the phone. Don't be that guy."

"You'll be sorry when I read you this text," was all Costa said, and did it anyway. "Yup. Just like I thought. The ladies are ready to mingle."

"Ladies?" Greg and Sweeney said at the same time. Both sat up. "Which ladies?" Greg added, not ready to get his hopes up yet.

"Yeah, because Cook is cute and all, but I heard a rumor she's spoken for," Sweeney added, which earned him a half-hearted kick from Costa.

"She's on some girls' night crusade with her friend Kara and the liaison woman."

"Yoga lady," Sweeney breathed.

"No, Legs," Greg corrected.

Costa looked at him, then at Sweeney and shook his head. "You're both right. Kara is the yoga and Pilates instructor, and 'Legs,'" he added with air quotes, "I can only assume is the liaison lady. I can't remember her name."

"Reagan," Greg said automatically, then glanced between the other two men. "What? I had that interview with her today. You did, too. Weren't you paying attention?"

"Uh-huh." Sounding unconvinced, Sweeney stood. "I'm one beer down, so you have to drive, Costa." He tossed Brad the keys to his SUV. "Let's roll, gentlemen. There are ladies waiting."

Brad joined him quickly. Greg waited a moment. He could stay here, or have them drop him off at the BOQ on the way.

But the thought of Reagan in those tight suits she wore, in those sweet heels that did impossibly sexy things to her legs, and what she might look like when she let her hair down off the clock had him jogging after them. "Wait up, I'm coming, too."

* * *

"I'VE missed this," Reagan said, finishing off her drink. "Okay, not the martini, maybe. That was terrible."

Kara and Marianne both laughed. "I warned you not to order anything they had to mix," Marianne said with a grin. "This is strictly a bottle-or-tap sort of place."

"And yet neither of you strike me as the brewski type," Reagan said, setting down the martini glass and pushing it away. Lesson learned there. "So why pick here?"

"It's a hub for adorable men," Kara said matter-of-factly. "In fact, Marianne's mom likes to come here and scope out the scenery a few times a week."

Marianne simply rolled her eyes.

"Oh." Reagan glanced around, but mostly only noticed Marines out of uniform. They were impossible to miss. The oldest male who wasn't with a woman looked like he would barely pass thirty. "Uh, how old is your mom again?"

"Old enough to drive me crazy," Marianne muttered. "She's been happily married for almost thirty-five years, and yet, is still boy-crazy. But can we please not spend our girl time out talking about my mother of all people?"

"Yes, let's talk about the ever-adorable, slightly brooding Bradley Costa," Kara said with a smirk. She sipped her beer with dainty movements that made Reagan think of a queen at high tea. "How are things with you?"

"Things are good. Great, actually." Reaching for her own beer, Marianne froze and watched Reagan. "Sorry, is this weird? Hearing about one of the teammates and me, personally? I can stop if it's a conflict of interest or something."

"No, not at all. As long as it's something I can use for media," she added. Counting to three, she burst out laughing at the twin jaw-drops on Kara and Marianne's faces. "Oh, come on! I'm kidding."

Marianne shook it off and grumbled, "I knew that."

Kara just smiled serenely. "So how about you, Reagan?

Any guys waiting for you back in . . . where was it you said you were from again?"

"Wisconsin. And no, absolutely not. There was nothing for me back there." And she meant that literally. "I mean, I had to come all this way just for this tiny job. Clearly, things were not happening in my hometown. Which works well for those who live there by choice. Me, not so much."

"And this is your first job post college, right?"

Reagan nodded, flagging down the waitress to ask for a beer. "Yeah. I know I have to start at the ground floor, and frankly I'm glad I even got this job with zero work experience. But sometimes I think—"

"Hello, pretty ladies. Can we buy you a round?"

Marianne's eyes grew soft as she glanced over Reagan's shoulder. "Don't look now, ladies, but we're about to be invaded."

Reagan glanced at Kara, who shrugged and scooted her chair over. If they didn't mind girls' night being invaded by a male, who was Reagan to argue? She was the outsider in this group.

But it wasn't just any male who slid into the chair beside Marianne. Brad Costa, Marianne's boyfriend, took the seat and draped an arm over the back of her chair in a proprietary, "This Is Mine" sign to any other men at the bar. The way he leaned over her while talking into her ear was about as obvious as if he'd whipped it out and peed on her to mark his territory.

The imagery both horrified Reagan and made her smother a chuckle, which ended up coming through as a snort that choked her a little. She coughed, then flew forward as a large hand thumped her on the back. Catching herself a half second before her chest flew into the table's edge, she barked out another cough to clear her throat. Glancing behind her, ready to give hell to whoever thought that was amusing, she found herself eye to eye with none other than Gregory "just Greg" Higgs.

"Sorry about that," he said sincerely, sitting beside her. "Didn't mean to hit you so hard. I thought you were choking on an olive or something."

There was no way to be mad at a guy who'd had noble intentions . . . even if she might be sore in the morning from his *help*. "It's okay. I'm fine."

"Good." He hesitated, then took his hand off her back. Was it her imagination, or had he grazed his fingertips across her shoulder?

Pull yourself together, Reagan. You're an adult, act like it. He was just being helpful.

Graham Sweeney—who Reagan only recognized because he was another of the main team leaders—sat down beside Kara, who scooted over a few more inches to give him space. If he noticed the subtle don't-touch-me vibe he didn't say so. Kara, for however sweet she was, definitely had the ability to put on her Cloak of Solitude when she wanted to.

"So what's everyone drinking?" Graham asked. Kara and Marianne immediately held up their beer bottles as Brad waved down their server.

"Did you want another martini?"

The question, so close to her ear, made Reagan shiver. His breath was warm, warmer even than the air in the bar. She turned to answer him, only to find Greg's face a mere two inches from hers. She could actually lick his lips right now without moving.

And again with the poor thoughts, Reagan.

She settled back in her chair and shook her head. "No, definitely not. That thing was . . ."

"Bad?" Marianne suggested.

"Horrible," was Kara's offering.

"Lethal," Reagan decided on. "Lethal, with a deadly aftertaste. I'll just have a diet Coke."

"Driving home?" Greg asked as they gave their orders to the server, who jotted them down without a word and left the same way. "We can drop you off if you want to grab another drink or two. I hear it's a special ladies' night out."

"Of which it is no longer just ladies," Kara said pointedly.

"Sorry," Marianne said with a flushed smile. "I told him where we were and, well . . ." Brad nuzzled against her neck and whispered something in her ear, which made her smile grow and her flush deepen.

Greg snickered, Graham rolled his eyes, and Kara and Reagan chose to look at each other rather than the new love-birds. Kara's lips rolled in, as if trying to keep from smiling.

Of course they wanted to spend time with each other. If Reagan had a boyfriend as cute as Brad, she'd be with him, too.

Brad's phone rang, and he reached into his pocket for it. Graham booed, and Greg threw a napkin. "We just got here, man. Put it away."

"Could be important."

"Could be his mom," Graham said with a grin. "Tell her I said hi."

"You know his mom?" Kara asked, surprised as she turned to Graham.

"No, but that's not the point. It's just a thing." Graham started to say something else, then froze as he watched Brad's face turn from jovial to grim. "Hold on, looks like we've got a problem. What's up, man?"

"Jesus H.," Brad muttered. "Someone slashed Tressler's tires outside his barracks." He stuffed the phone back in his pocket. "And according to him, his wasn't the only one hit. Two of your guys got slashed too, Sweeney."

"Any of mine?" Greg asked, standing beside Reagan.

"Didn't say so, but who knows? Let's head out there and see what's up." Brad went to the bar to grab their tabs.

"Looks like it's back to ladies' night," Graham said with a shrug. "Sorry for busting in and running out again." He bent down to give Marianne a kiss on the cheek, then waved to Reagan. For Kara, he tipped his head, then headed for his car.

"I'll go pay my tab and be right there." Reagan stood.

Greg grabbed her elbow, stopping her from moving. "There's no need for you ladies to call it quits. Stay."

"If it concerns the team, it concerns me. Maybe it's nothing, but with everything else that's gone on, I want to make sure of it." She gave his grip a pointed look, and he released her. She took two steps, then turned back around. "Uh, where exactly are the barracks on base again?"

Marianne laughed. Kara groaned. Brad came back to give Marianne a quick kiss. "You can follow us, if you want," he added to Reagan.

She bit her lip. "I just have to pay the tab and I'll meet you outside."

He nodded and followed Sweeney out.

She waited for Greg to go, but he didn't. Instead, he followed her to the bar while she paid for her one drink and left a tip. Finally, when he stalked her out to the parking lot, she halted by her car door. It occurred to her then, as he pressed in close to her side, that she was almost an inch taller than him in her heels. "What? Why are you playing the creeper game?"

The corner of his lips twitched, but he gave her a serious look. "Know where you're going?"

"I'm following you, I guess. Past that, I'm pretty much clueless."

"Okay then." He went to open her car for her as soon as she'd hit the unlock button, waited for her to slide in, then jogged around to the other side and got into the passenger seat.

"Uh, hi?" Reagan stared at him. "Going somewhere?"

"You don't know where you're going, it's dark, and you could easily lose Brad driving Sweeney's SUV. So I'll just ride with you and make sure you get there okay."

She glared at him a moment. "Purely out of the goodness of your own heart, huh?"

He held his hands up, a boyishly innocent face on. "Hey, I'm a civil servant, what can I say?"

Right. She twisted to put her purse in the back, recoiling a little when her breasts brushed against his biceps. Her car was small—read: affordable—and he was, well, he wasn't the biggest guy but he was still an imposing male. Plus, her boobs were larger than the average woman's, so this had all the hallmarks of a disaster.

"Just head for the main gate—you know where the main gate is, right?"

She shot him a look that warned him to lock down the idiotic comments ASAP.

Smart man that he was, he heeded the call. "Get to the main gate and then we'll go from there. Shouldn't take us more than ten minutes, fifteen if there's weird traffic."

"The back gate isn't anywhere close to here, is it?" she asked as she pulled into reverse and backed out of the parking spot.

"Not even remotely."

"So why is this bar called the Back Gate if we're so close to the front gate?"

"Someone's idea of a joke, I guess."

"Some joke."

"No kidding."

GREG'S nerves were on high alert and had been since the second he'd ever-so-smoothly thumped Reagan's back. That delightful move had earned him the Dumbass of the Night award. And the hits just kept on coming. But fate had thrown him a bone and given him a very good reason to get the luscious Reagan Robilard alone in her car.

"Just keep driving straight now," he said as they pulled through the main gate and past the sentry.

"There's nowhere to go but straight," she pointed out.

"Could turn right here for the hospital."

"I don't want that," she said, her voice tight.

"So keep driving straight."

She growled a little, the sound so cute and feminine he wanted to lean over and kiss the tip of her nose. But he resisted. One stupid move a night was his limit . . . hopefully.

"Did you have a good night out?"

She smiled, which he couldn't see so much as hear in her voice. "I was, until a few weirdos came and crashed all the fun."

"Weirdos?" Ready to defend her honor, despite being too late, he sat up straighter. "Who? What'd they look like? Did they bother you?"

"That would have been you three," she answered with a smug grin.

Oh. Right. He let his head thump back against the headrest. Damn. She had a wicked sense of humor on her. "How's the job working out?"

"It's far more action-oriented than I imagined, that's for sure. I never thought I'd be driving out in the dark to inspect slashed tires, or figuring out who keeps vandalizing the gym. I feel like I stepped into a Nancy Drew book instead of my first real job."

"First real job, huh?" She flushed slightly, the tint barely perceptible thanks to the street lamps. "Just graduated, I take it?"

"I did, yes." Her voice deepened when she wanted to sound more professional, he noted. "Took me a little longer because I had to work full time while I went through college, and I couldn't always take a full course load. But I'm a proud graduate and ready to use my degree."

"Good to know." How long had she practiced that defensive little speech in her mind in case someone asked? He settled back in his seat. "You'll turn here, then make another and the barracks will be dead ahead."

"Gotcha."

She finished the drive and pulled into a space at the back of the lot next to Sweeney's SUV. "I should have brought a camera or something," she said, looking around her car. Her voice was higher again, telling him she was nervous. "I don't know if I'll need photos but . . ." She bit her lip, and he put a hand over hers on the gear shift between them.

"Don't sweat it. We've all got cell phones with cameras. Between all of us we'll have plenty of photos."

"Oh. Right." She closed her eyes for a moment and took a deep breath. A breath that pushed her more-than-a-handful breasts against the tight confines of her shirt. "Sorry, I'm nervous. This isn't the sort of thing they cover in marketing class."

"You're fine. You've got it." He stepped out, then debated going to open her door. She was, for all intents and purposes, on the job now. Would she see that as stepping over a boundary? Be angry he'd done something she could do for herself?

While he internally debated, she opened her own door and stepped into the warm night air, smoothing her dark pencil skirt down over her hips as she did so. And thank God for skirts that hugged those curves. She was a damn work of art, a true hourglass. He let her get a step in front of him as she walked toward the group congregated on the sidewalk in front of the building, just to give himself another minute of appreciation at the way her hips swung while she walked.

CHAPTER

3

" Good evening, Marines." Reagan's voice deepened into a husky, sexy tone that had Greg fighting an erection in the parking lot. "Problems with some tires, I hear?"

She listened as the guys explained having made it home with no problem, parking, then finding the tires slashed when they'd come out to get dinner. She took notes on her phone, getting everyone's license plates, makes and models, which tires were slashed and where they'd been parked in the lot.

"And nobody else's tires were slashed? The people who'd parked next to you, for example?"

"Only tires we see slashed are from the team's," Tressler said, looking supremely pissed and ready to brawl with anyone who gave him a wrong look. The hothead was in for a rude awakening in the ring if he couldn't keep himself together and shield those emotions better. "Except Chalfent, his got hit, too, but he didn't make the team. He leaves in the morning."

At Brad's growl, Tressler's eyes widened. "Which, I

mean, he should have," he finished, then shot Chalfent a look. "Sorry, man. That's not what I meant."

"I know," the tall, gangly man said quietly. "It's okay."

"So what you're saying is the person who did this appears to have enough information about the team to know who to target, but not enough to know who was cut this afternoon," Reagan said quickly, cutting off any potential problems at the knees. "Someone who must not have that much of an inside track to know better."

"Yeah, that's what we've been thinking. You're good." Tressler nodded and grinned, which made Greg take a protective step toward Reagan's back. She glanced over her shoulder with a grouchy expression, but he didn't back up.

Tressler caught his eye, narrowed his brow slightly, then shrugged. At least the kid wasn't a total moron, even if he was a cocky little shit. He picked up on the subtle back-off vibes fast enough.

After she'd gathered all the official documentation, she asked who had called the authorities. The younger Marines all looked at each other, each one shaking his head in turn.

"Nobody?" Reagan glanced between them, then fisted her hands on her hips. "Not one of you thought to report this? Your insurances alone will require that much."

"We thought we should wait to see what these guys wanted to do," another Marine—one of Sweeney's, Greg thought—said. "We figured it was their call, because things are so weird right now with the gym and the training room getting trashed."

"Can't fault them for thinking it through," Greg muttered by Reagan's ear. "Cut them some slack. They're babies."

She turned to cut him a frosty glance. "Half of them are just a year or two younger than me, and a few are my age."

Whoops. He hadn't considered that. She'd mentioned being a recent graduate, but he'd simply assumed she'd gone back to school after working for a few years. So she was what, twenty-four? Twenty-five?

Not that he cared. He was only twenty-eight himself. But she gave the illusion of being older than she apparently was. Probably the same way she gave the illusion of being taller, more in control, more sure of herself. She projected it perfectly with wardrobe and attitude.

In full control now, Reagan started to pace in front of the group. "Let's go ahead and talk to the . . . the . . ." She waved her hand in the air. "The base law enforcement . . . military police."

"MPs," Greg added quietly by her ear.

"Thank you. MPs," she said, not looking at him. "Let's talk to the MPs and get that situated and on the record. While we're waiting for them, we need to make some calls for rides to get you guys to practice tomorrow. Once that's done, we'll make appointments for you to get your tires replaced at whatever place your insurances will approve. We'll stagger the repairs so we can get them fixed without jeopardizing your training schedules."

She started tapping at her phone, and Greg nearly had to pick his jaw up off the floor. He had the distinct feeling she'd left Reagan in the car and brought Ms. Robilard with her to work. Night and day difference.

And the other men noticed it, too. They scrambled to follow her directions, making calls or looking information up on their phones, taking photos and texting people about rides.

The woman knew how to light a fire under a group of Marines.

With a satisfied, if a little grim, smile, Reagan nodded and clapped her hands once to get everyone's attention. They stopped talking immediately, and Greg nearly laughed at the image of a kindergarten teacher getting the attention of a dozen five-year-olds. "Right, I'm going to take some photos before I go, and then I will see everyone tomorrow." With a steely stare, she added, "This does not excuse anyone from practice in the morning. You've got plenty of time to arrange for a ride, so do it."

Most mumbled a quiet, "Yes, ma'am," before she walked off to start taking photos of each car's slashed tires. Greg followed behind, hands tucked behind his back to keep from thrusting her against one of those vehicles and kissing her senseless. That was, without a doubt, one of the hottest things he'd seen in years. Her ability to take charge in the blink of an eye, command a group of hard-ass Marines, and do it in a sexy pair of heels and body-hugging skirt . . .

She did a dainty little squat, keeping her knees primly together as she angled her phone toward the rear tire of a pickup truck. Her skirt stretched tight over her curvy ass.

Come to think of it, maybe that's exactly how she commanded their attention so well. Hmm.

"Did you need something else?"

His concentration broken, Greg blinked and uttered the ever-intelligent, "What?"

"You were staring." Reagan took another photo, the flash momentarily blinding him, then looked over her shoulder. "Did you still need something?"

"A ride back to the BOQ would be nice."

"Your friends are still here. I assume that's why. You could go with them." Snap, snap.

"But then how would you get home?"

"GPS," she answered easily. "It's easy enough to key in 'Home' as my destination from an unknown place. Not so easy to key in the address of 'Barracks, Camp Lejeune.'"

Okay, she had a point there. "It wouldn't be very gentlemanly for me to ditch you now."

"You're not ditching, you're going home to get some rest. I'd actually prefer that, to be honest. The more rested you are, the better you train." She stood, teetering for just a second before he grabbed her arm to steady her. The short-sleeve blouse she wore gave him the chance to feel the soft skin of her forearm under his thumb. He brushed once over the pulse on the inside of her elbow, felt it hammering and knew she wasn't nearly as cool as she played.

"You want me to go home and get some beauty rest?" He lowered his voice, stepping in, wondering if she was ever without those damn heels—which yes, did great things for her ass—so he could actually look down at her instead of up an inch. "I don't think you do."

"And that's why I'm the brains of this operation," she said lightly, stepping back. "Someone has to think about the greater good. Besides," she added, picking her purse up from the side mirror she'd hung it on to take photos, "you'll need your strength for battle tomorrow."

"It's training, not battle."

"I wasn't talking about practice. I was talking about dealing with me." And with that sassy parting shot, she slid between two cars and disappeared to continue her photo documentary.

"Higgs, let's go man. This day's a big cluster and I'm ready to hit the rack." Brad appeared by his elbow and tugged lightly on his neck. "Sweeney's dropping us back by the BOQ on his way home."

"Oh, joy." He followed along, not at all willingly.

REAGAN watched through the lens of the digital video camera, taking in as much of the action in the mock training ring as she could without losing definition and focus. The equipment was primitive at best. Though at this point, she should probably be glad she was given a digital anything. God knew, she could probably have expected a VHS recorder to take video with.

"Getting any good shots?" Coach Ace walked up to stand beside her. "I know my guys are preening like pretty peacocks for the camera."

Reading between the lines, she closed the lens and picked up the tripod she'd paid for herself. Oh, how many pairs of shoes she could have bought for the price of that tripod . . . "You think I'm distracting the men."

"Not think, know. They're all under thirty, most of them single, and they are pumped up on adrenaline and testosterone and ego from having made the team. Hell yes, you're a distraction." Coach Ace scanned her from head to toe in a gesture that was definitely meant to be derisive rather than sexual.

Reagan placed one hand over her chest and fluttered her lashes. "Ooh la la. If only I'd remembered to wear my frumpiest outfit to disguise my feminine wares so as not to distract the menfolk from their important endeavors. However shall I earn your forgiveness, good sir?"

The head coach snorted out something she hoped was humor, then crossed his arms to watch the men spar. Another group worked cardio upstairs along the catwalk with Coach Cartwright, while a third was in the adjoining weight room with Coach Willis. Though she would rather bite off her own arm than admit it, she knew Greg Higgs was with the group in the weight room. That shouldn't matter. She was here for the team, not one Marine.

One very fine, very delicious, very funny . . . Marine.

"Coach Ace," she said slowly, packing up the camera in the case at her feet, "I have a job to do. I know you do, too. But we have to work together, not constantly butt heads."

"It's not hard to avoid that." He picked up the case when she reached for it, taking it over to the side where she'd stashed her tote bag full of folders. "You stay out of the way and do your PR voodoo magic outside the gym."

Tread carefully, Robilard. "That might have been how it worked in the past—"

"It was," he agreed firmly.

"But that's not how I plan on running things."

She watched the coach, trying her best to gauge his reaction based on his expression. She would have been better off trying to guess what a brick wall was thinking. His face curiously blank, Coach Ace shrugged and walked to his office, closing the door quietly behind him.

"Was that acceptance, or denial?" she muttered as she packed up the camera.

Getting along with the coaching staff wasn't specifically required, but it would be a hell of a lot easier on everyone if they could come to terms over the parameters of her job. She refused to run back to her own supervisor and tattle on the uncooperative coaching staff. So it was up to her to figure out how to get everyone on the same page.

And add that to the ever-growing list of things she needed to do better. She really had to pick up her game.

"Hey."

"Eeeee!" Reagan bobbled the camera bag, nearly dropping it to the floor. She grabbed the handle just as a large pair of hands swooped under to shield the bag from the floor.

Heart pounding, she turned to find Gregory Higgs standing there, grinning. She started to speak, then realized her mouth was dry. To cover, she took the bag back from him and set it gently on the floor. When he only continued to smile, she stiffened her shoulders and met him square on. "What?"

"Do you ever wear anything smaller than three inches?"

That had her taking a step back in surprise. "Three inches of what?"

"Height." When she blinked, confused, he added, "The heels. I've never seen you in anything shorter than three inches, give or take. Just curious if you ever wear flats."

"Not if I can help it." She bent over to pick up the camera bag again—now that her hands had stopped shaking and her heart rate was nearing normal—but he beat her to it. She accepted the bag with a slight nod and started toward the gym's main doors. If she headed back to her cubicle in the main athletics office, she might be able to catch the travel coordinator.

Greg missed the hint and jogged beside her to keep up. "Luckily I like a girl with some height to her."

She faltered just a little, glancing over at him. "I have a

lot to do, so if you don't need anything, I need to keep moving."

"I can move. We're on lunch break."

Oh, yay. She snorted and kept going at the same pace. He kept up. "So are you free?"

"Free for what?" she asked, huffing a little. She realized then she'd been all but sprinting to the parking lot, hoping he'd ditch her and move along. She restrained herself so she could breathe properly. Time to use the gym facilities herself.

Or, maybe, she should just try not outrunning the fastest guy on the team. There's a brilliant idea.

"Lunch. We've got two hours."

"Oh." She reached her car and nearly winced when he did a double take at it in the daylight hours. "Don't mock her."

"What's her name?"

"Name?" Reagan tried to play it cool as she slid the camera bag into the passenger seat, then set her purse on the floor. The passenger door creaked as she closed it again. "Whose name?"

"The car's." Greg did a circle around it, taking note, she was sure, that the color of the vehicle was more primer than silver. And of the industrious way she'd duct-taped the taillight cover on. "A car like this always has a name."

She mumbled something, but he cocked his head. "Sorry, didn't catch that."

"Dolly Madison," she bit out. "Her name is Dolly Madison. Happy?"

He snorted, then chuckled, then laughed so hard she thought if he'd been a cartoon, he would have fallen to the ground and rolled around on his back. "It wasn't meant to be funny."

"I'm . . . I'm sorry," he gasped out. "Your car is named Dolly Madison, and it's *not* a joke?"

"She's a mature, distinguished gentlewoman," Reagan shot back. "You don't mock the first lady."

"The first lady's been around the block a few times," he added, which only set his oh-so-humorous chuckles off again.

"Go eat your lunch. I've got work to do. Unless . . ." She waited until his laughter had slowed and his attention was fully on her.

"Unless?" He inched closer, and she could smell the sweat from his workout. How was sweat appealing? That was impossible.

"Unless you want to come back with me and . . ." She glanced to the left, then the right. He hunched in, shoulders rounding as if to protect the secret she was going to impart. "Finish our interview for the PR packet I'm putting together."

He straightened and stepped back as if he were a vampire and she had garlic breath. "Forgot I had a lunch date with Costa and Sweeney."

"Uh-huh." Reagan crossed her arms. "I'm getting the information I need from you, don't doubt it."

"Whatever you say, Legs." He jogged away a few feet, then waved over his shoulder. "See ya around."

"Yes, you will," she muttered under her breath. "Cocky Marine."

"That's redundant."

"Eeeeek!" For the second time that day, Reagan let out an embarrassing shriek, tossing her keys three parking spaces away and shielding her face. When she peeked through her fingers and found Marianne Cook staring at her in amusement, she groaned. "I hate my life."

Marianne just smiled. "Sorry you didn't hear me over all the pheromones you and Higgs were throwing at each other."

"Phero . . . no. You totally misunderstood the situation." Reagan straightened her jacket, then smoothed straight down the skirt she wore. "We're becoming professional adversaries. It's not a personal thing."

"Right." Marianne's tone said, *You're full of shit.*

Time to change the subject. "What's redundant?"

"Cocky Marine. They're all cocky. The attitude is issued

with the uniforms once they sign on the dotted line. It's survival." She glanced down at Reagan's feet. "I thought I told you to stop wearing heels like that in the gym."

Reagan looked down at her adorable, so-on-sale-they-basically-paid-her-to-buy-them peep-toe pumps, then kicked one out to the side just a little. "But they're so cute."

"They're a death trap. A walking death trap, literally. You're going to slip on the smooth floorboards of the gym floor and snap an ankle." When Reagan opened her mouth to protest, Marianne shook her head. "Never mind, that's not why I'm out here. I wanted to make sure everything's okay from last night."

Last night. She'd completely forgotten she'd ditched Marianne and Kara to get started on work. "I'm so sorry, I should have texted or called when I was finished to see how things were."

Marianne waved her hand at that and leaned against Reagan's bumper in a casual slouch. Reagan prayed to the patron saint of automobiles that the bumper didn't give way on the spot. "No biggie. We all get the whole career thing. I'm not a stranger to weird calls late at night."

"But how . . . you know what? Never mind." Reagan opened her driver's side door and shook her head. "Don't want to know. Now, you and I need to schedule a time to meet this week, too."

"Meet for what?" The trainer stood, and Reagan winced mentally at the rust spot on the hip of her friend's khakis. She prayed it would come out in the wash later.

"Meet to go over the travel arrangements, plus any potential interview questions you might get in the future. Standard PR prep."

"I'm the athletic trainer. I'm not exactly high profile . . . and that's how I like it." Marianne gripped the door frame as Reagan slid in. "Have you interviewed everyone else?"

"Almost."

"How chatty were the Marines?"

Reagan grinned at that. "Some were extremely chatty."

Marianne raised a brown. "And others?"

"Bradley was very short," Reagan said, answering the question she knew her friend wouldn't ask. "And very smart on how to answer questions pertaining to your affiliation with the team, your relationship, and how that plays out. He's got it covered. So will you, after I've had my hands on you."

"Why, Reagan, we just met." When Reagan's eyes widened and she started to explain, Marianne laughed. "Go to lunch, PR queen. I'll see you later. In flats," she added in a firm voice, then shut the door.

Flats. Reagan shuddered—as did Dolly Madison as she pulled out of the parking spot and headed toward the main offices. Some things were just not worth arguing.

CHAPTER

4

Greg walked into the BOQ, salad container in hand, and heard Costa on the phone in his own room. They shared a common entrance, but had small individual sleeping quarters. His roommate was probably talking to Marianne, since those two couldn't seem to go more than three minutes apart without talking to each other. He gave it a three-count, then burst into Brad's room and yelled, "Costa! Put your pants back on and get that stripper out of here!"

Brad whirled on him, fully dressed, phone to his ear, with a death stare. "No, *Mom*, that's just my soon-to-be-dead roommate. No, I don't have . . . *Mom*! Come on."

Whoops. Greg swallowed back a laugh. Cook would have found the whole thing funny. His roommate's mother was an unknown quantity in the joke's equation.

"No, he didn't say stripper, he's got a weird slur. Yeah, I know. It's a sad situation. I think the coach kept him on the team out of pity." He walked over and punched Greg on the shoulder, then pushed him out of the room and slammed the door. Chuckling, Greg walked to the small table in the common room and sat down to eat. He mentally counted out the minutes, and after five, Costa appeared.

"I hate you," his roommate said succinctly. He walked over to the tiny kitchenette they shared and opened the fridge for a bottle of water.

"I thought you were on the phone with Cook. My bad."

"Because telling my girlfriend I've got a stripper in the room is much better than telling my mom." He settled down in the seat across from Greg and sulked. "Your humor needs improvement."

"I get that a lot." He dug into his salad, fork freezing halfway to his mouth when Costa stared. "What?"

"You're eating salad."

Greg stared at the plastic container for a moment. "What? No way. Those grocery people lied to me. They swore this was a cheeseburger."

"You've never willingly eaten anything healthy. What's wrong?"

"I'm eating a salad, so clearly it must be cancer." Put off of his impulse salad, he set the fork down for a minute. "Maybe I got sick of you harping on my diet. You're always nagging me about 'fueling the temple,'" he said with air quotes.

"And here I thought you didn't care about that." Looking smug, Costa sipped his water.

So maybe he cared a little. The entire boxing gig had only been a game to him at the start. He hadn't even asked to be sent for the tryouts; his commanding officer simply called him in and told him he'd be going. Each additional day he was at training camp was another day he didn't have to show up for regular work. Past that, boxing wasn't a passion for him.

Fighting had simply been survival, once upon a time.

"Sorry about that whole mom-on-the-phone thing." He reached into the mini fridge behind him for a soda. Some habits died harder than others. A health nut was not built in a day.

"No big deal." Costa smiled a little and looked at the phone sitting on the table. "She'll laugh about it later. Next time I walk in on you talking to your mom, though . . . payback."

Greg smiled, but couldn't work up a laugh. Instead, he stuffed another bite of lettuce and other assorted healthy crap into his mouth.

Fat chance of Costa ever catching him on the phone with his own mother, since Greg hadn't seen his mom since before his first birthday. Couldn't describe her if his life depended on it. He carried no memories of his life before his mom dumped him with the state, and for that he was grateful.

But each and every foster "mother" since he was about four? He could sketch them from memory. All fourteen.

"Have you finally unpacked?"

Costa's question broke his contemplative eating and thinking. "Yeah, figured my name on the roster was the sign I'd been looking for. Time to act like it's real."

"It's been real from the start."

"Ah, there's that stick-up-the-ass roommate I've been missing." He grinned when Costa scowled.

Greg had come into the adventure hoping to make new friends and have some fun. Really wring the experience dry. Costa had been eagle-eye focused on the prize from the start, willing to sacrifice the option to make friends in order to get ahead. Thank God he'd loosened up, mostly due to meeting one flaming-hot athletic trainer named Marianne Cook. She'd snapped the stick in half and forced him to be a social human.

He checked his watch and stood, closing the take-out box on his still mostly uneaten salad. "I've gotta go get my two guys from the barracks whose tires were slashed for afternoon practice. God, I hope their cars get fixed soon. I'm not in the mood to play taxi service all week." He dumped the container in the trash, which landed with a satisfying thump.

"Must have been a good salad," Costa said with a raised brow.

"Tasted like I'd rather be fat."

"YES, of course I'll hold." Reagan tapped her foot on the linoleum floor of the training room, the sound echoing in the currently empty room. Currently empty, until Marianne walked in and gave her a *What's up?* look.

"Newspaper," she mouthed to Marianne, who shrugged and headed for her desk. Reagan watched as Marianne sat down at her desk and began typing on her laptop. From what Reagan could see, it looked like another pamphlet.

Marianne was in a very committed relationship with pamphlets. If pamphlets would take the next step, Reagan was pretty sure they'd get married.

A voice spoke in her ear and she straightened, pacing while she spoke. "Yes, I'm still here. Uh-huh, right. We'd love to do an interview. Do you want to speak with the whole group or . . . okay, sure. I'll pull out a few representatives. Full team photo? I'm sure we can manage that, unless you . . . of course. Yes, I know your photographer has other things to do. No problem." Reagan reached the end of the training room, spun around and nearly walked into a table. She skirted the furniture and paced to the other side. "I'll look forward to it. You have my number. Thanks again."

"Gonna break an ankle," Marianne sang in a told-you-so voice.

"My ankles are fine. It's my hips that are in real danger here. There are tables everywhere."

"I know. What were we thinking? Tables in a training room. We should have done our decorating with your comfort in mind." Marianne leaned back in her chair and swiveled to look at her. "Newspaper? Which one? The base paper?"

Reagan blew out a breath at that. "Of course not. That's not even up for discussion. Getting in the base paper is a given. It was the Jacksonville paper. They'll be doing an interview with the coaches and a few of the guys tomorrow morning."

"Hmm." Obviously uninterested, Marianne went back to her laptop. A scruffy-looking young man who was probably only a few years younger than Reagan walked in, gave her a once-over, then kept moving until he reached the storage area of the room. Without a word, he pulled a sleeve of disposable cups down and left again.

"Chatty fellow, isn't he?"

"That's Levi, one of my interns." She grinned over her shoulder. "I have interns. I'm a real adult."

"Congratulations on your adulty-ness." Reagan paused a moment. "When does the adulty-ness kick in, exactly?"

"Still feel like you're playing pretend?"

"Still feel like I'm pretending, and nobody else has caught on yet. I'm waiting for someone to walk in one day, point their finger and yell 'Aha! We know you're just a kid. Who do you think you are, playing at being an adult?'" She rubbed at her temples. "That sounds stupid."

"Sounds normal to me." Marianne stood and looked out toward the gym where the Marines were running through circuits. "I can admit I've led a pretty cushy life. Hardest thing for me so far was staying awake during my fourth year finals before graduating college." She nodded at a group of young men who jogged by in a line of twos, several of whom gave her a quick wave of acknowledgement. "Working with these guys sort of puts things into perspective. For me, this is what I do. For them, this is a very short, very well-earned break before they go back to being the finest fighting force in the world."

Reagan felt a squeeze in her chest. "Hoorah."

Marianne winced. "We'll work on your pronunciation."

"That we will. For now, I have to snag a few guys for some interview prep." She took a few steps, then looked back toward Marianne. "How amenable will Bradley be to my asking?"

"Not very, but he'll do it." She gave Reagan a wicked smile. "Better let me ask. I have ways to persuade him. He'll be much more relaxed about the whole thing."

"I so did not need to know that," Reagan said, walking toward Coach Ace to plead her case.

"WHAT'S the deal now?" Sweeney asked, hopping onto one of the tables in the training room. "Are we being given another group to look after?"

Costa winced a little as he lifted himself—all arms— onto the next table. He settled the ice bag in his hand over his knee before answering, "I doubt it. Probably something PR related. I saw Ms. Robilard talking to Coach Ace before he pulled us aside."

"She's a hot number," Sweeney said casually. "Not entirely my type, but definitely a looker. Those legs, in those heels?" He made a burning sound, flicking his fingers together as if they were singed. "Ow, hot."

"I'm more partial to polo shirts and tennis shoes lately," Costa replied. Both Sweeney and Greg groaned, and Sweeney threw his paper-covered pillow at Brad. He caught it and tossed it back with a grin.

"Boys, don't make a mess of my training room," Marianne called out, walking in with her two interns trailing behind. The lanky one with hair that reminded him of Justin Bieber before the singer went wild stopped short when he noticed the three men sitting on the tables. The female intern, with eyes that constantly roamed over the Marines like a cat on the prowl, hustled over to Sweeney's table.

"Can I help you with anything?" she asked eagerly. It was like watching a puppy scrabble and paw against someone's legs, waiting to be picked up.

"Uh, no. We're good, thanks." Greg nearly laughed out loud when he noticed Sweeney inching back and away from the intern.

"Then why are you here?" the guy snapped out. Greg saw anger in his eyes before his bangs covered them again. Quickly putting two and two together, he assumed the kid had a crush on his co-intern . . . and wasn't a fan of the attention she paid to the Marines.

Frankly, the Marines weren't often fans of the attention, either.

"We're waiting for . . . her," Greg finished, swallowing back the urge to whistle as Reagan walked in, clipboard in hand. Her hair was up today, in some complicated twist thingie that left a few strands artfully sticking out. Her suit had pants this time—damn—but somehow the creased legs of the pinstripe suit only elongated her legs that much more. Of course, it could also be from the huge platform heels she wore.

The woman loved her heels. And Greg was seriously debating making a move to get her into bed so he could see her in nothing *but* those heels. One round in the sack for every pair she owned.

That could keep them busy for weeks by his calculations.

It was good to have goals.

"Gentlemen," she said, her voice that deep, formal tone she used for business. "Thank you for coming."

"Didn't have a choice," Sweeney said simply.

"Oh." She blinked, momentarily caught off guard. "Right. Of course. Well, thank you anyway. I have here some mock interview questions, and suggestions or guides for your answers." She walked by each table and handed all three of them sheets. "A reporter from the Jacksonville paper is coming tomorrow and would like to interview a few of you for an article."

"Why us?" Costa asked, voicing what all three were thinking. Of all of the Marines, they were the oldest, which meant they really were the least likely to want the attention an article would give them. The younger guys would fight each other for the chance to do it.

"Because you are the leaders. I've spoken to Coach Ace and he's fine with taking an hour out of your practice time tomorrow to sit down with the reporter."

"I'm sorry," Costa interjected. "We're losing practice time for this?"

"I'm sure as hell not giving up personal time for it," Sweeney shot back, then flushed. "Sorry, ma'am," he mumbled.

"Not a problem." Totally unfazed, Reagan went on. "You three are the most mature and the least likely to go off into tangents thật might, shall we say, highlight potential problems."

"Potential pro . . . oh." Greg nodded. "You want us to forget the vandalism and stuff."

"I do, yes. Someone might see it as a challenge to play copycat, or one-up these childish pranks. No need to give them fuel." She let out a deep breath, then put on one of the fakest smiles he'd ever seen. "Positivity, gentlemen. Keep it positive."

All three flashed her their own equally fake grins of the grin-and-bear-it variety.

Her smile faltered, but she fought to keep it. "Excellent. So review those, and then I thought we could do some role-playing."

Role-playing? He could get behind that. Mentally, Greg dressed her up as a sexy librarian. Not hard, really, just slipped some cat-eye glasses over those pretty eyes and maybe undid a button or three on her shirt. Or maybe stretch reality a little and go for a naughty nurse routine. Some white heels with those stockings that ended mid-thigh with the garter? Or they could try—

"Wake up."

He jolted, slapping the sheet of paper down on his lap to cover his obvious erection as he looked up into Reagan's not-so-amused eyes. "I'm awake."

"You're first," she said, motioning for him to follow her

out the door. One more chance to watch that sexy ass in motion. He followed, grinning over his shoulder at Costa and Sweeney.

"Dibs," he mouthed. Brad rolled his eyes, clearly uncaring. Graham narrowed his, but didn't look overly put out.

"Are you coming?" she asked tightly.

"On your six," he said with a grin and followed her out.

"SHOULD we be worried about that?" Graham asked as he settled back against the wall.

"Worried about what?" Marianne leaned back in her office chair and turned to observe Brad as he iced his knee. She did her best to give him space, but a girlfriend was supposed to worry, wasn't she?

"Hell no, I'm not going to worry." Brad shifted the bag a little to the right and laid down, lacing his hands over his stomach to wait out his twenty. She'd set the timer on her phone the minute he'd put the ice on. "I'm going to enjoy it."

"Enjoy what?" Feeling three steps behind, Marianne made a note in a file and turned to put it back in the drawer.

"She must be sick on love for you or something." Graham gave Brad a nudge with one fist. "Because otherwise I don't know how she missed all the sexual daggers those two were throwing at each other."

"I have her well and truly shielded from any other man's daggers." His tone smug, Brad nudged Graham back. "This is giving me so much chance for payback. He busted my balls all the time over Marianne. Now I get to return the favor."

Marianne sighed and rolled her own eyes, turning toward her computer. "Think I should make a pamphlet on testosterone poisoning and the early warning signs of impending male stupidity?"

"No," both men said in unison.

* * *

HE followed Reagan out to the gym, over to a side farthest away from the locker rooms and training room. In short, they were alone in the empty gym.

She waved to the wall. "Have a seat."

He sat, then waited for her to do the same. Instead, she paced away, then back again. Then repeated the lap three more times. From this position, he had a world-class view of the way her hips and butt moved beneath the snug black pinstripes. Not bad.

"Okay, let's start with an easy one. Where are you from?"

"All over," he answered automatically.

She glanced up from her clipboard. "Military brat?"

"No."

She crossed something off, then continued her pacing. The slim heels of her shoes made a hollow clicking sound. "Care to elaborate on the 'all over' statement?"

"No."

"Tell me about your family."

"Pass."

Exasperated, she whirled. The hand holding the clipboard fisted at her side. She shook the other at him like she was preparing to deck him one. "You're not cooperating. You're not even *pretending* to cooperate."

"This isn't what I signed up for."

"It is now."

"Says who?"

"Says me." With a sigh, one that said she was exhausted, she straightened her suit jacket, then slid down the wall to sit next to him. In what he considered the most unladylike thing he'd ever seen her do, she let her legs sprawl in an ungainly fashion. Probably because she was wearing pants for once. He had no doubts if she wore a skirt, she'd have her knees locked together tighter than a munitions supply chest . . . or not have even tried the move in the first place.

In a conversational tone, she added, "You're making my job difficult."

"My job is to box. Pick another talking monkey."

Though he kept his face turned forward, he could tell she was watching him. His right side tingled from the stare she shot him. But she didn't say a word. Just kept staring for so long he actually felt himself shift a little.

Now that she'd stopped wearing a hole in the floorboards, he could take a moment to appreciate her scent. Fresh, like she'd just showered and then walked through a field of daisies before coming into the gym.

He should have showered and changed before the meeting. His sweat was probably disgusting her.

"Fine," she said after the world's longest stare-down. "I give up."

It was exactly what he'd hoped for, and yet, perversely, he hated it the instant she uttered the words. Because if she gave up, he wouldn't have a reason to tease her, torment her, be around her like they were now. He turned to watch her toss the clipboard and pen in front of her and shut her eyes. "Tonight."

She tilted her head just a little to watch him from beneath sooty lashes. "Tonight what?"

"I'll be coached tonight, at dinner." He smiled a little. "In exchange, I'll play the monkey."

She blinked a few times, then reached over for her clipboard and flipped through several pages. "I don't have anything scheduled for tonight. What dinner?"

"The one I'm taking you out to." He grinned when she just kept staring at him in confusion. "Should we go out or stay in?"

"I . . . don't . . ." She blinked, and he could actually see her mentally brushing away the cobwebs of confusion. Her voice firmed, deepened, and she said, "Out. Definitely out."

"Fine. We can stay in on date number two. I'll pick you up at seven. Text me your address." He hopped up and left before she could argue. Right now, he had the upper hand in the battle because he'd caught her off guard. But she was quick, and the more time he gave her to catch up in the battle, the more ground he lost in the war. She was a challenge, and he liked it.

Liked her. She hadn't been what he'd expected when he'd thought of meeting new people, when he'd thought of having fun, but . . .

Plans could adjust.

He popped into the training room just as his roommate tossed a bag of mostly water into the large stainless steel sink in the corner of the room. Graham looked as if he were taking a nap, propped up against the wall.

"Hey, Sweeney."

His friend sat up, mumbling. "What?"

"Remember those steaks we talked about grilling tonight?"

"Hmm? Oh, yeah. Right. Steaks." As if still dreaming, Sweeney nodded and let his eyes drift closed again.

"Keep mine in the freezer. I've got new plans." He slapped his palm down on the plastic cover, the sound cracking in the quiet room. Graham jolted, nearly falling off the table entirely.

"Wha . . . huh? Steaks?" He glanced at Greg, then at Marianne, who was laughing quietly; and Brad, who was smirking.

"See ya."

"What plans?" Sweeney demanded as he left the room. Greg just kept walking.

CHAPTER

5

Reagan walked straight into Kara's apartment the moment her new friend opened the door. "I didn't know where else to go. I'm sorry."

"That's okay." Kara closed the door behind them and stepped toward her, then froze. "Did you grow?"

"Heels."

"You're always wearing heels," Kara pointed out. "Those are not heels. Those are stilts."

"I needed the confidence boost," Reagan said defensively, then began to pace. "I'm freaking out."

"What's wrong? Do you need wine? Should we call Marianne for reinforcements?"

She shook her head, then let her purse drop to the couch as she walked by. "Your apartment is cute."

Kara looked around. "Thanks."

"Homey, you know? Like you could live here and be comfortable, but not so lived-in it loses its cuteness." Reagan shook her hands, which were now cramping. She wanted to rub them on the thighs of her dress to get rid of the cold sweat but refused to ruin the dress she was wearing. God, she was a hot mess. "It's perfect for you. And now I'm talking in circles."

"I think you're *walking* in circles," Kara added dryly. "You're going to make yourself dizzy."

"No way. I was a cheerleader. I can do the splits at thirty feet. I don't get dizzy." Reagan felt the cold sweat start to run down her back. Awesome. Now her gorgeous black dress would have a weird wet line between her shoulder blades.

"Reagan, what's wrong?"

"Nothing. Everything. No, nothing. Ugh! I don't know!" She stopped in place, squeezed her eyes shut and tried to picture a calm, serene ocean in her mind. Hear the waves, see the waves, feel the waves . . .

And now she had to pee. Fantastic.

"I'm meeting a guy here in fifteen minutes. If he's on time, that is." She mumbled, "His kind tend to be late."

"Meeting who? And why here?"

"Because I *can't* meet him at *my* place!" Reagan just stared at Kara, who stared back with a complete lack of understanding.

"Mom?" A boy of about nine or ten stepped out from the hallway and slid in close to his mother. He wore a hoodie with the front pocket partially ripped off, a pair of jeans with two grass-stained knees and socks that flipped out when he walked. In short, he looked like any other nine-year-old she'd ever met, including her brothers when they'd been growing up. "Who's that?" he asked.

Kara smoothed a hand over his head, and looked into his eyes. Even from their profiles, Reagan could see they were basically clones of each other. "Ignore the crazy lady, Zach, and go finish your homework."

He ran off without a backward glance. Reagan couldn't blame him. Nor could she fault Kara's "crazy lady" comment. She *was* acting crazy. But there were reasons for her elevated craziness.

"Okay, time to stop walking yourself in circles and come sit down." Using a firm grip, and a firmer tone, Kara took hold of Reagan's wrist and pulled her to the couch. They sat down and Reagan was immediately filled with a moment of peace. Must have been the lavender-scented candle on the coffee table. Or maybe the way Kara mothered her without smothering her. She'd needed it.

"I'm meeting Gregory Higgs for dinner." She waited for Kara's exclamation of disbelief or excitement. Something. Anything.

She was met with a calm stare and patience.

Okay then. "Greg Higgs, the Marine? One of the boxers?" When Kara showed no signs of recognition, she added, "Brad Costa's roommate? He showed up the other night with Brad and the tall one, Graham."

"I know," Kara said easily. "And that's what has you so worked up?"

"What if it doesn't go well?" Reagan paused, then voiced the worse option. "What if it *does* go well? Oh my God, I don't know how to date like an adult. I'm only twenty-four!"

"When I was twenty-four, I had a five-year-old. I might not be the person to freak out to about this."

"You're right." She covered her face, doing her best to not smear her makeup in the process. "I'm sorry, you're right. I'm pathetic."

Kara rubbed her back quietly for a moment, just lending the support Reagan desperately needed.

"You're not pathetic, you're having a pathetic moment."

Reagan peered at her through her fingers. Kara shrugged. "What? It works on Zach."

"I've been reduced to a nine-year-old."

"Ten last month."

"Even better."

As the door thudded with a knock, both women startled a little. Kara watched Reagan. Reagan watched the door.

After a minute, the knock came again. Kara asked, "Should I tell him you're not here?"

"No." With a sigh, feeling like she was on her way to meet a firing squad, Reagan picked up her purse.

"I've got it!" Zach slid up to the door, skidding past it just a little in his sock-clad feet.

"Zach, no!" Kara called, but it was too late. Zach opened the door to a very handsome, very confused-looking Greg.

He glanced down at Zach, then leaned back to check the number above the door of the apartment. "Is this 3F?"

"Yeah. Who are you?"

"Zach," Kara scolded as she stepped up beside her son. "Hi, Greg."

He raised a brow. "Hey, Kara. Hold on." He looked at his cell phone, and Reagan assumed he was searching for the text message she'd sent him. "Yup, it says 3F here." He looked at Kara and smiled, and Reagan could feel her knees melt just a little. He wore simple slacks and a button-front shirt. No tie, no sports jacket. Just clean, fresh Greg.

He raised a brow at his phone. "Reagan sent me the wrong address. Do you know hers?"

"I'm here." Reagan clutched her purse and stepped up beside her friend and her friend's son. "Sorry, I knew I was coming over here first so that's why I had you meet me here."

"Huh." Greg shrugged, then handed her a bouquet of flowers. She nearly wobbled on her now-putty legs. "These are for you." He grinned, then shifted them to Kara. "Or maybe they're for you, since you own the place."

"Rent, but that works." Kara took the flowers. "Reagan, I'll put these in water. You can get them when you're done with your . . . whatever," she finished, then pushed Reagan out the door and closed it behind them.

GREG stared open-mouthed at the closed door. He'd only met her a few times, but in his limited knowledge of the woman, she'd been sweet as pie. He hadn't known she'd had a son, but he also wasn't shocked. The lady was a looker, and with that aforementioned sweet disposition, it stood to reason she'd be taken. But that send-off was definitely not sweet.

"She's annoyed with me," Reagan explained, pushing at the hair she'd left down for the evening. It was the first time he could remember seeing it down. The entire thing was a thick curtain of rich chestnut and oak, and he wanted nothing more than to tunnel his fingers through it to feel how heavy it was. How sensitive her scalp was.

In the weak light of the apartment hallway, he took his first look at her. And nearly had to roll his tongue back in his mouth, cartoon-style.

She wore a black dress that hugged her curves in all the right spots, fell loose and swishy where it mattered, left her shoulders and arms bare, and was capped off with the highest damn heels he'd ever seen in his life.

"Those aren't actually real shoes, are they?"

Reagan tipped her left foot to the side just a little. "Why does everyone think I can't walk in these? They're just shoes."

"Honey, on you, those are definitely not *just* anything. It's like the cherry on top of a gorgeous sundae . . . only upside down."

She smiled at that. "Thank you. I think."

He held out his arm, and she looped hers through it. With the stilts, she was now at least two inches taller, and he'd bet his next paycheck she'd done that deliberately. "No flats, huh?"

"They're at the dry cleaners."

"No problem." He walked her to his rental and opened the door for her. His breath hitched a little as the skirt rode up while she arranged her legs in an artful little bend. "Luckily, I'm a guy who doesn't mind being topped by a beautiful woman."

When she glanced at him, shock on her face, he added, "Height-wise, I mean." With a wink, he closed the door. Let that one marinate a little.

* * *

"TELL me about yourself," Reagan asked the moment the waiter took their menus and abandoned their table.

He'd driven them down to Wilmington, partly because he wanted the privacy. But mostly because he wanted an extra hour in the car with her. She'd surprised him by singing along to several songs on the drive, belting out a particularly interesting rendition of Taylor Swift's "Blank Space." He couldn't fault her for trying, or for having some fun.

"That's going to take more than the single drink I'm having with dinner." He saluted her with his glass of draft beer.

With an exasperated sigh, she picked up the wine he'd urged her to order and took a healthy gulp. "You promised to let me coach you if we went out to dinner. I'm coaching. You're not holding up your end of the bargain."

"Hey, call me old-fashioned. I just thought we could get through appetizers before we really got down and dirty with it. Maybe at least wait for salads before grilling me?" He smiled as the waiter set down their stuffed mushrooms. "Still not sure why you think anyone from the Jacksonville newspaper is going to give two rips about any of us individually."

"Human interest is the backbone of our society."

"That sounded suspiciously like a line out of a marketing textbook."

She bit delicately around the edge of one mushroom. Her mouth fascinated him. The way her teeth nipped into the soft skin, how her lips pursed together as she chewed and the way her tongue darted out to catch just the smallest crumb. "You probably already know this, but some people are not all that violent-sport friendly."

"So they shouldn't buy tickets to come watch." He took another mushroom, then froze with it halfway to his mouth as he caught her eyes widening. "What? There's plenty more."

"That's exactly the wrong thing to say." She brushed her hands off on her napkin then dug through her tiny matchbox-sized purse and drew out a notepad.

She'd brought a notepad. On their date. A *notepad*.

Maybe she didn't consider it a date. He'd been vague when getting her to agree because he'd known she would have automatically said no at the D word. But she had to have picked up on that fact by now, hadn't she?

When she pulled a pencil the same size as the ones they gave you with your golf club at Putt-Putt courses and started to write, he realized no. Definitely not.

He waited until she pushed at her hair for the third time before he reached over and looped one lock of mahogany strands behind her ear. She jolted, then looked up at him as if surprised to remember he was still there.

"Sorry." She gave him a sheepish smile and slid the notebook to the side. Not away, he noted, but to the side. "I get a little caught up. This is just the sort of thing I really like."

"Making goons like me look good?"

She blinked like an owl then shook her head. "No! Oh my gosh, no, that's not what I meant."

He laughed and caught her hand, holding it in his against the table. "I'm joking. I know. I can see when someone's excited about their work."

"Is that like you and being a Marine?" She looked at the plate of mushrooms and he saw her hand twitch, but she held back.

He scooped two more, set one on her plate before she could argue and took a bite out of his. "Not really. The Marine Corps is a passion for some people. It's an escape for others."

"What is it for you?"

"A job."

She wrinkled her nose at that, and he nudged his chair closer to hers. "What about yours? How did you get into PR?"

"Oh, I love talking. My mom says I was born talking." As if remembering some long-forgotten memory, she smiled.

"She says her mind has me coming out of the womb talking, though logically she knows that's not right. But from the start, I was chatting and trying to get to know people."

"Stranger danger?" he asked, enjoying this little private piece of her life she gave him.

She scoffed. "Didn't exist. Literally. In my town, there were no strangers."

"Tell me about yourself." He settled back a little as the waiter brought their meals, disappointed he didn't have a clear table to lean over so he could see her better.

She opened her mouth, then shut it again and glanced at her notebook.

"You need cue cards to answer the question?"

She laughed. "No, it's just that I'm supposed to ask *you* that question. In fact, I already did."

"So show me how it works." When she raised a brow while cutting off a piece of her steak—praise Jesus, a woman who ate real food on a date—he gave her his most innocent grin. "I'm observing. Show me the way, great leader. Teach me."

"Stop, stop." She held up her fork as if she were about to flick a piece of broccoli at him. He wanted her to do it. This was the most relaxed, the most unwound he'd ever seen her. He loved it. "I'll tell you. But you have to promise to try in return."

"Tell you what." Greg reached across the table and stabbed the piece of steak she'd just cut off for herself. When she let out a huffy breath, he chewed and swallowed on a moan. "Yup, that's good."

"I know. That's why I ordered it." She scooted her plate closer to the edge, as if that could stop him if he wanted another bite.

He'd rather have a bite or two out of her.

"I'll answer one question, of my own choosing, if you hand me the list. But first, you have to answer the 'tell me about yourself' one."

She thought about that for a moment, one finger tapping

her chin. "Your interview is tomorrow, and you'll only let me help you with one question."

"If you hate how I handle it, you'll know not to let me do the gig tomorrow." Which would be a solid win for him, as far as he was concerned.

"And if I don't agree?"

He watched the heat in her eyes, how they fired up at the mere hint of a challenge.

He leaned forward just a little. "I suggest you do."

OH, that arrogant, cocky, egotistical, sexy . . .

No, not sexy.

Okay yes, sexy.

Reagan glared at Greg across the table. "You suggest I do?"

"It's either one question, or none." He lifted one shoulder and let it drop again, as if he couldn't care less. But she had a suspicion his lax attitude was really a front. That if she called him on it and made him answer a question, he'd sweat through it.

"Fine. Deal."

He held out his hand for the notebook, which she grudgingly handed over. Luckily it was brand-new, so nothing personal was scribbled in the margins or anything embarrassing, like "Pap smear, 2 pm Thursday." She shuddered.

"Cold?" He glanced up, then reached out a hand to rub down her arm while he kept flipping through the questions.

Another guy would have made her sure the whole arm-rub thing was a move. But Greg barely seemed to register the action, which made it all the more sweet in her mind. These were the little touches she watched Marianne and Brad exchange. The light caress over the back of Marianne's neck while she was hunched over her desk. The simple brush of fingertips across his knee before he iced. Covert, second-nature things that kept them connected.

But Brad and Marianne were actually in a relationship. Reagan was simply on a nice business dinner. So really, she should grow up and move on.

"You can start now with the whole answering thing." He looked up at her, finger marking the place he'd left off on her list of potential questions. "Tell me about yourself."

She folded her hands in front of her plate and cleared her throat. "I was born and raised in Wisconsin, with my mother and four brothers. I—"

"Do you do that on purpose?"

She stopped, then looked down at her hands, at her lap and back up at him. He studied her, and she had no clue what he meant. "I don't understand."

"Your voice. Do you do that voice thing on purpose?"

One hand flew to the base of her throat automatically. "What's wrong with my voice?"

"Nothing at all. It just gets deeper when you're in business mode." Greg's eyes danced as he watched her. "It's sexy."

"My business voice is sexy?" Panic wanted to fight its way in. Was this how men were viewing her when she made professional phone calls? As a sex kitten? Did they think she was doing it on purpose? "Oh my God."

"Don't freak out." He laid a hand over her forearm, thumb caressing over the skin inside, up to her wrist and back again. "Seriously, it's not a bad thing. And frankly, I'm probably partial because, well." He winked. "You know."

"You're a horndog?" she said dryly, then gasped and covered her mouth.

He laughed. Then when she thought he was done, he started chuckling and built right back up to a belly-shaking laugh.

Reagan glanced around, saw people watching their table with avid interest and kicked him under the table. "Shhh! People are staring!" she hissed.

He finally quieted down enough to wipe at the tears at the corners of his eyes. "You kill me. Seriously, you do."

"Such a compliment. However will I resist," she muttered as she stabbed her steak with something akin to rage.

"I'm hoping you don't."

He saw by the way her eyes widened for just a second before she looked back down at her plate that she'd heard him.

CHAPTER

6

"I 'm not sure how you did it," Reagan said as they walked to Greg's car, "but I didn't actually get any answers out of you."

"I'm good, what can I say?"

"Maybe you should be the one in PR. Oh!" Realizing she'd left her notebook behind, she turned to go. Greg caught her wrist and pulled her against him.

"I've got your notebook."

Thanks to her heels, she was nearly two inches taller than him. She expected to feel awkward, or maybe powerful, with the height advantage. But her knees were nearly water as he nuzzled his nose against her jaw. Maybe her brain was liquefying, too, because she actually felt herself lean into the caress. His warm breath against her neck sent a tingle of gooseflesh racing over her exposed skin. And as his arm wrapped around the small of her back to pull her tighter against him, there wasn't a single protest in her mind. He could have laid her down on the asphalt and it wouldn't have occurred to her to voice an alternative.

"We should get going."

He stepped back, and she was left to blink at the immediate lack of warmth. "Going . . ." was all she could say.

"Long drive home, and we've got work tomorrow." He shifted his hold on her wrist lower to lace his fingers with hers. "Besides, I have to be well rested for my media debut, right?"

"Uh-huh," she said stupidly, following as he walked to the car. Had she really been so naïve to think he'd start putting the moves on her in a parking lot? No, that would be ridiculous. And she was nothing if not practical.

In everything but footwear, anyway.

When he opened her door, she turned. It was wrong, and she shouldn't press, but she had to know. "Why did you stop?"

His smile was slow, and it sent alarm bells ringing in her head, but she wasn't quite sure which ones. The alarm that said *Run now!* or the one that said *Supper's on, come and get it!*

"You were expecting it."

"I . . . okay." She crossed her arms over her chest and leaned against the back door. "So what if I was?"

"When I kiss you the first time, it's not going to be expected. And it's not going to make you feel the way you *think* you should feel."

Reagan turned that over in her head for a moment as she got in the car. She let it marinate while he drove them out of the parking lot, and half the way home.

"How do you know what I think I should feel?"

"Legs," he said without taking his eyes off the road, "you've got TTBP all over you."

"I'm almost afraid to ask, but . . . TTBP?"

He grinned, his face illuminated in the headlights of a passing truck. "Trying to Be Professional. You play the starched business lady during the day, and you tried to bring her out tonight. But you've got a wild streak you're trying to keep hidden for one reason or another. When you're ready to let that loose, then we'll see."

"That's insulting," she said with a huff, staring straight ahead. She couldn't even get into lip-syncing along with the radio. But curiosity had her asking, "And how do you know I even have a wild streak?"

"Shoes," he answered quickly, without hesitation. "And partly because of your endearingly horrible lip-syncing on the way down . . . but mostly the shoes."

"Why does everyone comment on my shoes?"

"Because they make a statement. And you know that, or you wouldn't pick them. You'd wear some flats or plain ones with just a tiny heel. Or you know, some white running shoes with those scrunchy, puffy socks that come halfway up your calves."

"Uh, the eighties called. They want their working woman stereotype back."

He just snorted.

"And you never answered an interview question."

"That's because all these interview questions are boring." He reached into his pants pocket—which took a little maneuvering—and tossed the notebook on her lap. "Who cares where I'm from or why I'm in the Marines or why I joined the boxing team? They should care about my stats or how I box or what I do when I'm down and have to rally for a come-from-behind victory. What matters is on the mat."

"You want to get to know my wild side, away from my work persona. Why is it so weird to think others might want to know you beyond the ring?"

"Because nobody cares."

She watched him—difficult as it was—in the darkness for a bit, and realized he wasn't being facetious or difficult for the sake of being annoying. He honestly believed it didn't matter.

"I care," she said softly.

"To peddle some human interest story?"

That stung, but it wasn't completely unwarranted. "I care because I like you. And this dinner—"

"Date."

"This dinner—"

"Date," he said more firmly. "Can you just call it what it is?"

"I'm sorry, I don't recall you asking me on a date. I remember being bamboozled into coming out in order to get my job done."

"Well, I did. You must have slept through it." He reached over and squeezed her knee. "Damn shame. It was a good story. One for the grandkids, I'm sure."

"Uh-huh." She took a chance and put her hand over his. When his fingers curled up and caught hers, she smiled. He couldn't see, so it wouldn't hurt anything. "You still have to answer one of the questions."

"My prematch routine," he said, in a monotone voice like a seventh grader reading a report off of cue cards as he answered one of her questions, "includes lots of protein that morning, a light workout to stretch and establish muscle memory and some mental moves before I step into the ring."

She waited a beat. "Wow. That was inspirational."

"You want inspiration, you pay a thousand bucks and go to a business conference. You said one question, I answered one question."

And he picked the single most impersonal one to give, too.

"Fine." She settled back in her seat and prepared for the rest of the drive home.

"Fine . . . what?"

The barest hint of trepidation colored his question. She bit her cheek to keep the smile from her voice. "Fine, that's all. You're a smart guy. I'm sure you can handle yourself tomorrow at the interview."

He seemed to take this news with slightly less happiness than she thought. "You're giving up? I thought we talked about that this afternoon."

"Not giving up. No, just looking for a new angle." She grazed her thumb over the back of his hand. His fingers tightened on hers in response. "What will it take to get you to let me coach you?"

"Another meal, another question."

The answer came so quickly, she knew he hadn't come up with it on the fly. "If you want another date—"

"You said it was dinner," he teased.

"Date," she repeated firmly, using his own word now, "then why don't you just ask? Drop the game and let me coach you, then we can keep them separate."

"Not as fun."

"Why does it have to be fun?"

He lifted her hand to his lips and pressed a kiss to her fingertips. "Fun's the reason for everything."

FUN is the reason for everything?

Reagan tossed her keys on the kitchen counter and let her purse slide across it until it hit the microwave. Since her kitchen was the size of a shoebox, that slide was approximately seven inches long. She opened the refrigerator, hoping there was still a bottle of water in there. The door stuck, and it took her three tries to get it open before she could check.

Stupid landlord. The damn man was supposed to look at that. And the broken window she'd had to board up herself. And the toilet that flushed only when it was in the mood. And the hot water heater that should be more aptly called the whatever-temperature-I-want water heater.

The place was a hole, no doubt about it. But it was all she could afford, thanks to an entry-level salary and student loan debt that would make a mortgage look like small potatoes.

And that was exactly why she didn't want Greg picking her up at her place. He'd either be scared off, or he'd feel sorry for her. That was definitely not what she wanted.

Toeing off her shoes, she picked them up and walked

them to the closet, placing them reverently in their shoebox and sliding them out of sight. It was the only way she could justify buying the expensive heels . . . she took excellent care of them and expected them to last her years.

Her clothing she dealt with a little more recklessly. It landed in a heap somewhere close to but not really by the hamper. Good enough. Slipping into some comfortable sweatpants, she went to her laptop—another post-graduation splurge—and decided to do some digging on Greg Higgs.

That was totally legit, right? Not only was he someone she needed to know more about for professional reasons, but she was, apparently, dating him.

Did one date count as "dating?" Maybe. Or maybe not.

Either way, it wasn't sketchy. It was just good business, no matter which angle she came at it from.

Not that it did her any good. She came up empty. His Face-book page was so generic—funny *SNL* skits, memes and posts about sports—that she couldn't glean much of his personality from it. He either didn't have a social media profile on any of the other major platforms, or he was so good at his privacy settings, he was all but invisible by regular searching means. From a PR standpoint, that was a pretty good deal. Guys who kept a low social media profile were often the least worrisome. From the dating standpoint . . . dammit. She wanted more information.

So she went back to the tiny desk she'd found at the local thrift store for fifteen bucks and brought back to her place, found the files of the team members and did exactly what she'd been doing the last few nights.

She opened Greg's file and stared at his ID photo, along with the mere trickle of information he'd listed on his form. The exercise was pointless. It wasn't as if his photo was going to magically start talking, Hogwarts-style, and give her all the answers she sought. No mysteries of the universe lay in that file folder. But it didn't stop her from looking at it every night and wondering, just a little, if this was for her.

This job. This area of the country. This man.

He'd asked her out on a date. He'd charmed her. He'd enticed her. He'd made her laugh. And yet, in the end, he'd kept her at arm's length when it came to the physical.

Cautious? Or callous . . .

Her gut said cautious. Reagan set the file down, forcing herself to slip it back into the pile. But she could only continue on for so long—both professionally and personally—without some give on his part.

For now, she had to get some sleep. There was an interview to prep for, and it certainly wasn't going to prep for itself.

GREG watched as Reagan tapped her foot on the floor outside Coach Ace's office. She checked her watch, leaned her chin into her palm and stared off into the distance, with that damn toe sending an SOS signal across the floorboards. Brad was inside the coach's office, talking to that reporter. Sweeney had already had his turn. Greg knew he was next. Knew that any minute, Reagan would walk across the floor in those sinful heels and skirt to tap him on his sweaty shoulder and ask him to follow her.

Where he would sit in near silence with a reporter from the local paper who likely couldn't wait to get out of there and go write about something actually interesting. Because Marines who boxed couldn't be all that fun.

Coach Cartwright walked up behind him and pushed at the back of his head. "If you came for the scenery, we should have had you buy a ticket at the door."

"Sorry, Coach." He went back to his speed bag, but kept one eye on Reagan when he could.

Her cute little agitated movements caught his eye again and again. The dangling foot jangle. The watch-checking. The switching of which hand her chin rested in. The hair debate. Up in the clip, down around her shoulders, half-back . . . she'd done it all in the last ten minutes.

When Greg saw the door open and his roommate step out, shaking the hand of a guy in his fifties with a bit of a paunch, wire-frame glasses and a graying beard, Greg felt his gut tighten. He was next, and there was nowhere for him to hide. So he turned his back on the whole thing and prayed they'd forget about him.

When he heard Reagan's voice behind him, he knew he wouldn't be so lucky.

"They practice here at least twice a day," she said, leading the reporter through the different stations set up. "And typically have at least one cardio session as well, either here or on the outdoor track."

"Hmm," was all the reporter said. He didn't even write anything down in his notebook that Greg could see.

Pay attention, dude. You're lucky she's giving your ass the time of day.

Reagan's determined smile was in place as she pointed to a group of Marines running along the catwalk upstairs. "As you can see, a lot of their training has nothing to do with the ring itself. It's a great deal of discipline and will of mind. Training the entire athlete. It makes boxing and the Marine Corps a perfect sort of fit, I think."

"Ah."

Greg could all but hear her back teeth grinding as the guy stuffed his notebook in the bag he had looped over his shoulder. The reporter wasn't even trying, the bastard.

"And not to disparage our fellow service members and their own boxing teams, but I feel confident saying we have a winning squad here." She pointed toward the catwalk. Several Marines—Greg included—followed her gesture with their eyes. Up there stood three of the younger Marines, holding what looked like string. "You're also here for a special moment."

"Oh?" the reporter asked, as if she'd just told him she'd had salmon for lunch.

"Yes, we're unveiling the new banners for past wins at the

All Military games. The old ones were faded, and we wanted to move them in here so the guys could see them while they practiced." With a grin, she cupped her hands around her mouth and shouted, "Let them go, boys!"

She was in her element. Despite the reporter's lack of enthusiasm, he could see Reagan was enjoying herself. This was something she loved. The nerves from before were gone, and she could have been speaking to the president himself with the poise she showed.

Time in the gym stopped, everyone froze and they watched as one the unveiling of the banners. The ones that would list the previous years the Marine boxing team had taken top place in the All Military games. Their past, which would stay in the gym as a daily reminder of the legacy they had to live up to.

He heard a quiet countdown from the three Marines above, then, at one, they released the strings they'd been holding and the banners unfurled over the gym.

The first thing that came to mind was, *Wow, those are intense.*

The second thing that came to mind, Brad was already voicing behind him.

"Are those . . . aww, shit."

CHAPTER

7

SPLAT!

Reagan shrieked, several Marines cursed or yelled, and the reporter gasped as the gym floor exploded in color. Greg barely covered his face before he felt the slick slime of thick, wet . . . whatever coating his skin.

"Shit," he muttered, keeping his face covered until he knew it was over. After another few seconds, he risked looking.

The gym—and most of its inhabitants—were covered in paint. Red, yellow, blue and green for the most part. Greg looked up, and found three Marines standing frozen on the catwalk above, mouths gaping open like guppies. Something told him they were just as shocked as the rest of them down below.

Someone coughed, and he turned to find Reagan and the reporter. Her face was largely untouched, as it seemed she'd protected herself as best she could, but the rest of her was covered in green and yellow paint. From her hair to the shoes she worshipped so much, she looked like she'd been on the wrong end of a paintball war.

The reporter hadn't been as quick on the draw. He slowly reached up and removed his glasses. His eyes—the only part of his face not covered in paint—reminded him of a raccoon in reverse. And Greg did his damndest not to laugh, going so far as to turn around and wipe a hand over his mouth—in the pretext of removing paint—to keep from bursting out. Most of his reserve came from knowing Reagan would shove those paint-covered shoes straight up his ass if he did.

"I am . . . so . . ." Reagan's hands shook as she reached out for the reporter's glasses. "So sorry. I don't even know how that happened."

"Marines!" barked Coach Ace. "Get your asses down here *now*!" He coughed and spit a little as some paint dripped into his mouth.

Coach Ace on a normal day was something to behold. Coach Ace, livid and covered in red paint?

Greg wouldn't have traded a million dollars to be in those three Marines' shoes.

The three young Marines scrambled toward the staircase, likely fighting each other to not be the last one down.

"Is this sort of . . ." The reporter coughed out a little paint as he took his glasses back from Reagan. ". . . spectacle how you welcome the press? Or is it just your idea of fun?"

"I can assure you, sir, this was not intentional." She handed him his glasses back, looking around quickly before taking one of his arms. "Let's just head into the locker room—the ladies' locker room should be empty—and get some towels."

"If it wasn't intentional, then what was it?" The man stood his ground, looking around.

The three Marines burst through the stairwell doors and immediately slipped on the paint. One landed flat on his ass; the other two slipped around a few feet before gaining purchase.

"Coach, that wasn't us!" one insisted before he managed to skid-slide his way to where Coach Ace stood.

"It was a booby trap!" the other insisted.

"Just like the slashed tires and the wrecked training room!" the third, still on his hands and knees attempting to get up like a man who'd fallen at an ice rink, put in. "Someone's out to get us!"

"Slashed tires?" Showing the first signs of life since he'd walked into the gym, the reporter's paint-coated eyebrows rose. "Booby traps? What's this all about?"

"Oh, just some young Marines with silly imaginations." She laughed, though to Greg the sound was high-pitched enough to border on hysterical. "Let's go get cleaned up first, then we can see about finishing that last interview. In the meantime," she added, talking over her shoulder, voice raised, "Coach Ace is going to get things under control out here!"

They all waited, frozen, until the outer door to the never-used women's locker room shut. Then it was as if someone had opened a box of drunk magpies. Everyone began walking around—or sliding, depending on the traction they could gain—chattering at once, accomplishing exactly nothing.

"Quiet," Coach Ace said, and the tone carried more than the sound. Everyone settled down, even the three moronic Marines who had blurted out that junk in front of the reporter. "You three, in my office now." He watched as they made their way toward his door. "And don't sit on anything!"

"I'll go call maintenance," Coach Cartwright said.

"Coach Willis!"

"Back here, Ace." The short man, who resembled a bearded Danny DeVito, held up a hand in the back of the gym. He stood in front of a group of men who had been in the weight room, sheltered from the paint splatter.

"Avoid the paint, take those guys out back and have them wait outside while we get this figured out. Nobody leaves," he said in a deadly voice. "The rest of you, do your best to track as little paint as possible outside. We're hosing off."

* * *

REAGAN sent the reporter on his way, after lying through her teeth, repeatedly, about sabotage in the gym. It was her worst nightmare. She'd expected questions about violence in athletics. About wasting taxpayers' money on sports when they should be training for combat or downsizing the budget. About a dozen other potentially negative-seeming stories any media might throw at her, to give it all a positive spin.

But no. She didn't get to do any of that. She got to wipe paint off a newspaperman's face and apologize profusely, then lie outright about not having a clue what had happened or why.

Well, not entirely a lie. More of a fib. She certainly had no clue why the boxing team was being targeted, or by whom. But when he'd asked about the slashed tires and the wrecked training room . . .

Oh, everyone has to deal with a flat tire now and then. I had one last month! Yes, yes, the training room was broken into, but nothing was stolen. Just some mischief. The MPs— that's military police—yes, of course you know that—are on it, but think it was just teenage pranks.

Okay, she'd evaded with creative storytelling. That sounded better, didn't it?

She stared at herself in the mirror of the locker room. Her eyebrows were crusty with dried paint, her hair was a crunchy mess around her shoulders, her suit was definitely ruined, and her shoes . . . Oh, her beautiful shoes. She rose on her toes, experimentally, and then settled her weight back down. The squish echoed through the empty bathroom. They were full of paint, despite having wiped them down with damp paper towels.

No, nothing about this sounded better, no matter how she spun it.

She took a deep breath, then stepped out into the gym. And realized the men had completely vacated the premises. She walked over to a maintenance worker who was on his hands and knees, wiping up a trail of paint close to the exit. She didn't envy him his job. "Excuse me, did you see where the boxing team went?"

He looked up for a moment, then hooked a thumb toward the back exit of the gym. "Out back."

Okay, they were still here. She still had time to ream three baby Marines and give the entire team a crash course in What Not to Say 101. She hustled toward the back, wincing as each step squished a bit. Ew.

And opened her door to what might be considered the single girl's paradise.

Marines, stripped down to their skivvies, were hosing each other down in the employee parking lot. The few who hadn't gotten paint-bombed were manning hoses while wearing their gym shorts, barefoot. Those they blasted with water stood on towels as the strength of the garden hose power washed the paint away. Nearby, others toweled down from a recent spritzing. Their clothes lay in heaps of color, soaked.

As she watched, the Marines rotated and still-paint colored men took their places on the towels while the others shuffled off to dry.

The door behind her opened and closed again, and she heard Marianne laugh. "Where's a girl's camera when she needs one?"

"It's like a freaking calendar out here. There's February," Reagan said, nodding in the direction of one Marine who bent at the waist and tunneled his fingers through his hair to rinse it out.

"Looks like he's giving September a run for his money," Marianne added, using her elbow to indicate a good-looking man whose dark skin gleamed while he toweled from the feet up.

Brad wandered over, walking carefully over the pavement in his bare feet. "Are they grabbing our bags from the gym?"

"Yup." She patted his cheek—blessedly clean—once, then looked at Reagan. "My interns are gathering up everyone's bags, which should have their street clothes and hopefully some shoes.

"Good idea." Reagan fought to keep her eyes on the men's faces as they moved around her. Hard . . . so hard. "Whose idea was this to come back here instead of using the locker room?"

"Coach Ace's. Said he didn't want to cause more a mess than we had to." Brad vigorously rubbed a towel over his short-cropped hair. It dried almost instantly. Not fair. "Cold, but effective. Plus, saved the drains in the locker room. They already suck. I can't imagine what putting this much paint down them would do."

"Considerate," Marianne added. "Oh, look, November's getting started."

"Huh?" Brad turned—well, they *all* turned—to watch the Marine Reagan thought was named Tribalt step into the spray. "Oh, Jesus H. You've got to be kidding me."

"Don't worry. You're the only calendar I want, January through December," Marianne said with an amused gleam in her eyes.

"Better be," Brad muttered.

"But I have to help Reagan build her own calendar. Just because I'm a one-man planner doesn't mean she can't diversify her months." Marianne laughed as Brad growled, dancing out of the way as he threatened to toss his sopping wet towel at her.

"I'm good being a one-man planner, myself," Reagan said absentmindedly, watching Greg take his turn under the water. It was like he didn't even feel the icy blast, the way he turned around, his movements economical and efficient. He was a get-in-get-out shower taker, she guessed.

But that didn't mean, for the short time he doused himself off, she couldn't marvel at the scenery.

The way his biceps bulged as he stretched to wash off all the paint, how his fingers disturbed his almost too-long hair, spiking it up as he scrubbed through, the way his butt tightened under the black boxer briefs when he turned to wash his front . . .

"Uh-huh." Marianne snorted. "I think you found your calendar already."

Reagan chose to say nothing, lest she incriminate herself. She patted her flaming hot cheeks. "It's so warm out here."

"Right. I often think fifty-nine and partly cloudy is so warm, too." With a dry voice, Marianne added, "It's not the weather that's got you all hot and bothered."

Coach Ace walked over, his own tennis shoes squishing a little as he came by. He was dripping wet but still wore all his clothes, as if he'd chosen to keep them on while hosing off. "How pissed was the reporter?"

"Not too much," she started, then shrugged when he lifted one brow. "Okay, very. I have a feeling our byline at this point will be less than complimentary."

"Don't care about that too much, as long as it doesn't affect the team."

"But it might," she pointed out. "If the boxing team is considered a liability, they could always shut it down without warning." And that would be the worst-case scenario for Reagan. Her first adult job, and she'd managed to run the entire program straight into the ground. "Or they could change up coaching staff, or make you start all over with new Marines, or—"

"I get the point. We need to remain in the good graces of the reporting population." With a heavy sigh, the coach crossed his arms. Arms that were, in Reagan's opinion, more like tree trunks than limbs. "What next, PR expert?"

She almost argued at the "expert" label, then decided not to. "Before they leave, I need to speak with all of them. Very quick, just a short spurt on how to handle this little"—she looked at the colorful pile of abandoned clothes—"snafu, shall we say."

"We shall." His voice said he caught her sarcasm.

"From there, I'll meet with everyone individually this week and do a quick coaching session one-on-one. I'd only planned to do that with the guys who were getting the most airtime, but thanks to a few somebodies," she added, staring daggers at the three idiots with big mouths who stood off to the side, handing out towels, "we need to be more proactive. I'll try not to disrupt your practices too much."

"I think we're past that." With another heavy sigh, he pushed away from the wall and walked toward the center of the drying Marines. "Gather round, everyone. You, too, once you're finished rinsing him off," he added to the last pair using a hose.

After another three minutes, they all waited. "Ms. Robilard has some stuff she needs to share with you. You're going to listen, you're going to absorb and you're not going to make another mistake on sharing the inner workings of this team with an outsider again. Understand?"

The group gave a combined "Oo-rah!" in answer, and Reagan felt the hairs on her arms stand. She loved it when they did that.

Coach Ace stepped to the side and motioned for her to take his spot. She did, cleared her throat, then realized she was now speaking to a group of mostly naked, dripping-wet Marines.

This was so not covered in her public speaking courses.

"You know," she began, going on instinct, "when people say to picture your audience in their underwear, I don't think this is what they had in mind. If they did, we'd never get through our speeches."

The group laughed, and she caught Greg watching her with an approving gaze. He winked at her, and she knew she'd made the right call to start with humor.

If he kept looking at her like that, she might think she could do just about anything.

GREG set down his laundry basket and groaned. That paint had been a bitch to get out of his clothes. Three rounds in the washer—not including the prerinse in the bathroom sink—before he'd been able to dry them.

He caught himself about to put them in a duffle under his bed, hesitated, then started to put his clothes in the drawers instead. Not two weeks ago, he would have repacked it in his suitcase, just in case. There was no sense of permanence with the team, with these men. Just fun. Now, he'd be damned if they sent him home.

A quick knock on his bedroom door heralded his roommate. Turning, he pushed the drawer closed with his hip and found Brad, hair still wet from a shower, watching him. "How long did it take you to get the paint out of your ears?"

"Ears were no problem. It was the gap in my waistband where it seemed to seep in and make its way to unfortunate places."

Greg sucked in a breath. "Ouch."

"Yeah. No kidding." With a shake of his head, Brad wandered around Greg's room a bit.

Greg waited, but his roommate said nothing. "Need something?"

"You used to do this to me all the time. Just returning the favor." With a smart-ass smile, Brad plopped down on the bed and crossed his ankles, making himself comfortable. "Plans tonight?"

"Yes and no."

"Sounds like you haven't asked her out yet."

"Her?" Greg went for innocent, maybe slightly confused, but one look from Brad had him giving up the charade. "I haven't called her, no. She's got a lot on her plate with the paint and the reporter and fixing that whole issue."

"Damn big issue. Gonna take her longer than one night to get to it."

"No kidding." Greg waited a beat. "What's your point?"

"My point is, a night off's not going to kill her. Call her."

"Hey, Captain Cupid, who are you and what have you done with my roommate?" He ducked the pillow Brad threw at him. "Come on, man. I just made the bed."

"Good Marines make their beds when they first get out of them."

"I'd state the obvious, but I won't."

Brad seemed to shrug that off. They both knew he would have just made fun of Brad's anal retentive tendencies. "She's smart, she's hot—"

"Watch it," Greg growled.

"Oh, piss off. You know I've got my own woman. Just stating a fact. And for some reason, she isn't totally repulsed by you."

There was more between them than just "not repulsed." But he kept quiet.

"So go call Reagan Robilard and take the lady out. She could probably use a good distraction tonight after the day she's had. Let her get loose. She'll have enough shit to deal with tomorrow."

"She'll just bitch at me about some conflict of interest or other bullshit."

"We thought that. Marianne and I hid our dating for way longer than necessary. And now you have no excuse."

"Damn," he muttered.

"Afraid of rejection?"

Greg threw the pillow back at his smirking roommate. "I think I liked you better when you were a standoffish jerk."

"Me, too. But here we are. And it's your fault I'm more chatty, anyway."

"I'm asking her, I'm asking her." Greg pulled his cell phone out of his pocket and waved it. "But if she says she's tired, I'm not pushing. She's had a rough day."

"I don't doubt it." Brad waited a beat. "But she won't say she's tired."

That made Greg think twice. "Why?"

Brad stood, and Greg noticed him favoring his knee just a little on one side. "Because you'll find some way or another to convince her to throw caution to the wind. To seize the moment. To carpe diem. It's what you do. You're the social one. So"—he finished as he went to the door—"go be social." With that, he closed Greg's door behind him.

"Go be social," he mocked. After letting his thumb hover over the call button on his phone, he switched to text and sent her a message.

Coward? You betcha.

She responded less than sixty seconds later, exactly how he'd guessed. Tired, overworked, needed some rest and time to go over notes.

Greg: All work and no play makes Jill a dull girl.

Reagan: I can handle being dull. I can't handle putting work off. Thanks, though.

See, Costa? You don't know everything. She was going to reject his offer. But at least he'd put it out there.

Just as he was about to put his phone down, he tried one more thing.

Greg: You can ask me one more question, if you let me buy you dessert.

There was a long pause, to the point where he wondered if she'd put her phone down and didn't hear it alert with the text. He gave up and set his on the bedside table and went to the drawer where he kept takeout menus.

And nearly broke land speed records racing back to grab it when it beeped with a text.

Reagan: Dessert only, my pick and we call it quits early.

Bingo. Before he could stop it, he felt a smile creep across his face. The one thing destined to get her out of her work funk was . . . work.

He could choose to be offended by that, and see it as a negative that she only wanted to spend time with him if she could call it productive. That being out with him wasn't reason enough. Or he could see it as a positive that she was *too* tempted by him, and using work as an excuse made her feel better about stepping over that boundary.

He was an optimist, after all.

Greg: DEAL.

CHAPTER

8

Reagan waited in the back corner of the popular café-style yogurt bar. She'd arrived early, notebook ready, and scoped out the offerings. Frozen yogurt was the least of the dessert sins she could think of. There was a fat-free, dairy-free yogurt that looked tempting . . .

Oh, who the hell was she kidding? That thing looked like pink glue.

But hey, anything fat-free, dairy free, shame-and-guilt free had to be good for you, right?

"This is an interesting choice."

She jerked her head up as Greg slid into the small chair across the tiny bistro-style table. Why did the man have to make a simple polo shirt and jeans look sinful? "What's wrong with it?"

"Nothing, I guess. I just thought you'd be someone to pick something a little more . . ." He glanced around the room, at the bright lights, brighter colors and several tables full of screaming kids. "I don't know, adult?"

"Frozen yogurt is very adult," she said, biting the inside

of her cheek to keep from smiling. "It's practically a health food."

He stared at her. "Uh-huh. And that's why you can dump a bowl of peanut butter cups on top of it and they weigh it by the pound? Because of the health benefits?"

"Exactly." She left her purse and notebook there—the café was small enough she didn't worry about it—and went to the starting line where the cups were. "Have you been here before?"

"A few times. You?"

"First time here. But there was one near my apartment in college. Very popular place." She'd gone there a few times to study, when the lights in her apartment had gone off for nonpayment. The owners had been sweet and let her sit at a corner table to work even though she almost never bought anything.

Greg waited for her to grab the provided cups—which were big enough to hold three baked potatoes—and pick out her flavor. She let three seconds' worth of pink glue plop into her cup and walked to the register. She passed by Greg, who was on flavor number two, when he snagged her elbow.

"What the hell is that?"

"Strawberry," she answered defensively.

"That is definitely not strawberry. That's nothing. There's, like, a thimble-full in there. Go get more."

"I don't need more." Really, the man was exasperating.

He finished the flavor he was on—cookies and cream—and stepped over to layer on some key lime pie yogurt.

"Uh, that combo doesn't sound appetizing," she pointed out, in case he had misread the sign.

"That's half the fun. Coming up with some weird combination that will make the employees gag."

She stared at him blandly. "You were one of those children who enjoyed putting some of every soda in his cup at concession stands, weren't you?"

He winked. "Bet you can't top this one."

She could. But really . . . "I'm good."

"Oh, man. And here I thought you'd be more creative than me." His disappointed voice grated against her nerves.

"Sucks to be wrong. Oh, well."

"Look, it's not *that* disgusting. There's worse combinations out there."

He looked her in the eyes, nearly nose to nose, and whispered, "Prove it."

Something inside her clicked, and suddenly she was seven years old with her two older brothers double-dog daring her and her younger two brothers betting she would chicken out.

Oh. *Oh*, it was so on. She pulled away from him and started the hunt for the most repulsive combination of flavors. No, not just flavors, she reminded herself. They had syrups and toppings, too. The nastiness could not be avoided.

Ten minutes later, with her massive cup nearly overflowing with yogurt, she put it on the scale at the register. Next to hers, Greg set his own malformation of dessert. They both burst out laughing as the cashier made a Mr. Yuk face at their creations.

"Now the trick is," Greg said as they carried their beloved treats to their table, "we have to eat this thing without choking."

Oh, God. She hadn't actually thought that through when she'd been swirling vanilla fudge with tropical punch and topping it with Jujubes, hot fudge and making what first looked like a smiley face in whipped cream but now that it had melted, sort of resembled a phallic symbol.

"Your face," Greg said on a gasp. "Seriously, priceless. We don't have to eat it."

Well, now it had become a thing of honor. She did her best to brave the coming storm, scooped up a healthy bite and tasted.

"You don't have to—"

"Oh," she breathed. "That's not bad."

He raised a skeptical brow. "That's a joke, right?"

"It's not my first choice, but it's not as horrific as I thought it would be." She grinned and took another bite. "Try yours," she added, pointing to his concoction with her spoon.

He didn't look convinced, but she could tell he wasn't about to be shown up. So he closed his eyes, took a heaping spoonful of yogurt and toppings, and put it in his mouth.

And nearly gagged. He managed to swallow what he had in his mouth while the plastic spoon clattered to the table top and his eyes bugged out.

Reagan tried—she really did—to keep a straight face. But she couldn't help the snort that squeaked by. Then the chuckle. Then the laugh that came from so deep down she thought she might pee her pants before she got control of herself again.

She wiped her eyes, aware there were more than a few parents staring. One shushed her daughter and forced her to look the other way. *Don't go near the crazy lady, sweetie. Just leave her alone.* Totally worth it.

Then she caught the way Greg watched her. Like he was a starving man watching a waiter put down a porterhouse steak. He took ahold of her hand, calloused fingertips brushing against the inside of her wrist. There was no way he could miss how her pulse thundered under his touch.

"Told you there was a wild side under there."

She furrowed her brows at that. "Mixing gross yogurt combinations equals having a wild side?"

"No, but taking up the challenge to try does. Lying to me and making me think you enjoyed yours to get me to eat mine is a close second."

She flushed. "Caught."

He picked up her hand and nipped at her knuckles, then pressed a kiss to the same spot. "I'm impressed." He let her go—why did her fingers instinctively curl to keep his hand with hers?—and settled back for another small bite of yogurt. "Not so bad, if you concentrate on one flavor at a time."

She wrinkled her nose and pushed hers to the side.

"How did the Great Paint Spill end up after we left?" He took another bite, and she watched his tongue lick the last of the yogurt from the curve of the spoon.

That tongue could do wicked, wicked things to the curves of a woman's body. Say, her body, for example . . .

"Earth to Reagan."

She blinked. "Sorry, what?"

"The paint spill thing. What came out of that?"

"Ruined shoes, and probably a ruined suit, too." She was still smarting over that. It had taken her months to find those shoes on sale. Months. She grabbed the yogurt back. Even the gross flavors were better than thinking about those shoes. "Otherwise, a very upset reporter, and a big bucket of ice in my belly over how he's going to write up this little piece of 'mischief.'" She used air quotes on one hand—the one not gripping the spoon that was currently going in for another bite.

"How are you still eating that thing?" Greg looked appalled.

"It's not as bad, if you try to stick to one flavor on your spoon at a time." She scooped out some fudge brownie with a little whipped cream. "See? Yours was all mixed up. I kept mine in nice, divided sections."

"You couldn't even go wild without putting order to it." Looking disgusted at her lack of spontaneity, he grabbed her spoon and licked the yogurt off. "Serves you right."

"Probably." Plus, she didn't really need all the added calories. Gross taste or not, it all stuck straight to her hips. She'd be a walking cello if she wasn't careful. "What's your favorite part about boxing?"

He blinked, then settled back in the wrought-iron chair that looked too small to hold his weight. "Where'd that come from?"

"You said to be able to ask you another question and coach you through it, I had to go out with you again." She spread her arms wide. "We're out, dessert and all."

She saw the moment he realized she had him. He scowled, then stabbed his spoon into his yogurt and pushed it to the side. "I'm good at it."

"You are," she agreed. Then when he said nothing more, she prompted, "And?"

"And . . ." He shrugged and used the handle of the spoon to push his yogurt cup around the table. "I like to win. I like to have fun. Winning is fun, so . . . yeah."

Reagan tapped her finger to her lips. His entire demeanor changed when she questioned him as Reagan Robilard, Team Liaison than when they were simply chatting. Was that a good thing, or bad? "If a reporter asks, you'll need more. That answer will come off in print sounding cocky, though I doubt that's actually how you mean it. Try something like, 'I took to the sport of boxing naturally, and as I became better, my enjoyment for it grew.'"

He sneered. "That sounds like twisted PR crap."

"It *is* twisted PR crap. But it's my job to twist the crap until it can't get you into trouble in any way." She stood and tossed her yogurt in the trash behind her. "I've got to get back to my place and start figuring out how to play serious damage control. Plus, I've got an interview with the head leader guy of the MPs to figure out exactly how people keep breaking into the gym—if that's what is happening."

"The head leader guy?" he asked, lips twitching.

"Whatever." She scowled and stood. "Military jargon is still ninety percent lost on me."

He stood and followed her out toward her car. One large hand patted the trunk of Dolly Madison fondly. "If nobody is breaking into the gym, how else could all this crap be happening? A ghost?"

"Someone with a key, maybe an old employee who never turned one in. Or a roommate of an employee who made a copy. Someone who currently works with the Rec department and has access. Or even someone on the team."

That stopped him in his tracks, and he gripped her elbow

so she flailed to a halt a step ahead of him. "Nobody on the team would pull shit like this."

She wouldn't warn him about the language right now. He was worked up. "I can't discount the possibility that—"

"Nobody," he said quietly, his voice carrying the clear hint of temper. "Nobody on this team would pull a stunt like that."

She watched his eyes, those beautiful golden eyes, and nodded slowly. "Okay."

He didn't release her, but pulled her just a fraction closer. They were nose to nose today; her replacement heels for the ones paint had coated weren't as tall as she normally liked. But he never seemed to mind her height. If anything, he almost appeared to like them on equal level.

He pulled her so close, her breasts brushed against his chest as he breathed in, then out. Their breath mingled. And she knew he would kiss her, there, in the parking lot of a yogurt cafe where they'd just laughed over disgusting creations.

But then he stepped back, a small smile on his face. "Damn, you're a temptation."

She wanted to point out he didn't have to resist, she was perfectly happy to make out with him then and there. Temptation solved. But that wouldn't have been very worldly or mature of her.

Screw maturity, her libido screamed. *Grab the guy and let's do this!*

"You're not ready yet. Still too wrapped up with work to give it your all. Almost," he added, with a wistful sigh. "Just not quite."

She rolled her eyes and dug her keys out of her purse. "This little game you're playing with yourself, on the timing of our supposed inevitable tryst? It's only going to leave you with blue balls and a broken heart."

He waited for her to open the door, let her slide in, then blocked her from closing it with his knee. "Broken heart, huh?"

"Yeah." She went for a sad, almost pitying expression. "I would have been the best thing for you. But you keep backing off so . . . oh, well." She'd meant the words to sting—like his insistence she wasn't ready yet, as if he could read her mind—but he only laughed.

"I like that little bit of fight in you." He drummed his fingers on the top of her car. "How about tomorrow, you invite me over for dinner at your place."

The thought of him in her small, embarrassing apartment had her fighting back a rise of panic in her throat. "How about not? I can't cook." That was true, anyway.

"I can."

"Then I'll come over to your place."

"Which is the BOQ, with a roommate."

Oh, right. "Restaurant, then. There's a nice—"

"I'll work something out." He closed her door for her, then motioned for her to roll her window down. Reagan started the car, then prayed hard the window would actually cooperate—as it only did three out of four times. Luck was on her side this time, and the window rolled down without protest.

Greg leaned down to eye level through her window. "Just keep in mind, I don't give up. And I'm not playing a game. I'm doing what I think is best for us. Both of us. We're not going to rush this." He gave her another long look, one in which it was impossible to miss the heat between them, and patted her door one more time before stepping back to let her drive off.

Infuriating man. Infuriating, funny, sexy man.

GREG awoke with a jarring thump as something thick landed an inch away from his family jewels. Sitting up straight, he glanced around his still-dark room. "What the hell?"

"Read it, then tell me if we should weep."

"Costa?" Eyes still adjusting to the dark, he glanced at

his bedside clock. "It's five thirty in the freaking morning, you asshole. What the hell are you doing in my room?"

"Lights on," was the only warning Greg got before his retinas felt like they were burning from overexposure.

"Ah, Jesus!" He buried his head in the pillow and moaned. "What is wrong with you?"

"Our paint debacle is in the paper today."

"Super. Will it still be in there an hour from now, when I was set to wake up?"

"It's bad."

Costa sat at the edge of his bed, and Greg knew that was the end of pretending to have a shot at sleep again that morning. He cracked open one eyelid and glared at his roommate. "Why don't you sleep with your girlfriend like a normal guy? You've got a hot, available chick fifteen minutes away and you're not even with her."

"She likes her alone time now and then. So do I. It works."

Greg let his silence do the talking. It said, *You're full of shit.*

"Fine, she had an early morning breakfast date with Kara and kicked me out last night. Fuck you." He pointed at Greg's lap. "Read."

"I'm hitting the head first. Open it to the sports page and find it while I'm gone."

He stepped into the main area of their shared space and over to the tiny bathroom to take care of necessary morning duties.

"It's not in the sports section. It's front page."

Greg paused in washing his hands. "Front page? An article about Marines and boxing? What, slow news day?"

He walked back into the room, found a pair of shorts and pulled them on before sitting with his back against the headboard and the paper in his hands.

"Not about boxing. About vandalism and something about protests against the intertwined double helix of violence, with killing machines playing bloody war games inside a roped arena instead of in a desert sandbox." When Greg glanced up at Brad, brow raised, Brad held up his hands. "Just quoting the article. The dude has serious issues with us, it sounds like. And makes the paint and slashed tires—which yeah, he talked about—sound less like petty vandalism or teenage pranks and more like more serious protests that are gathering strength."

"Protests about what?" He scanned down the below-the-fold article. When he saw Reagan's name, he slowed down and read the paragraph more fully. Then read it again. And again. "Oh, hell. Reagan's gonna be pissed."

"Coach Ace and the other coaches. Marianne, the other team members, the athletic director . . ." Brad shook his head. "This is so, so not good."

Greg set the paper down. "They made Reagan sound like an idiot. Like a naïve idiot."

Brad cleared his throat. "Is it telling that you care more what the article said about our team's liaison than what it said about us as a team ourselves?"

"What did it say?" He picked up the paper to read it again, but kept coming back to the part where the reporter called Reagan "a country bumpkin with her head so far buried in the sand as to the realities of the team she supports she couldn't see the truth in front of her face."

His hands fisted around the paper until he felt the pages start to crinkle and tear.

"Right. Well, if you missed it, I won't draw your attention that direction." Brad pried the paper away. "This is bad. They could shut down the team. Hell, they could shut down the All Military games."

"Based on one idiot's article? No way." But the idea put a clutch in Greg's belly. He wasn't ready to leave yet. He liked his team. Wanted to see what they were made of.

Wanted to see what he and Reagan were made of, too.

"Maybe not, but it doesn't help, that's for damn sure. We have to figure out who's vandalizing the gym." Brad stood, folding the paper like an efficient businessman on a commuter train and tucking it under his arm. "Time to keep our eyes peeled for anything suspicious."

Greg gave him a sarcastic salute, which Brad ignored. After his roommate left, he grabbed his phone and thought of texting Reagan. Just to see if she was okay, if she'd heard yet, if she even got the paper delivered.

Of course she got the paper delivered. Or had an online subscription, one of the two. She'd consider it part of her job, or something.

There was no hiding it from her. Not that she'd appreciate him sheltering her from it, or give him any credit for it. She was one hell of a puzzle for him. So independent, so focused on making things happen all by herself. Putting out that serious I-can-do-anything businesswoman front. But he sensed the fear, the worry, the absolute uncertainty lurking behind the four-inch heels and starched suits.

The time for mussing up those sexy suits and kicking off those mouth-watering heels was coming soon. He couldn't rush it and ruin their work up to it. She'd never take him seriously if he did. But God, waiting was a pain in his ass.

He'd rather be a pain in *her* ass.

But in the end, he knew without a doubt she had to deal with the article herself first. She'd need to absorb, let the hurt and the anger rage, and then let it all go before she stepped foot in the gym. It'd be her way; presenting the cool ice-princess act, as if nothing were different. He'd give her that. And later that night, when he got her alone, he'd let her crumble if she needed to. Let her stay strong if that was her choice. But he'd be there for her, either way.

CHAPTER

9

Reagan paced the narrow confines of Marianne's training room. "What the hell is wrong with journalism these days?" She shook the paper in her hands, wanting to rip it to shreds. Only then, she'd have to buy another one and no way was she doing that. "What kind of pompous asshole reporter uses the phrase 'double helix' in a story about Marines and boxing?"

"Someone who is low on his word count?" Kara suggested not so helpfully. When Reagan glared at her, she stuffed a piece of apple muffin in her mouth.

"Don't get crumbs on my table," Marianne warned as she sat at her desk with her own plate of muffins. Kara had baked them and met them early, as they'd planned. Since Kara was leading a yoga lesson that morning, it made sense to just head to the gym early and be there for work rather than head to a restaurant and wait.

Plus, bonus, Reagan didn't have to pay restaurant prices for a calorie-laden muffin. She could get one for free. Only half the guilt. Except there was no way she could choke down anything right now. She was too upset to swallow anything.

"Calm yourself down. There are no crumbs." Kara leaned over into a graceful stretch on the table, her nose touching the knees of her yoga pants.

"I hate that she can do that," Reagan muttered and kept pacing. If nothing else, she was burning calories.

"You're going to kill yourself in those shoes. Stop wearing a hole in my floor and sit." Marianne kicked over another rolling chair and Reagan sat, because her feet were killing her. "I've warned you about those heels in the gym."

"I needed the armor." She pulled down on the jacket of her most professional, starchy suit. She hated the thing—made her feel forty instead of twenty-four—but it also gave her an added boost of professionalism.

Neither woman asked for clarification. They understood what she meant by "armor."

"I have to do some serious damage control. I've got to call my supervisor, then probably *his* supervisor. I've got to speak to the editor of the paper—aka the moron who let this article run as-is. And then I've got to find some more positive PR for the men."

"And how will you fit all that in between dates with Greg?" Kara asked with a smile. "Come on, dish. I never got to hear how dinner was the other night."

"Or yogurt last night." When Reagan glanced at Marianne in surprise, she shrugged. "He told Brad. Brad told me."

"Those gossips." She blew out a breath, and realized a few stray hairs had escaped the tight, schoolmarm bun she'd pulled it into. Digging through her bag, she found her travel-sized hairspray and gave it a little spritz. "Greg is not my main concern right now. Avoiding getting fired is. Doing my job. Not failing at this career before I even get started."

"I hardly think going out to dinner for an hour or two will cause anyone to get fired or fail. You're spinning this out of control." Kara hopped down, a graceful act that barely caused a ripple in the air. Reagan never even heard her soft tennis shoes land. "It's okay to be nervous, but you're letting it control you." She arched her back and stretched some more. Reagan tilted her head to the side, watching her friend nearly bend in two.

"Why are you stretching now if you're just going to stretch again in an hour?"

"Muscle memory. Don't change the subject."

"What's the point? He's just going to leave after this is all over. He isn't stationed here." As soon as she said it, she winced and looked toward Marianne. She was in the same position, only deeper. She and Brad were a fixed, unquestionable couple. But Brad was stationed in California normally, and Marianne lived here, in North Carolina. "Sorry. That was insensitive."

"No, it wasn't. It's a reasonable logistical consideration. However, I'm only here temporarily, too. Once the team is done, my job is done. I can look for a job out there in California just as well as I could here."

Reagan thought about that for a moment. "You'd move around with him?"

"His job isn't flexible on travel. Mine is, at least for now." She shrugged, as if it didn't bother her one bit. "I don't look at it as following him . . . too passive for my taste. I look at it more as choosing my relocation based on the needs of my heart."

"That was really lovely, Marianne." Kara smiled approvingly and moved into some sort of lunge thing.

It was nice, Reagan admitted to herself. Marianne was a strong woman. But she didn't seem to be bothered by the idea of her career being dictated by the needs of her lover's career. She didn't see it as a secondary place. It was encouraging.

"Well, it's not like it matters anyway." Reagan tugged at the hem of her pant leg, folding it around once, then letting it fall again to drape over her shoe. "I don't think he's interested, anyway. He hasn't even kissed me. He keeps putting it off, even when I've given him every signal that I'm good with it."

She glanced up in time to catch Marianne and Kara throwing a look at each other. "What? Seriously, what? What am I missing?"

"Well . . ." Marianne tossed her plate in the trash and brushed the crumbs off her red team polo. "I'm just thinking that if he weren't all that serious about you, he likely would have already made a move."

"Several," Kara confirmed. "He would have pushed, prodded, and forced the issue. If he didn't care about you in a more serious way, then he wouldn't care about making a better impression."

"But he didn't do that, which tells me he's fine taking his time, because he wants more than just a quick"—Marianne paused, peeking at the doorway before finishing—". . . fuck."

"Heard that." Brad walked in from around the corner, grinning. When Marianne scowled at him, he grabbed a bag of prepacked ice from the ice maker, bent down to brush a kiss across her forehead before leaving.

"Good riddance," Marianne muttered, but there was no heat behind it.

"Back to boys," Kara said, then snickered. "We're seriously in high school. I just said 'boys.'"

"Sounds about right to me." Reagan paced another minute, then stopped and sat down. She had to force her legs to not jiggle. "I've got calls to make. I have damage control to get started on. I've got to triple-check that the gym is good to use before the guys start practicing—"

Their conversation was once again interrupted, this time by Marianne's two training interns. The girl—and though Reagan was probably only a few years older, she couldn't help but think of her as a girl—wore her polo a little too tight, in her opinion. It strained across moderate breasts, and rode up to show about an inch of skin above the waistband of her short khaki shorts.

As the girl—Nikki, Reagan was nearly positive her name was—turned to toss her bag in a locker in the corner of the training room, Reagan saw the cause for the tight fit. She'd knotted it in the back and secured it with a rubber band. When she caught Marianne's eye, she nodded discreetly at the intern's back.

Marianne sighed. "Nikki, we've talked about the shirt situation."

Nikki turned, hands on her hips. "I don't work in a nunnery, Marianne. What's the point of being here if I have to wear baggy clothes all the time?"

The male intern—a skinny, tall guy with shaggy hair and a very quiet demeanor—stepped around her to put his own belongings in the locker, ignoring the scene unfolding.

"The point of you being here is to learn, for college credit. Or am I filling out those weekly reports for your advisor just for my own personal enjoyment?" Looking annoyed, Marianne stood and crossed her arms. "Pull the shirt out, Nikki."

Apparently willing to die on that particular hill, Nikki dug in her heels. "Baggy clothes make for an unsafe work environment. I could get caught on something, or—"

"Or distract a Marine from what he's doing and watch him get hurt," Marianne filled in.

"This isn't distracting." Eyes wide with practiced innocence, Nikki spun to look at the male intern. The poor guy was cornered by the locker, unsure of where to look. "Levi, is this distracting to you? Are you having trouble concentrating with my breasts like this?"

"I . . . uh . . ." He looked anywhere but at her, letting his shaggy hair drape over his eyes as some sort of modesty curtain. *Oh,* Reagan thought, *you poor, lovesick boy.* "I don't . . . I mean, it's not . . . I can't . . ."

"Levi, take the first jug of water to the catwalk upstairs." In a calm, very serious voice, Marianne added, "Nikki, stay and have a chat."

"But I have to help set up," she protested, starting after Levi.

"Stay." The word was said so calmly it wouldn't have

registered on anyone's radar who wasn't paying attention. But Reagan was paying attention, and heard the unspoken *Or else, you're fired.* Kara had, too. They met eyes, and by unanimous, unspoken agreement, grabbed their bags and headed out. Kara closed the door behind them.

"Oh, boy," she said, whistling softly. "That one's in deep shit now."

"She was rude" was all Reagan could think to say.

"Worse." Kara found a spot against the wall to set her bags. She'd be leading an entire team of Marines in under an hour through a yoga routine with some serious stretching. But they had another few minutes to chat first, before she started setting up. "Marianne prides her professionalism above everything else on the job. Getting in the way of that— especially if you're making it appear like you're here only to pick up athletes—is the quickest way to get on her shit list."

"So noted." Reagan checked the gym, found herself impressed it didn't look any worse for the wear. The maintenance staff had worked miracles, it seemed. The scent of cleaner was still sharper than usual, but it wasn't as bad as it could have been.

"Sounds like it looked like a color run in here yesterday." Kara smiled. "I know it's bad, but seriously, the image is pretty funny."

"I'm sure with some distance—say fifteen or twenty years—I'll think the same." As it was, she had some damage control to handle on that regard. "Thanks for breakfast."

"No problem. And hey, anytime you need to use my apartment for a date pick-up site, just let me know." Kara winked, but Reagan chose to ignore that and keep moving. Because otherwise Kara might ask why she couldn't just meet Greg—who was an all-around decent guy—at her own apartment.

She'd rather avoid that conversation as long as possible.

* * *

"SO, I'll be staying with Marianne tonight." Brad unlaced his second shoe, toed it off, pushed the pair off to the side and bent over to stretch out his quad. "Just in case you were wondering."

Greg shot him a funny look, removing his own shoes and lining them up next to Brad's. "Gee, Bradley, I didn't know we had that kind of relationship, but thanks for letting me know. Should I mention my plans for tonight, too? First, I intend to hit up Taco Bell for some dinner, then—"

"God." His roommate clutched at his belly. "God. Taco Bell . . . don't do that to yourself. You're in training, for God's sake. Jesus H."

"Nothing you say can dissuade me from my love affair with the Bell. So wrong, but so good." He made a delicious sound, just to watch Brad shudder. "Seriously, why are you telling me this? Do you want a bail out phone call or something?"

"He's telling you so you can bring back Hottie Hot Legs for alone time at your place if you want." Graham sat down next to them on the mat and began to stretch himself. "You idiot."

Greg felt his face burn, so he ducked down into a butterfly stretch to hide it. "How the hell was I supposed to know that? Can't you just say that?"

"And ruin how quiet you've been about the whole thing? Hell no. This is the first I've seen of you not being social and over-share-ish since we got here. I'm relishing." Brad kicked out, barely missing Greg's foot. "Plus, making you twist in the wind is fun."

"You got yours, so you can shut up now."

"Jealous," Brad said to Graham.

"Totally," Graham agreed.

"I'm right here," Greg offered.

"Don't care," they both said at the same time, then grinned.

"Assholes," he muttered.

"Okay, boys, time to stretch!" Kara, their graceful, beautiful yoga instructor, glided over. She really did glide everywhere, it seemed. If Greg checked the bottoms of her feet and found skates, it wouldn't have shocked him. She was simply born with an innate grace that seemed to carry through everywhere. "Grab a mat and some personal space. You know the drill by now."

Graham took a spot next to him, toward the back. Though the coaches were around the gym, they generally gave Kara the run of the show when she was holding a yoga class. For one hour, they were fully hers to twist and turn into devil dog pretzels. Which meant, by hanging out in the back, he and Graham could chat between pose transitions.

Kara took her spot in the front, on her own personalized yoga mat—a must-have, Greg assumed, for full-time instructors—and tossed off the sweatshirt she wore over stretchy yoga pants. The top was a halter that presented a good bit of her toned stomach. She twisted her auburn braid over one shoulder, closed her eyes and directed them to their first pose.

Greg started to move, then realized Graham hadn't budged. "You gonna join us, or just stand there? Because I'm no yogi but I'm pretty sure that's not a pose."

Graham blinked, taking his eyes off Kara—finally—and started to move, albeit without his normal athleticism. His motions were jerky, unsure, as if they hadn't been doing this three times a week for several weeks now.

"What's your deal?"

Graham just shook his head, then worked on his forward bend.

"Oh." Greg did another quick check at Kara, then back to his friend. "Oooh. Right. Okay then."

"Shut up," Graham muttered, sounding strained.

"Ohhhhh," he said again, a little quieter. Graham just

focused on folding himself as tightly in two pieces as he could.

"Easy there, cowboy." Marianne tapped Graham's back. "Don't overstretch or you'll pull something. Ease back, and stop when your body shouts uncle."

Graham scowled at him, then at Marianne, before storming off toward the locker room. Greg imagined he had a decent excuse worked up if someone asked. Had to take a leak, forgot to lock up my stuff, got bored and wanted a minute alone.

He knew better. His friend had the hots for the yoga instructor. And was none too happy about it.

A flash of light from the corner of his eye caught his attention, and he turned his head. Not easy in warrior pose, but he managed.

And found Reagan, camera in hand, taking photos of the group from different angles. When they transitioned, he sent her a quick wave, and she raised her hand in acknowledgment, but didn't smile or take her eyes off the shot.

He liked a woman on a mission. He just wished it didn't put such a pinched look on her face. He hated the thought that something wasn't working out for her. Hated more that he wasn't sure how to fix it. And knew, even as he thought it, she'd disagree there. She wouldn't want a man to fix something for her. She'd fix it herself. Rawr, woman power and stuff.

Fine then. But the longer she looked frustrated, the antsier he would get about stepping in and solving whatever it was that irked her. Starting with the damn reporter.

CHAPTER

10

Reagan finished typing the last of the editorial article she'd begged from the local paper to write. It had been a near thing, and she'd been ready to promise some sexual favors if it came to it, but luckily it hadn't. She had just enough space, plus one photo, to write up a rebuttal on the article from that morning.

David Cruise—aka Mr. High-And-Mighty "Journalist"—had dodged her calls all morning, and refused to call her back. Oh, but others called. A larger paper from the Wilmington branch, plus several touchy-feely blogs that dealt with anti-everything not fluffy kittens. They were against violent sports, violent hobbies, violent careers—military included, of course—violent acts, violent protests, violent thoughts, and violence.

Duh. Way to narrow it down there, bloggers.

She'd done her best there, working hard to make the reporter's story sound overdramatized without directly calling him a pansy-ass good-for-nothing. Fine line, but she was pretty sure she walked it well enough.

Hopefully the work she'd done that day, combined with this decent PR she'd written just now and would—please God—show up in tomorrow's paper, would help. Everyone wanted to see a softer side of Marines, right? She'd worked hard to strike the right balance between pride for the sport, a love of service and also some good-natured humor without overstepping any boundaries.

Her entire job was about fine lines, as it turned out.

Sliding her feet into the slippers Marianne kept in the office and said she could borrow, she turned in Marianne's desk chair and surveyed the training room. Marianne and her interns had packed up a bit ago and headed out. The gym was quiet now, with all but the emergency lights shut off outside of the training room. Reagan could have used Coach Ace's office, but his desk was a mess so she had borrowed her friend's room instead. And though she'd never admit it to anyone, she'd needed to get out of the heels. They were killing her.

Her phone beeped, and she glanced at the text message.

Greg: Hungry?

She rotated her head a little, stretching the neck muscles and giving her shoulders a bit of relief. She could so go for a cheeseburger right about now. But she still had way too much to do to contemplate leaving yet. If she went home, she'd just crash on the bed. Too tempting.

Reagan: Starving. But I've got too much work to worry about.

Greg: How about I bring the food to you?

She thought about it for a minute. But again . . . too tempting.

Reagan: Thanks for the offer, but I'll be okay.

Greg: Too late.

Too late? What did that mean? She hadn't even told him where she was.

"Knock, knock."

She shrieked and bobbled her phone a little. Catching it,

she put it down on the desk and glanced up to see Greg standing in the doorway, holding two brown sacks. Their bottoms were dark with grease, and her stomach rumbled just thinking of the deliciousness hiding inside.

"What are you doing here?" She thought for a second. "Actually, *how* did you get in here?"

"Marianne. When we were all leaving, I mentioned asking you to dinner and she said you were working late here. So she ran back by to let me in."

"Sneaky lady," Reagan muttered, pushing away from the desk and standing. The food smelled so good, her stomach actually started to rumble. She covered it with one hand. "Well, you're here now. Shouldn't let the food go to waste."

"That would simply be criminal," Greg agreed. He walked in and set the food down on one of Marianne's tables. Reagan winced, then silently vowed to wipe it down again with the disinfectant like she'd seen the interns do before. Good as new.

"You struck me as the kind of lady who would want a cheeseburger, but order a salad. Am I right?" He started pulling out paper sleeves of fries, a few plopping to the plastic table top as he did.

"That might have been insulting, but I'm too hungry to care." Her eyes strayed, though, from the fries on the table to the man holding the bags. He wore cargo khaki shorts, running shoes and a simple graphic tee. Nothing flashy or out of the ordinary.

But she started feeling a hunger of an entirely different sort after watching his forearms flex with each reach into the bag.

Down, girl. Not while you're working. She forced herself to walk with ease to the table and pick up a fry. He crumbled one bag, threw it in the other and set it down on the second table. So now she'd wash down both table tops before she left.

"Are we going to eat standing up?" she teased.

"Good for the digestion." Greg unwrapped a burger, checked what was in it, then handed it to her. "Just a plain old cheeseburger. You good with that?"

"More than good. Great. Thrilled, actually." To prove it, she took a healthy bite. "See?" she said around the gloriousness.

He smiled, then leaned in a little. Then a little more . . . then more . . .

Oh, God. He was actually going to kiss her now. A real kiss. And she had half a cow stuffed in her mouth. Her eyes widened and she froze as he inched in, as his fingers caressed her jaw and tilted her head, as his thumb brushed over the corner of her mouth . . .

"You had a little sauce there." He straightened and sucked the sauce from his thumb. "Good stuff." Then he unwrapped his own burger—twice the size of hers—and started eating.

Reagan's eyes narrowed, and she hoped he felt the daggers she was sending him. From the way his eyes danced above the massive burger, she knew he felt them and found them completely ineffective.

Finally able to swallow, she said, "That was low."

"No, *you're* low." He bumped her hip with his. "First time we're not eye to eye, or me looking up an inch or two."

Oh, crap. She looked down, and realized she was still wearing Marianne's slippers. And no, of course they weren't something adorable and sassy like leopard print or something. They were *Family Guy* slippers, Stewie on one, Brian on the other. Ugh. She actually debated rushing back to the desk for her heels when he wrapped one arm around her waist and squeezed.

"Don't. You're comfortable. I like it."

It took everything she had not to do it, but she managed to resist the siren song of her heels. When was the last time she hadn't been in heels in front of a man?

That was embarrassing to admit, so let's not go that direction.

"I think," Greg went on, picking up a piece of fallen bacon, "that you in heels is sexy. I like your suits. I like your hair up in that tight school-principal bun. You make business look sexy." He winked. "But you make slippers look pretty damn hot, too. You're not a one-trick pony."

"Hmm," was all she could manage. Finishing off the burger—her thighs were so not going to thank her for that— she dug into the fries. Then she grabbed the bag off the other table and rooted through it. "Ketchup, but no mayo?"

He blinked. "I'm sorry, mayo? Wasn't there mayo on your burger? Which, I have to point out, you've already polished off."

"I was hungry, shut up. No, not for my burger. For the fries." When he just stared at her, silently chewing his food, she sighed. "Does nobody outside of the Midwest know this? You mix the mayo and the ketchup and then dip your fries in it."

He swallowed another huge bite of burger before asking, "Could they think of anything more disgusting?"

"Don't knock it until you've tried it."

"Okay." He wrapped the last three bites of his burger up and tossed it in the bottom of the bag. Grabbing the fries from her hand, he tossed those, as well as his, into the bag, too.

"Hey! I was going to eat those!" *Sorry, thighs. We'll do lunges later, okay?* "What's the deal?"

"Get your shoes on, unless you want to walk out in your slippers."

"Not mine, Marianne's." She hustled at the excuse to put her heels back on. "Where are we going?"

"Just come on." He grabbed her hand and, barely waiting for her to lock up the training room, pulled her to the parking lot. He impatiently waited again as she locked the gym itself, then pulled her to his car and opened the passenger door for her. When she was settled, he tossed her the bag and raced to the driver seat.

Reagan held the bag up a few inches off her lap. Much as she loved the food, the grease did not agree with her wardrobe. "Are you going to tell me now where we're going?"

"Going to get some mayo."

"All this, for mayo?"

"The lady wants mayo, and I live to serve the lady."

REAGAN sat on Greg's bed, looking supremely pleased with herself. "Tell me I'm right."

He hedged, wanting to play it out longer. "I dunno . . ."

She kicked at him with one bare foot. He'd gotten her to dump the heels once they were in the privacy of his bedroom. No slippers necessary here. He grabbed her foot and squeezed. She closed her eyes briefly, but opened them again. "Tell me."

"As shocking as it is, you were right." She kicked with her other foot. He dodged easily. Using the non-foot-holding hand, he swiped the last two fries through the mayo-and-ketchup creation she'd made for him and popped them in his mouth. "I wouldn't use it every time, of course, but it's definitely not bad."

"Not bad." She snorted. "The first bite, your eyes lit up. Don't lie."

"Unexpected," he went with.

"Unexpected that I kicked your ass in the taste department." When he just stared at her, she shrugged. "Call 'em like I see 'em."

He squeezed her foot once, then let it fall to the bed. "How was your day? You know, besides the whole kicking-my-ass thing."

Her smile dimmed a little, and he regretted that. But he also needed to know if she was ready to start trusting him, talking with him about her day. If she was ready to let loose on everything that built up inside her.

"It was . . . hard." She set her drink on the nightstand and stretched her arms up. The hem of her shirt rode up to reveal a delicious strip of pale skin, marred by pink lines from her waistband. He wouldn't mind kissing those marks away. "It was harder than anything I thought it would be coming into this job."

"What'd you think?" When she gave him a blank look, he rephrased. "With the job, what were you expecting?"

"Fluff," she answered immediately, then blushed. It was adorable. "That's probably rude to say, but it's true."

"Well, it's a well-known fact Marines are the fluffiest of the services." When she laughed, he shook his head in mock disgust. "We're just so cuddly and lovable. About as innocent as a teddy bear and a bedtime story."

She laughed at that, sitting up enough to clutch at her belly. "Oh yeah," she said through gasps. "You're regular stuffed animals, all of you. So harmless, so tame."

"Exactly." When she'd calmed down, he added, "No fluff jobs closer to home?"

"Oh, there's fluff, but . . ." She picked at the edge of his pillowcase for a moment. "I needed to get out of there. Suffocating family, you know?"

He didn't know. He couldn't even begin to fathom what that felt like. To not only know who your family was, but to feel their presence so keenly in your life that you wanted to escape it. "Yeah," he said, throat tightening. "Sure." To buy him time, he added, "What's so fluffy about this job?"

"Oh, I don't know." She picked up her drink, set it down again. "Keep you all in line, make sure you didn't completely lose your minds when traveling, arrange simple media stuff, not screw up ordering the travel bus for the right day. Basically, idiot-proof junk. At least, I *thought* it would be idiot proof."

"Is that what you wanted?"

"No." She gritted her teeth, then sighed. "If I tell you this . . ."

"It stays here." He did some halfhearted attempt at a cross. "Confess your sins, my child."

She groaned, turned her face into his pillow, then popped back up again. This playful side of Reagan, in his bed no less, was seriously turning him on and making him think decidedly unpriestly thoughts. "I only took the job because I couldn't get anything else. I wanted to be Olivia Pope from *Scandal*. I wanted to be out there, tackling the world's toughest, most ugly PR scenarios. I wanted to be hiding a politician's love child behind my back while kicking the bra he wore last night at the drag show under the bed with my foot and smiling through it all for the press."

"That's . . . an interesting occupation aspiration." He wasn't sure what to say about that. "Do people actually act like that?"

"Of course they do. They just have Olivia Popes to hide it. But of course, Olivia Popes don't come from Nowhere, Wisconsin, with a 5-point-5-year degree and zero experience. So . . ." She let her arms lift, then fall into her lap. "Here I am. And as it turns out, the moment this job turns into more than fluff, I'm floundering."

She looked so disheartened, he wanted to change it immediately.

"Well, if you ever have to hide Coach Ace's bra, please tell me where you put it." She snorted a laugh, and he grinned. "I'm glad you took the job."

She sighed and let her head loll against the headboard. "For all I thought it was just a filler . . . I'm glad, too. Half the time, I think I'm in over my head. And the other half, I'm running so hard on adrenaline that I'm pretty sure if I got enough of a running start, I could leap off the catwalk and fly." She patted her stomach. "Apparently, a belly full of comfort food makes me mushy."

That tired contentment, the sight of her sighing in happiness and exhaustion in his own bed, surrounded by his things, after they'd spent an evening together, filled him with his own brand of contentment. Crawling to her, he hovered over her. She blinked her eyes open and waited very still for him to say something.

"I'm really glad you took the job," he repeated.

CHAPTER

11

Reagan waited for him to move . . . what felt like a lifetime of waiting. She'd have sworn it had been years since she first wanted to feel his lips on hers . . . not weeks. But he didn't move in, didn't push any farther.

And then it occurred to her. He was giving her the last bit of control. He wanted her to come to him, to give that last seal of approval on the act. To show, without a doubt, it was what she wanted.

She raised her hands to cup his jaw. The rasp of his five o'clock shadow under her fingertips excited her. Despite having shaven that morning, he already had a good head start on a beard. She explored for a moment, the trail from the tip of his earlobe to the slight dent in his chin, invisible to the eye but so easy to feel with fingertips. He watched her, warily, lips barely parted. His chest heaved, and she wondered if it was from excitement, or the effort to give her this chance.

Maybe both. It's why her own heart was thundering loud enough to drown out a herd of stampeding mustangs.

Following instinct, she traced over his lips, to that sweet

cupid's bow in the middle of his upper lip, up to the tip of his nose. There, she grinned as she pushed in. "Boop."

As if that were all the invitation he needed, he rolled her over to straddle him. He was flat on the bed now, the pillows pushed to the floor in his haste. And though the suit rode uncomfortably tight in the back due to her unbusinesslike stance, she'd never felt more powerful than when she looked down between her arms and saw Greg Higgs looking up at her with hunger in his eyes.

And it was that power that gave her the strength to take what she wanted. It wasn't a surrender to temptation, she realized as she lowered her head to breathe in his clean, male scent. A surrender was too weak, to mild sounding. No, she was claiming what she wanted. She was making it hers. That was a power in itself.

"I'm claiming you," she whispered as she nipped his lip. His eyes widened a little—in fear? No, in surprise—and he licked his tongue over the spot she'd bit.

"Is that so," he murmured. "I won't get in your way, then."

"You won't," she agreed, then kissed him fully.

It was exactly what she'd needed. The immediate release of pressure, like letting the cork on a champagne bottle fly free, gave her limbs a weightless quality. Or maybe that was just Greg's arms as he steadied her.

He lay quiet beneath her as her hands roamed his upper body, while her lips explored his. Though his muscles quivered while she touched and stroked, he allowed her the time to get to know his body. Let her make each new move against his mouth. When she chose the tilt of her head, he accommodated her and adjusted. When she swept her tongue against his lips, he opened invitingly.

And he never once pushed her for more, never demanded she move faster to suit his pace, or slow down more. For once, he gave her the option of choosing.

It was like stepping into a cage with a lion. The lion might allow you to pet its head, run your hands over its powerful, rangy body, make the first move to play. There was no escaping the knowledge, though, that in an instant, the lion could make the final move, swipe his big paw once and it would all be over.

But for that moment of control . . . what a rush.

When she pulled back enough to see if he was just as affected as she was, she couldn't help the catlike grin that spread.

Greg's eyes were half-closed, as if drunk on lust, and thanks to the way she draped over his body, his erection was impossible to miss. It lay thick and hard against her thigh, making her very much want to reach down and stroke it.

How much more would the lion take before swiping with that dangerous paw?

Before she could even find out, she was flat on her back. The lion, it appeared, wasn't as lust-drunk as she'd thought. He flashed her a quick grin before taking control and dazzling her with a kiss so skilled, she forgot to breathe.

She tore her lips away just before spots started to appear behind her eyelids. "You're . . . dangerous . . ."

"Me?" He did what she assumed was his best imitation of innocence. His best needed some work. "I'm just here with a beautiful lady, doing some sweet kissing. Nothing dangerous about it."

"You say that, but—" He interrupted her with another lip lock that took her several minutes to remember she'd been speaking. "You say that," she repeated, putting two firm hands on his cheeks to keep him away. "But there's nothing sweet about this."

He waited a moment. "Do you want me to slow down?"

"I want you to speed up, dammit!" She hooked a leg over the back of his thigh, her heel resting just below his butt. With a nudge that made him jolt, she brought him back to her. And when his hand started to roam down her body, finding all those spaces above the waist she loved, she arched into his touch.

But just as his hand cupped her breast through way too many layers of clothing, he was off her and across the room. He might have been yanked away with a wire like a stuntman if she hadn't been watching. She sat up, dazed and not entirely sure what had just happened.

"Why . . ." She moistened her lips, which felt sort of numb. Could really excellent kissing make your lips go numb? "Why are you over there?"

"Because you're in my bed," he said, as if that were a completely logical explanation. When she looked down at his crotch—yup, still saluting—he followed her gaze, then turned toward the door. "That's about all for tonight."

She scrunched up her nose. What the hell happened? "Did I do something wrong?"

"No. Hell, no," he emphasized when she didn't move. "You did everything right. Way too right," he added in a mumble.

She was starting to get a headache. Or maybe it was akin to altitude sickness . . . only with lust. Changing lust levels at too quick a speed caused the oxygen in her brain to lag behind.

"It's that I want you." He laughed halfheartedly. "Obviously. And that's not on the menu tonight so—"

"And why not?" She crossed her arms under her breasts, only to realize she was in the world's most unattractive sprawl on his bed. She sat up and did her best to position herself better . . . or at least more comfortably. "Why not? Oh." She glared. "You're doing that whole 'my way, caveman' thing again, aren't you? Exerting your control over the situation and the details."

"I'm doing what I think is right. You've had a rough few days, I've had a rough few practices, and the team as a whole got dumped on. I don't want you to look back tomorrow and think you were used. I want this to go right." He said it all slowly, as if he wasn't sure she wouldn't take a swipe at him.

With as much dignity as she could muster—not a lot,

sadly—she scooted to the edge of the bed and began to pull her heels on. "It appears as though I've overstayed my welcome."

"Ask me a question," Greg blurted out.

She paused in the act of putting on shoe number two. "A question?"

"One of your PR things." He shifted a little, and she knew it made him uncomfortable to offer. But he did it anyway, because it meant she'd stick around.

Brownie points for Greg Higgs.

She stood and turned a tight circle around his room. Nothing personal there. No photos of friends or family. No hints of the life he led outside of the gym where he trained with a dozen of his teammates. It was as if he existed for one thing only . . . to fight. "Tell me why you chose the Marine Corps."

"The Marine Corps is the baddest of the badasses."

She turned and watched him cautiously settle down on the edge of the bed. As if returning to the scene of the crime so soon might ignite potential feelings best left behind. "'The baddest of the badasses.' Very technical phrase."

"It's exactly what my seventeen-year-old mind was thinking when I chose." He smirked. "Seventeen-year-olds aren't known for their mature thought processes."

Seventeen. Not even eighteen when he joined. Still a baby, in all the ways that count. But something told her he'd hate hearing that. So she sat at the opposite edge of the bed, as far from him as she could, and nodded. "Okay. Keep going."

HOW did he explain it to her? She was a farm-fresh face with a loving family she actually wanted to avoid because they cared too much about her life. What was it like, he wondered, to hear from someone that the thing you dodged was the one thing someone else craved with every cell in their body? That the family she found smothering would have fulfilled every single childhood dream of his.

"I needed to pick a service, and I went with the one that sounded the coolest. When you're a seventeen-year-old boy, being a badass is basically the highest pinnacle to achieve."

"Seventeen," she murmured, and he could see the wheels turning. Did she ask, didn't she . . .

She chose not to. Wise, since he wouldn't have told her why, and he didn't want to lie.

And the truth was something he never wanted to discuss. Ever.

"Hey, so funny story . . . abandoned as a baby, foster system blew, got sucked into the wrong crowd, spent lots of time in juvie for fighting and other petty shit. Had a judge tell me it's either the service now—and he'd sign off on the early enlistment—or it's going to be the big time . . . adult lockup. So I picked the lesser of two evils."

Not exactly a sexy bedtime story.

"Anything else you want to add?" she asked, jarring him from the past.

He thought, then shrugged. Not particularly.

"What made you stay in?" She raised a hand, as if she wanted to reach out and touch him somehow. But she let it fall back. "You must have had to reenlist at least once between then and now."

"It's a good life." The only good life he knew. "I got my college degree thanks to the Corps, shifted over to the officer side, and just kept plugging away. Every time there was a chance to get out, I considered it. Any guy who says he doesn't hesitate, at least for a second, before re-upping is a liar. But in the end . . ." How else to say it? "The Corps has been good to me." A surrogate family, really. Like the team had become. He'd do whatever he could to keep it.

She nodded at that, folded her hands in her lap very primly and looked down. Eyes closed, she said, "Hmm."

Hmm? That's all? It was the most personal he'd been with her since meeting her—the closest he'd come to baring that true, vulnerable kid he'd been—and she said "hmm"?

"I wouldn't disclose what age you were when you went in," she began, eyes still closed, as if envisioning something.

Aw, hell. She was back in business mode. He straightened his shoulders and forced himself to be impartial.

"I would say that the military has provided you with a good life, a good and honorable living, and you feel it is your duty to continue to give back." She looked at him from under her lashes. "Does that meet your approval?"

He nodded, not trusting his voice.

"Good." She stood, picking up her purse from the dresser where she'd left it. "I'll leave you for now. Have a good evening."

Before he could stand up, she was gone. He raced to look for his shoes, slipped them on without socks and raced after her.

He found her, standing still, on the sidewalk outside the building. "I forgot . . . I rode with you." She turned, facing him with a blank expression. "You have to take me back."

The five-minute car ride back was quiet. He struggled for something to say, but nothing quite worked out. When he parked at the gym, he sighed in relief to see her car was still alone, unharmed. With the vandalism happening, he shouldn't have left her car there. Next time he'd be more careful. But before he could say anything, she slipped from his car and headed toward hers.

He barely caught up with her before she opened her car door. Damn, the lady could move with those long legs when she wanted to.

"Dinner," he blurted out, then felt like an idiot.

"Dinner," she said slowly. "We just ate dinner."

"Tomorrow. Your place." *Sentences, Higgs, use real sentences.*

She closed off at that. "No, thank you."

"Fine, back at my place then." He could make that work.

She shook her head. "Thank you, but no."

"Then at Sweeney's place. I'll kick him out. He won't care."

She hesitated, then asked, "He wouldn't mind?"

He might, but Greg wasn't about to tell her that. "Nah, he's good with it. Said we should make ourselves at home." Probably hadn't meant that for when *he* wouldn't be home, but Greg wasn't about to let the man take it back now. "Seriously, it's fine."

She hesitated, and in that hesitation he could see her true desire.

"Reagan."

Her eyes slanted to his. She nibbled on her bottom lip a moment, and he slid in for a kiss. With her heels on, and him in just his running shoes, he was actually reaching up an inch to make it work but that was fine. When she sighed and pressed into him, he knew he'd won over her resistance.

Breathing hard, he pulled away and pressed his forehead to hers. "Have dinner with me tomorrow. Let me cook you a real meal, let me sit with you on the couch and watch a movie. Let me cop a feel during the scary parts and whisper cheesy lines in your ear during the romantic stuff. Let's do the normal couple things that people do when they're dating that are hard for us here."

She laughed and let her head drop to his shoulder. "Okay. Fine, you convinced me. But only if Graham is okay with it."

"He will be," Greg promised as he shuffled her into her car and watched her pull away. He will be or else Greg would murder him on the spot and move into his house.

As soon as Reagan's car—God, that was a death trap on wheels—pulled out of the parking lot, he dug his cell phone out of his pocket and flipped through his contacts.

"Sweeney? Yeah, I need a favor . . ."

CHAPTER

12

"The article reads well." Marianne settled in her chair, Kara and Reagan in their by-now assigned positions on two of the training tables in the AT room. "I'm sorry about the protestors, though."

Reagan played with the homemade breakfast sandwich Kara had brought over. Zach, her son, was playing imaginary basketball in the gym while they talked in relative privacy.

Early that morning, Reagan had passed the small but determined group of protestors on her trek through the main gates. They couldn't step on base, but they huddled together just outside on the main road that led to the main gate, where a majority of the Marines would drive through. Holding up hastily created signs that ranged from generic military hatred—"Damn those who hide behind the uniform"—to ones that were more specific to the current kerfuffle—"Violent sports + violent men = more violence."

That one, she had thought with a private snicker, had been a truly moronic one. If you were going to take the time and energy to make a sign, at least create one that was original.

The smile died as she remembered children, no older than Zach, standing with their parents in the weak morning sun with their parents, holding hateful signs.

"I knew it would happen eventually. I just didn't think it would be so soon, and after just one article." Reagan let her sandwich fall back to the paper plate. Her appetite had taken a nosedive.

"It was a doozy of an article." Kara reached over and stroked a soft hand once down Reagan's arm. "They'll move on shortly. We've seen this dozens of times, right, Marianne?"

"She's right. It's not uncommon around here. We've seen it all."

"And when they're tired, or just bored, they'll move—" Kara paused, then yelled, "Zachary, get in here!" in a voice so fierce, Reagan jumped a little. That was, without a doubt, the Mom Voice.

Zach peeked his sweet face in the doorway. "Yeah, Mom?"

"Were you on the other side of the gym?"

He flushed, and even Reagan squirmed a little being witness to the Mom Stare. Kara had all the weapons of motherhood in her arsenal, and she was loaded for bear this morning.

The sweet woman with the elfin face and soft voice crossed her arms over her chest and glared. "And remind me, one more time, why you aren't allowed to cross the halfway mark of the gym?"

Zach sighed, the heavy sigh of the beleaguered. "Because the coach's office is on that side of the gym." When Kara only waited, he added, "And I'm not supposed to bother him, even if his door is closed."

"That's right. So you stay on this side, or I'll make you sit in here and listen to us gossip."

The horrified look on Zach's face had Reagan covering a snicker with a cough. "Fine, Mom." He sprinted away, and they could hear his sneakers echoing in the hollow, empty gym as he darted around invisible defenders on his way to make the game-winning basket.

"Stinker," Kara muttered, but she was fighting off a smile.

"He's awesome," Reagan said. "Reminds me of my brothers. They all turned out decent, for the most part."

"For the most part?" Marianne leaned in. "Which one didn't?"

"The ax murderer," Reagan said easily, appetite returning enough to pop another bite of sandwich in her mouth and chew before she added, "Kidding."

Kara and Marianne's twin frozen faces of terror made her snort.

"You guys are too easy. He's just a good kid, that's all I mean. Listens to his mom, pushes boundaries a little—but what kid doesn't?—and respects you enough to not argue when you rein him back in."

"He is pretty awesome, isn't he?" Kara's smile grew a little misty, and Reagan wanted very much to avoid waterworks.

"Yup. If only he weren't so ugly . . ."

"Reagan!" Marianne threw her napkin at her while simultaneously laughing.

The sound of men's voices drifted to their room, and all three women sat up a little straighter. Marianne checked the clock. "Must be an early group wanting to get some exercise in before practice."

"Zach!" Kara hopped off the table and rushed to the door of the training room. "Zach, come back in here now."

Zach rushed back, red-faced. The unmistakable sound of a basketball bouncing caught Reagan's ear. "Mom! Mom, they said I could play with them. They've got a basketball with them and they said they were going to get a game in before practice. Can I play? *Pleeeeeeeeeeeease?*"

The amount of pathos a child could pack into a single word was unbelievable.

Reagan could see the worry in Kara's eyes. Would her son get hurt? Would his feelings be crushed if they rejected him? Would he just be in the way? "I don't know. I think maybe you should—"

"Hey, ladies." Graham Sweeney walked over, a ripped T-shirt covering his torso—sort of—and a basketball under one arm. He slung the other arm around Zach's head, pressing the kid's ear into his rib cage. "We need someone younger and weaker to beat up on so we can feel manly before practice. Mind if we use this thing for a punching bag?"

Zach protested, fighting off the hold, but Reagan could see he was laughing. It was a totally guy thing to do, and Zach was loving it.

Kara looked unconvinced, but Marianne asked, "Do you promise to return him in nearly the same condition as you found him?"

"Which is pretty scrawny and not much to look at," Reagan added, which had Graham throwing her a brilliant grin. The man was truly Greek god gorgeous. If she hadn't been sitting down already, she would have felt the full impact in the knees on that one.

Kara reached out to stroke a hand over Zach's hair—a move Reagan had seen her do a dozen times. But this time, Zach dodged. Kara snatched her hand back, aware she'd nearly embarrassed her son in front of men he wanted to impress. "If you're sure he won't interrupt anything . . ."

"Nah. He's all good. Come on, fresh meat. Let's go rough you up a bit." He started to go, but then turned around. "Oh, and Reagan? You're all set for tonight. Have fun."

Zach laughed and followed, and then the sounds of a basketball bouncing, male grunts, groans and—along with Kara's winces—some swearing filled the gym. Marianne walked over and closed the door. "'Have fun'? All set for what?"

"Spill," Kara added.

"I might be having dinner with a certain Marine tonight."

Reagan took another bite, and forced herself to chew thoroughly before swallowing. The pained looks on her friends' faces told her she'd taken enough time with torture. "I'm going over to Graham's house tonight for dinner."

"But I thought you were dating Greg," Kara said, looking confused.

"Sorry, yes. We're borrowing Graham's house for the, uh, date." She shrugged. "Greg wanted to cook and obviously he can't do that at his place."

"Why not yours?"

Reagan swallowed another bite before answering, "My kitchen is horrible." No lie there. "I survive off cold cereal and granola bars." Also no lie.

"But you're not going to"—Kara checked the door before finishing—"do it there, right? Because in someone else's bed is just—"

"Ew. No!" Reagan recoiled at the thought. "We just wanted privacy for a meal and a movie." The image Greg had painted the night before as he'd said good-bye at her car drifted through her mind. She couldn't stop her lips from curving. "That's all."

"Privacy would be at your place, where you apparently don't want him to be." Marianne watched her thoughtfully. "So you either meet him at his place, where there's no privacy, or at Kara's place, where there's no privacy, or at someone else's house, where there's no hopes of getting busy because of the 'ew' factor. Sounds like you're cockblocking yourself."

"Or we're just in a unique situation that requires some extra thought before taking the next step," Reagan said primly.

"Bull," both women said at once.

"We've got a few travel gigs coming up," Marianne added. "Why don't you take advantage of them? Make sure your hotel room is right next to his or something. Sneak into his room after bed check."

"Could you make this sound any more juvenile?" Reagan

grumbled, then popped down and brushed her hands off on the napkin. "Guess today's the day I give a 'How to Handle Protestors' lecture."

Marianne smiled. "Want me to make you a pamphlet?"

FOUR hours later, Reagan sat at her laptop, trying to work in her apartment. She had two more hours before she needed to be at Graham's, and if she couldn't focus on something else, she'd go crazy with anticipation. But there was a problem . . .

The refrigerator was loud.

Not just loud . . . constant. The kind of constant noise that wormed its way into your mind so that long after the sound was gone, you still heard it because it had slowly driven you crazy.

Reagan threw an accusatory glance at the appliance. It didn't respond. Instead, it hummed the same hum it had been making all evening. The same hum that had buried itself into Reagan's brain until she could no longer concentrate on the task at hand.

Or maybe that was just her inner procrastinator talking.

Probably the latter. Not that she'd accept defeat to the fridge.

She focused, squinted at the screen, closed both eyes and tried very hard to remember all the different types of punches one could use in a boxing match.

She ended up with one: a punch.

"This is impossible," she growled, shooting one more glare at the kitchen before closing her laptop. How was she supposed to work with a bunch of boxers as their athlete liaison if she had no clue what they were doing half the time?

A small part of her mind reminded her this was exactly why she had misled her supervisor when she'd done the interview. That she'd done her best to sound as knowledgeable about boxing as she could without delving too deep into

the details. She'd memorized a few of the most famous boxers and what they were most famous for. But in reality . . .
she'd just needed the damn job.

Call your brothers.

They liked boxing. They liked all sports. It was the only
thing accessible for guys—that was legal, anyway—in their
backward town. Hell, the only reason she'd been a cheerleader was because it was either that or 4H for girls. Her
brothers had all played whatever sports they could get their
hands on, and watched what sports they could on the few
channels they had growing up. She'd been outnumbered four
to one when it came time to pick channels.

Calling her brothers, though, meant calling home. And
calling home was never something she could do lightly. Most
people thought of home as a safety net, a soft place to fall,
a nest one could be gently nudged out of, but always return
to when times were hard.

Reagan considered her home quicksand. Put one foot in
and it dragged you down until you couldn't breathe and lost
the light of day.

A dramatic image, maybe, but accurate.

But there was no way she was getting anywhere on her
own with this.

Call Greg.

She wasn't quite ready to admit her incompetence yet. She
would rather he—all the Marines, really—saw her as an independent businesswoman who didn't need assistance. Plus, she
was due to see him in a few hours. He'd consider her call a
ploy to hear from him, like a lovesick puppy. No, thank you.

Which left her with her brothers. Again.

Reagan stared at her phone with the same sort of disdain
she'd given the refrigerator. Finally, she picked it up and
dialed home, praying it was her youngest brother who would
answer and not her mother.

"Hello?"

No such luck. Reagan took a deep breath, then one more as her mother tersely repeated, "Hello?"

"Hey, Mom."

There was a brief pause. "Reagan?"

"Yeah, Mom, it's me." Swallowing, she tried to bypass what she knew would be a rough conversation. "I had a work question for Nick. Is he there?"

"And just what do you think an eighteen-year-old is gonna do for your fancy job?" her mother asked, voice tight with disapproval. "He doesn't have a college degree like you."

Reagan closed her eyes and counted to five. "I had a question about boxing. I know Nick watches it."

"They've got boxing here, if you wanted to work with a bunch of sweaty men. Remind me again why this job was so important you had to move halfway across the country? Away from your family?"

Because I couldn't breathe around you.

"Because that's where the job offer came from." Doing her best to be reasonable against all odds, she added, "I do miss you all."

"Not enough to call more often. Oh, I know," her mother added with the sigh of a woman truly put upon. "You have so much to do, being important, that you can't spare the time."

"Okay, so, I can call back later then."

"Always were too good for your family."

"No, Mom." She pinched the bridge of her nose and cursed whatever stupid idea had led her to this conversation. "That's not it. I just wanted something different."

"Which is code for better." Her mother sniffed. "You'll come back. They always come back."

If Reagan had had a nice, soft place to land, maybe. Sometimes people did need to come home to regroup. She could understand a home where you could move back when times were tough, get back on your feet quickly, and part with your parents once more on good terms.

She did not come from such a house.

"Hey, Mom? I actually have to run. The . . ." She fought for a good excuse. "Work is calling."

"Well aren't they special, calling you at all hours. See what reaching for better gets you? You're never off work. Never relaxing. Get yourself a solid job, and you can clock in and out and wash your hands of the place when you leave. Your brother—"

"I know, Mom. Sorry, love you, bye!" She ended the call and dropped the phone on the desk like it was a snake.

She could have stayed in her hometown, Reagan thought as she went back to searching boxing terms and watching instructional videos. Could have stayed there, married one of her boyfriends right out of high school like so many of her classmates had, been pregnant before twenty, become a mother before she could legally drink. Right now, she could have three under three, clinging to her legs while she cleaned the stove or something.

She shot her own stove an assessing glance.

Nope.

It wasn't that she had anything against those who got married out of high school. It was absolutely their choice, and she hoped they had a good life. It just wasn't *her* choice. She would have slowly died in that life. But that wasn't concerning to her family. What mattered was her turning her back on what her mother considered "tradition."

It hurt. Who would be able to say, "Yeah, rejection from my family? Great stuff." But you couldn't choose your family. Sometimes, you just had to live with it.

Her phone buzzed, and she checked the screen warily. It was a text message, but not from family.

Marianne: Don't you dare wear one of your suits tonight.

She grinned and texted back.

Reagan: I was thinking of going naked. Thoughts?

Marianne: I don't have bail money, just so you know. Put on some date-wear.

Reagan: Can you be more specific?

Marianne: Sexy, not slutty. Think shoulders, not tits. Think back, not ass. And nothing that will wrinkle, in case things get a little frisky.

Reagan: Hold on, let me get a pencil to write this down. It's pure fashion gold.

Marianne: :P Go have fun. Wear your hair down. And for God's sake, wear a heel under three inches. Your ankles and your athletic trainer are both begging you.

Reagan couldn't stop smiling as she walked into her bedroom to assess her wardrobe for anything "date-wear" worthy.

As she laid out three tank tops on the bed, she realized that no, you couldn't choose your family. But sometimes you could add on a brand-new branch, with friends.

She had a good start on that new branch with the friends she'd made already in Jacksonville. Time to focus on that.

CHAPTER

13

Greg stirred the sauce and kept an ear out for the door. Graham, the idiot, had left only minutes earlier, after razzing him ruthlessly about everything from his outfit—had the man never seen a pair of slacks before?—to the menu and mood music he'd put on.

Greg didn't take it personally. Clearly, his friend was jealous. He was about to spend the evening with a beautiful woman, eating decent food and hopefully doing a bit more of that kissing he'd gotten a taste of earlier.

Meanwhile, his friend was hitting up a movie and, well, he wasn't quite sure what else Graham had planned. As long as he stayed out until midnight, as promised.

The doorbell rang, and Greg turned the burner down to low and dashed for the door. When he opened it, he expected to find Reagan in his eye line. Instead, he realized he had to look down a few inches to find her. "Hey. You're here."

"I am." She stepped by, brushing her breasts against his arm as she moved into the home. "Nice and out of the way of Jacksonville back here."

"Not in Jacksonville at all, actually. It's Hubert. Don't blink or you'll miss it."

Reagan shrugged out of her light sweater and glanced around. "Coat closet?"

Greg couldn't move. He wanted to explain but couldn't. Instead of the starched, proper business suits he was used to seeing her in, she wore a tank top in deep emerald that cut low over her breasts with the thinnest of straps crossing over her shoulders. Her pants were black, but instead of the tailored business suit bottoms she normally wore, they were snug and cut off at just above the ankle. And foregoing her trademark heels, she had chosen flats instead, black again, with sparkly buckles.

And that didn't mention her hair, which she'd left loose and soft to fall in simple waves around those bare shoulders.

He realized he'd been staring as she pulled her sweater back against her chest. "Is something wrong?"

"No, no of course not. Sorry." He reached for her sweater and, after a moment of consideration, draped it over the back of the love seat. They wouldn't be using that piece of furniture anyway. He turned and pulled her into his arms, kissing her hard, and a little too briefly, before letting go. "You just look really good, that's all."

"I look different." She grimaced and glanced down at her bare arms. "Marianne convinced me to break out some 'date-wear.'" She used quote fingers on that one. "I thought I looked decent for work, but—"

"You do. This is just . . ." He hesitated, knowing he was walking right into a well-known man trap. "Different. A good different. A change. Variety."

When she only smiled, he hoped that was a sign he'd dodged the proverbial bullet.

She walked past, and circled around Graham's organized living room. "Does he live here alone?"

"He does, though he's got people over enough it probably doesn't seem like it. We all have an open invitation to hang out here if we need to escape the BOQ."

One finger trailed over a photograph of Graham with his sister—Greg knew because he'd razzed his friend on having a hot relative—and she grinned. "Either you picked up big time right before I got here, or he's a tidy fellow."

"The second. I struggle to keep my own box of a room neat, and I only have like two suitcases–worth of clothing with me." He took her hand before she could tantalize him any more with that fingertip-trailing thing she did and pulled her to the kitchen. "Come be my taster."

"Sounds like the best offer I've had all day."

He pulled her into the kitchen, then settled her on a bar stool and poured her a glass of wine. "I'm not great with wines," he admitted, "but the guy at the liquor store on base told me this one was good with a red sauce."

She lifted the glass, did a little swirl-and-sniff thing that made him doubt his ability to make a good selection, then took a tiny taste. He held his own breath, waiting. She burst out laughing when she looked at him. "I'm sorry, that was so pretentious. I know nothing about wine, either. I just know what tastes good."

His entire body relaxed, and he kissed her hard in retaliation. "Stinker. So is it at least good?"

"It is. Well done." She patted his cheek and settled back in her chair, waving a hand toward the stove. "Now go. Cook for me, minion."

"Yes, ma'am." He headed back to stir the sauce, dumped the pasta into boiling water, and double-checked his meatballs in the oven. After giving them the okay, he passed those to the saucepan and slid garlic bread slices into the oven in their place.

"The man can cook," she murmured, watching him over the rim of her glass. "Hidden talents."

"It's just pasta, and other than grilling some meat—which I have to add, I'm excellent at—it's all I can do. But it keeps me from fast food, at least part of the time. Meatballs go with a lot of stuff."

"What's the secret to grilling?"

He shook his head at that. "I can't divulge the secret without some give and take."

"Okay then." Reagan settled back, looking as relaxed as he'd seen her since the day they met. She let one wavy lock of hair twirl around her finger. "I'll bite. What do I have to do to get the famous grilling secret?"

"You've gotta pass on a recipe of your own. Simple trade."

"Easy enough. I'll give it to you right now." She leaned forward, which meant her breasts were shelved on the high kitchen island. It was as if the granite countertop was made to hold those gorgeous orbs of alabaster skin. "You open up a bag of that salad mix, pour it into a bowl, then dump some Newman's dressing over the top. Ta-dah. Salad."

He scowled. "That's it?"

"Sometimes, if I'm feeling really fancy, I buy that pre-sliced deli meat and toss it on top. Now you've got a chef's salad." She sat back, looking smug as she took another sip. "But that's really not for beginners. We'll work our way up."

"This isn't good," he said, stirring the pasta, testing a piece and deciding it needed one more minute. "Neither of us can cook more than two meals between the two of us. We're doomed."

"Hey, now. You haven't had my famous macaroni and cheese." She raised her brows at his skeptical look. "The blue-box recipe is extremely famous, thank you very much, Judgey Pants."

"I'm sorry. I should have worn my more humble pants this evening. Simple wardrobe mistake." He started to plate their dinner, stacking pans and pots by the sink to wash later. Or, should things go as anticipated, for Graham to wash later.

Sorry, buddy. You'd do the same thing.

As they sat down, he relished listening to her make pleasurable little sounds as she tasted a bit of each. "This isn't the garlic bread you buy in the frozen foods section, is it?"

He did his best to appear offended. "How dare you, madam."

She raised a brow, and he cracked like fine china. "Okay, fine. Normally I cheat and go that direction. But for tonight, I broke out the big guns and used a real French bread and did it myself. Much better."

"Mmm. Much." She took another bite of that piece, then set it aside. "Don't let me have another, or I'll never fit into my suits again."

"I hardly think that's an issue. But hey, if you're looking for a postdinner calorie-burn . . ." He waggled his brows suggestively, and had the pleasure of watching her groan while laughing. "I'm just glad you said yes to dinner."

"I'm glad Graham gave us the run of his house. You're sure he's okay leaving like this?"

Greg nodded. "He's fine. He's . . . do you want to get that?" he added, when her cell phone started to ring.

She glanced at her purse, sitting on the chair next to her. "No, ignore it."

The ringing stopped, only to start again a few seconds later. "Go ahead. Might as well get whatever it is out of the way."

She apologized, started to get up, then stopped and sat back down. "It's Kara. Normally I'd ignore but—"

"Totally okay."

He watched her worried expression as she answered.

"No, I'm not at my place, I'm already out. Why, what's . . . oh. Uh . . ." She looked down at her plate, then over at Greg. "Well . . . okay. Yeah, sure. I'll figure it out. How long will you need me?" She mouthed an *I'm sorry* to him. *Kara needs me.*

He motioned for her to hand him the phone. She hesitated, then said, "Kara, I'm actually with Greg and . . . no, it's okay. Please don't worry. But he wants to talk to you. Yeah. Okay, here." She handed him the phone. "She's got to run out and needs someone to watch Zach. It's a yoga-mergency."

Yoga-mergency? "Kara, hey. It's Greg Higgs."

"I'm sorry about this." Misery and embarrassment were both plain in Kara's voice. "I completely forgot you two were spending tonight together. If I'd remembered, I wouldn't have barged in like this."

"You need someone to watch Zach?"

"One of my clients—the one you don't say no to because she pays way too well—called for a last-minute private before she leaves the country. Apparently she can't go on vacation without one more round of sun salutations. My normal babysitter can't make it."

In the background, he could hear Zach's small voice yell, "I don't need a babysitter!"

Kara sighed. "I can't get ahold of Marianne, and her parents are on vacation themselves. I'm so sorry, but—"

"Stay there. I'm sending reinforcements. And trust me, Zach will definitely not complain. Just trust me."

"I'm not comfortable leaving him with a stranger," Kara warned.

"You won't be. Just hold tight." He hung up, handed Reagan's phone back to her, then whipped his own out to start texting.

After a minute, Reagan said, "Okay, curiosity is winning. Who are you sending over?"

"Graham." Satisfied, he stuffed the phone in his pocket. "She knows him, Zach likes him, and he planned to stay out of the house for a few hours anyway. He'd been debating a movie, but this is going to be more fun. He's good with it."

"I know, but—"

"Hey." He put one hand over hers, let his thumb caress the side. She opened under him, laced her fingers with his. "Has Kara ever been one to shrink in the face of motherly duties?"

"Of course not."

"So she's going to let us know if it's not okay." He took a sip of water, not wanting to let go of her hand just yet to eat. "Plus, I added that kid likely has a good video game collection, which means she'll have a hard time getting rid of Graham."

"Men." Reagan smiled a little before pulling her hand away to twirl some pasta on her fork. "They're just boys who eat more and kept getting bigger."

"Exactly." He tugged the back of her neck so she leaned in for a sweet kiss. "But you ladies tolerate us. Bless you."

KARA wrung her hands, caught herself doing it, and forced them behind her back. Then in her pockets. Then clutching the straps of her yoga bag, she walked back to her son's room.

He was exactly where she'd left him ten minutes earlier, sprawled on the bed, arms extended straight up, holding a graphic novel above. If he fell asleep for even a second, that book would fall and smack him straight in the nose.

She knew because she read the exact same way, and had woken up more than once when she'd dropped her book—or worse, her e-reader—on her face.

"Remember, Graham's in charge."

"Uh-huh," Zach said without looking away from his book.

"I won't be gone long."

"Uh-huh."

"And you know your list of restrictions."

"Yeah."

"The main EpiPen is—"

"With the rest of the meds, like it's always been." He put his book over his stomach and gave her an irritated glance upside down. "Mom, I'm ten. I think I've got this."

Her little boy, all grown up. Or at least, he thought so. "I know. I'm just being a mom. You'll thank me one day."

His snort as he picked up the book informed her he considered that outcome unlikely at best.

The knock on the door had her turning, just before she leaned back to say, "I love you, Zach."

"Uh-huh."

Boys. Shaking her head, Kara went to answer the door, and let in the babysitter.

The babysitter, of course, was the most gorgeous man she'd ever met. Graham's dusky skin and perma-shadow from stubble made her think of pirates sailing the high seas. His hair was always a little longer than most, and probably skirted the edges of regulations. And he was tall, so tall. She'd also seen the man move. He was a true athlete, even with a yoga mat. He made her feel smart, listened to what she said and treated her like a lady.

He must be kept at arm's length at all times.

"Graham." She opened the door all the way and let him in. "I'm so sorry you got roped into coming over here."

"No big. I had to be out of my place for a while, anyway." He stood inside her tiny living room, making the room shrink just with his presence. He turned a three-sixty to take in the small space. "Nice."

"It's small, but it works for us," she said, biting her tongue at the defensiveness. He'd just complimented the space, hadn't he?

"Hmm," was all he said, and stuffed his hands into his jeans pockets. "Where's the squirt?"

"Zach's in his room, reading. He might come out, or not. He's big on reading though, and when he goes into the zone, it's hard to break." She waited for some taunt, some egghead joke, something that she could take and mull over, something to make her not like him so much.

"Cool. Lucky you, getting a kid who likes reading."

Dammit. Would the man stop being so damn perfect? With a frostier tone than was warranted, she pointed toward the kitchen. "Emergency numbers are on the fridge. He has an EpiPen in the medicine cabinet, which I put a Post-it Note on so you don't have to dig for it. He knows how to administer it himself, but the instructions are on the box. If you have a minute and want to read through them, that would be great. I also put a list of his allergens on the fridge next to the numbers. He hasn't eaten dinner yet, but he can make his own. Please don't feed him anything from outside the house. If you're hungry though, you can order a pizza or whatever. Just make sure he doesn't get tempted and have any." It was the same spiel she'd given all his babysitters since he was fourteen months old and popped positive on his first allergy test for, well, almost everything.

Graham looked offended, his dark eyes flashing. "I'm not ordering a pizza to eat it in front of him when he can't have a slice. That's cruel. I'll have what he's having."

"You might regret that. It's going to be sun butter and jelly on special, not-normal bread," she warned. No matter what, she still couldn't get used to non-peanut butters. But she ate them for her son's sake. Too bad they were twice as expensive.

"I'll make the squirt make me a sandwich. If he can eat it, I can eat it. Guys can eat anything." Walking back to the door, Graham opened it. She tried hard not to notice how the short sleeve of his polo shirt gripped around his biceps when he did that. "Off you go. The menfolk will be fine."

"Yeah, Mom." Zach, emerging from his cocoon, stood beside Graham. "We're good." As if in agreement, Graham laid his other hand on Zach's shoulder, united in pushing the lone female out of their cave for the evening.

Her son's chest puffed out just standing next to the Marine. He looked so happy to be in the company of another male, even if he was being—ew, ick—babysat.

"Fine." She debated for a half second, then left without trying a hug. It would only embarrass him. So she just added a thank-you for Graham, and closed the door.

Instinct had her pausing on the doorstep for a moment. She heard her son shout with joy as he yelled, "Come see what I've got in my room! Mom just got me a new game," and Graham's more deep-voiced answer, then nothing.

If his father were around more . . . *No, shake that one off, Kara.* His father chose to not be around, except in very limited doses. So these moments of male bonding were all she had to offer currently. As he grew, she'd have to intentionally find more opportunities like this.

But for now, it would be enough to hang out for a night with a sun butter–eating Marine and some unwise video games.

CHAPTER

14

"How have you not seen any of the Harry Potter movies?" Greg asked, rubbing her upper arm as she jerked against him, startled by the action on the screen.

"I'm a purist. How have you not read any of the—oh!" Reagan covered her eyes as something jumped out from the shadows. Her startle reflex was terrible. "Not read any of the Harry Potter books? They're classics."

"Not much of a reader."

She didn't hold it against him. Some might automatically make the leap into "stupid jock" territory, but that was short-sighted of them. Ten minutes with Greg and it was easy to see there was nothing dumb about him.

"Are you looking forward to your meet next week?"

"Shh," he said, squeezing her closer to his side while they watched Harry and his friends battle through the dungeon looking for the Sorcerer's Stone.

"You've seen it, and I know how it turns out," Reagan pointed out, which had Greg sighing and turning the volume down. Score one for female logic. "Are you excited?"

"To go beat up on a few guys in South Carolina?" He made a noise of disagreement, but she could feel his muscles tighten. Or at least the ones pressed against her. He rotated so that his back rested against the arm of the sofa, and her back leaned flat over his chest. She laid her head back and listened to his heartbeat while he thought. "I mean, Paris Island's team is probably pretty decent. It's not like us, but it'll be a good show for the crowd. Good practice for us." He thought for a moment, then let his hand drift to the nape of her neck, let his fingers slide in just a little to her hairline and play there. "Maybe worried for some of the younger guys."

"Worried they can't keep up?"

"A few. Others, worried they'll do too well and won't know when to pull back."

"You're supposed to treat this like a real match. You're not meant to pull back." Or at least, that's what her packet of information had told her. "Everyone goes in giving one hundred percent."

"Yes . . . and no. A few don't know when to pull back. You give the full goods, until you know the other guy's done. Now, if it's a real rival, like during the All Military games, then hey, play on." He chuckled. "I'm not gonna pull you off an Army guy. But when it's one of our own, you don't go for the throat like you would otherwise. When he's down, he's down. No need to keep at it so he stays that way."

"I see." She didn't fully, if she were being honest with herself. Sports weren't really her thing, ever. But she was doing her best to catch up. "Either way, are you excited to be traveling and seeing new competition?"

"Excited to get out of the BOQ. . . and into a new BOQ, sure. And ready to see some new blood. We'll stop there with 'ready.'"

He seemed so blasé about the whole thing. So matter-of-fact. "I have to go with you. It's my first time traveling like this for work. Can I tell you a secret?"

He wrapped an arm around her, just under her breasts, and squeezed gently. "Shoot."

Why did he have to make her feel so safe, so secure, so dainty when he did that? It scrambled her mind like an egg meant for an omelet. "I'm nervous."

"Nervous about what?"

"About messing up. About making the wrong step. I've already made mistakes with this whole prank-war thing going on. And now there are protestors, and that stupid article that seems like it's going viral . . ." She sighed and snuggled tighter against him. He pressed his lips to her temple, and she was ready to tell him her entire life story, even the embarrassing parts. "I'm worried I'm failing, and I won't know how badly until I walk into work one day and there's a pink slip in my mailbox."

"That's not gonna happen."

"Oh, really?" She smiled at the fierceness in his voice. The absolutely certainty he could stop it from happening by sheer will and determination alone. "Who's going to stop it? I was going to ask 'you and what army?' but since the answer would clearly be 'the Marines,' I'll let that one stand."

"You're not going anywhere. I'm just getting started with you." He slid her down just a little, then did some fancy leg work so that she rested on her side, her back to the back of the sofa, their faces an inch apart. He blocked her from rolling off the couch with his own body. "I'm not letting you get away that easily."

"You look at me the way you do," she said, tracing a finger over one of his brows, then the other, "and you say the things you say, and you make me feel not so much . . ."

"What?" he asked, his voice all but a rumble in his chest.

"Not so alone out here."

As if that were the answer he'd looked for himself, his eyes glowed hot an instant before his mouth came down over hers. He rotated them once more, so she lay flat on her back, and all that kept his weight from pressing into her were his elbows and one knee. The man was a master at the ground work. He should have been an MMA fighter instead.

Wrapping her arms around his neck, she pulled him more firmly to her. "I want to feel you," she whispered. He shook his head and tried to prop himself back up, but she nipped his lip. "I'm not a flower, I won't get crushed. Please. I need to feel you."

Tentatively, he rested his body more fully on hers. Oh, God, she needed that. Needed to feel the full weight of him across every inch of her. The hard, thick length of his every pound of muscle pushing at her softness was so delicious she moaned into his mouth. He returned the sound with a groan of his own, pressing his thick erection into the cleft between her legs before letting his tongue sweep in.

He tasted like the ice cream they'd had after dinner, and his hands rasped over her skin as he pushed her tank top up to sit right below her breasts. It took everything she had not to suck in her stomach, to flex, try to make it feel flatter as his fingers traced over her torso.

But if he noticed she wasn't exactly a thin lady, he didn't seem to mind. With every stroke of his fingers, calloused tips rasping over her skin, he seemed to thicken against her thigh more. One thumb brushed just under the wire edge of her bra, but no more. It was as if he were teasing them both, holding out until they were nearly burning with the urge to touch everywhere.

She was thirty seconds away from unhooking her own damn bra when he sat back, relieving her of his weight entirely. She blinked up at the ceiling, jarred from the quick movement. "What . . ."

Greg stood, on what looked like not-so-sturdy legs, and did a quick once around the living room. She noticed while his back was turned, he shook out his right leg more than once . . . to relieve the pressure against his erection, she assumed.

"What happened?"

"Nothing," he said quickly, back still turned to her.

"Then get back here. You changed the channel right when it was getting good."

"I want to, but I won't." He said it through strained vocals, like he was talking around a lump in his throat. He cleared it, then faced her. The massive bulge in front was impossible not to stare at. "Eyes up here, Robilard."

Without even a blush, she met his gaze. "You're not going to tell me you don't want me, right?"

"No. And from the way your high beams are flashing, I know you're feeling the same way."

She instinctively reached down to cover her breasts, then realized there was no point. So she brushed her tank top down and hoped to look nonchalant about the whole thing as she sat up. "Is there something the matter?"

"I'm just thinking," he said, and started to pace, "that maybe we're not ready for this step yet."

"Second base," she said dryly. "We're not ready for second base."

"You don't have to say it like that." His voice, like his gaze, was dark and not altogether friendly.

"Greg," she said with a sigh, "there are high schoolers who move on to second base faster. I know you've got your training schedule, and that keeps you busy. And I've got work, and all the weirdness that goes with that. But I thought . . ." She held up her hands, then let them fall again. "I thought we were past that. Aren't we past that?"

"It's not you . . ." he started, and she stiffened. He rushed over to kneel in front of her just before she could stand. "Stop. Don't move."

"If you finish that sentence with, '. . . it's me,' I will punch you," she warned. "I've been watching you guys practice. I could put some heat behind it."

He snorted, but did his best to keep his face straight. Other than a slight twitch at the corner of his lips, he managed it. "I wasn't. Hear me out?"

She waited a moment, just to make him sweat. But then she settled back into the couch cushions and put her hands in his when he held his out. "It better be good. I dried my hair for this, you know."

"I know, and it looks beautiful." He started to speak again, then just leaned in and kissed her once more, on the lips. "I needed that."

It amused her that he took the kiss like another man might take a shot of bourbon just before doing something unpleasant. For courage, or for encouragement, maybe.

"I'm not great at this whole . . . thing. This slow build to a relationship."

Neither was she, clearly, but she let that pass.

He ran one hand over his short hair in a gesture so obviously self-frustrated, she wanted to tell him it would be okay. But that would be helping, and he didn't want help, so she waited.

"I don't want to mess this up. I wasn't sure if I even wanted to be on the team, but now I am. And I wasn't sure I wanted to tangle with a woman, but I do. And I wasn't sure I wanted that woman to be you, but she is, and I'm glad, but it's fucking terrifying."

Maybe some women wouldn't be impressed with a speech that included the word *fucking* but for her, for Greg, for that moment, it was raw and real and it was the exact right thing she needed to soothe her nerves. She cupped his face in hers and kissed him, long and hard, so he knew where her head was. "I get it . . . I think. You want to make sure that we don't move so fast that we burn out physically before we reach the next step emotionally."

"No," he breathed. Then, "I mean, yes."

"Poor guy," she murmured, rubbing her lips over his. "This has you all twisted up, doesn't it?"

He grumbled something adorably grouchy.

"Can I tell you a secret?"

He nodded, their noses bumping.

"It has me pretty twisted up, too."

When his shoulders dropped, just a fraction of an inch, she knew she'd worked her way into that soft spot she'd been searching for the whole time. Not sure how much longer he'd keep it exposed, she added, "I'm not all that brave at this. Combination of reasons, I guess. But I'm willing to open myself up more, if you are, too."

He nodded an agreement, kissed her again.

"So, are we the real deal?"

"Hell yeah, we are." Greg kissed her, pulling her against him so that her knees were spread wide and her crotch pressed to his stomach. "But we're still not going to second base tonight."

"Maybe before the homecoming dance," she teased, and let him kiss her again.

REAGAN inched forward in line to pass through the front gates, doing her best not to glare at the steadily growing number of protestors. The first day, it had been maybe four or five families plus a few more single people. No more than a dozen, total. Today, the head count was probably closer to fifty.

She snail-crawled past a mother with three kids, the youngest in a stroller. The youngest held up a sign written on what looked like construction paper. Clearly, he hadn't written it himself, as he was probably no more than two. But the sight of that child holding up a sign saying "Fighters go to hell," made her stomach drop.

Apparently her article in the paper, doing her best to debunk the myths surrounding the Marine Corps boxing team, either hadn't worked, or had induced the opposite result.

Gasoline on the fire.

At least they were peaceful, she reasoned as she inched forward another few feet. Cardboard signs with pithy sayings and half-hearted jargon wouldn't make anyone driving through these gates do anything but roll their eyes and take another drink of their morning coffee. But it still felt like a physical reminder of her failure.

Ten minutes later, she walked into the gym and headed straight for Coach Ace's office. She had calls to make, confirming their bus down to Paris Island for their matchup with the Marine drill instructors. And she had a text message on her phone to call her supervisor ASAP.

The moment she closed Coach Ace's doors, she dialed her supervisor.

"Robilard!" Andrew Calvant barked.

"Yes, sir?" She sat down, instantly regretting the choice. Even if he wasn't there, he might feel her intimidation. She stood, ready for the offense.

"What the hell kind of article is this?"

She blinked. Hadn't he read it yesterday when she'd emailed him? "I'm sorry, I thought you read it already. It was my response to the first article about—"

"Not yesterday's thing," he snarled. "Today's paper. Did you read it?"

Did she admit she hadn't read that morning's paper, and look lazy? Or did she act like she had, and fly blind for the rest of the conversation?

He made the choice for her. "Front page, above the fold this time. Lovely title, though I'll let you read that for yourself. I especially like the alliteration. But the article is a true gem. It talks about how we're attempting to make a bunch of killing machines—that would be our athletes, if you aren't keeping up—look like, and I quote, 'pansy-ass candy sticks' and trying to pass them off as 'an enlightened bunch of kangaroos.'"

She let that sink in for a moment.

"Anything to say?" he bit out.

"People like kangaroos."

There was silence on the other end.

People like kangaroos? That's the best you can come up with?

She was so getting fired.

"Robilard," he said, in a voice so low and menacing she'd need to check if she was bleeding somewhere from the sheer venom alone, "make this go away. Make it all go away, very quickly, or you will be exiting stage right." That was the last she heard before the line died.

"Right," she said, her voice shaky. "Good to hear from you, too, sir." She sat down and let her cell phone drop to the desk. Would anyone notice, she wondered, if she crawled under the table and just cried for a few minutes? Nothing more, just a couple good sobs to clear the system . . .

Yeah, probably not a good idea.

Doing the best she could by rote, she called the bus barn and confirmed their transportation, then went online using Coach Ace's computer—holy molasses, Batman, the thing moved at the speed of a snail—and checked what the local paper had to say.

After she found it, she felt her lip sneer. It was the same reporter from the other day, that David Cruise. The one who had written that stupid, overly verbose crap about the double helix of violence and whatever else. The poor guy had been paint splattered, and she knew that wasn't a great first impression. But come on.

There was a knock on the door, and she went to open it. Coach Ace stood there, and she started to apologize, but he shook his head. Then he stepped back, and two MPs took his place. "Ms. Robilard?"

She nodded, her tongue too thick to speak.

"We were told you were the athlete liaison for the team. Is that correct?" the same one asked.

She again nodded.

"We'll need your assistance, ma'am. We're conducting an investigation into the events that have taken place leading up to the paint incident."

"Oh." She blinked, then looked back at the coach. "Uh, can we use your office?"

"You've got it. Let me know if you need anything." He stepped aside so the two young Marines could walk in and sit down. Before he left, the coach bent down closer in the guise of grabbing the door handle, and added, "You need anything, you come get me. All right?"

So grateful for the show of immediate support after she'd just been dumped on, she nearly teared up at that. But it would only embarrass them both, so she nodded quickly and turned to go sit behind the desk.

"Gentlemen," she began, forcing her most professional tone of voice. "What can I do for you?"

CHAPTER

15

Greg worked the heavy bag, keeping one eye on Coach Ace's door. Nobody else was getting a damn thing done in the gym, either. When the MPs started calling in one Marine at a time, you knew it wasn't good. And it definitely was a big kick in the nuts to productivity.

The whole thing sucked. He swung, punched, punched again, then said "Fuck it," and let his fists fly, forgetting the training pattern the coaches had handed down. Channeling his frustration, his anger, his inability to help Reagan into the heavy bag, he felt the soothing burn up his shoulders, into his back. Felt the way his knuckles started to tighten, his wrists ached. Knew he was getting out of control, but couldn't stop.

He had no idea how much time passed while he worked the bag. Could have been a few seconds, or an hour. That anger, the frustration of the day worked its way out through his fists. And he let it control him until he felt the tap on his shoulder. In instinct, he swung around, fists still cocked, and found one of the younger Marines backing away, palms up.

The younger man was sweating bullets. Greg knew it wasn't

just from the pretty mild workout they'd had. He shook his hands out and relaxed his stance so his teammate wouldn't worry. "Sorry, got in the zone."

"Yeah, I noticed." He glanced at the bag behind Greg, then back at him again. "You okay? I thought you were going to pull something the way you were working it."

"I'm fine."

"Okay." His eyes darted toward the coach's door. "What's going on in there? Why do they keep calling people in? I don't get it, we're the ones who keep getting targeted. We're the victims here. Why are they after us?"

Greg sighed. For some people, the police—in any form— were something they could never associate with the good guys. Either prior experiences or the way they were raised ingrained in their minds that all law enforcement were out to get everyone, were all crooked, were all bad. He'd seen enough of it himself in the numerous foster homes. Kids— usually older and more jaded than him—would tell him stories that could raise the hair on his arms. Cops that took bribes, that ran drugs, that bought into prostitution rings.

He was fortunate enough, he supposed, it didn't stick. There were dirty cops, just the same as any other occupa- tion. But the sunny optimist in him believed most cops were out there doing their job.

"Calm down, dude." Taking a break from the bag, he wrapped an arm around the younger man's shoulders and took a quick walk with him around the perimeter of the main floor. "They're just trying to fill in the blanks on what's been going on. Nobody's in trouble here."

"B-b-b-but I l-l-let the balloons f-f-fall," he stuttered. "My f-f-fault."

"No way." He shook the man a little as they kept walking. The other man's gait was decidedly stuttered as well. His sneakers squeaked over the waxed floorboards. "There were three of you, and trust me, we all saw your faces. You were just as shocked as the rest of us. You're good."

The other man started to shake. Greg cursed under his breath.

"Want me to come in with you?"

The young Marine gripped his forearm so hard, Greg thought he'd have a bruise in the morning. "Yeah? You would? Please say yes."

"If they let me," Greg answered by way of promise.

"Garrison, Christopher," one of the MPs called as he stepped out of Coach Ace's office. "Christopher Garrison, please."

"Okay. Here we go." Greg walked with him to the office and stood by the MP as Christopher took a seat inside. In his most quiet voice, he said, "The guy's scared shitless. I said I'd sit with him. I won't say a word."

"Name?"

"Gregory Higgs."

"You're next anyway. Just stay quiet and don't say a word while he's talking." The MP headed inside, leaving Greg to follow.

Greg waited while they questioned the younger man, paying more attention to the MPs than to his teammate. If they were all that interested in Christopher as a suspect, they damn sure hid it well.

But Greg was pretty sure they didn't suspect anyone from this team. If anyone, it would be auxiliary at best. Maintenance staff or something like that.

They finished up their questions, then freed him to go. Greg shifted into the chair Christopher had vacated and crossed his fingers over his belly. "Second verse, same as the first?"

"We'll ask the questions," one of the two older men said in a biting tone.

The other rolled his eyes.

Greg decided he liked the one with a sense of humor more.

"Seen anything suspicious lately?"

"Other than threats on walls, paint balloons and slashed tires? Nah."

The first looked unamused. The second fought off a lip twitch.

"Is there anyone who you believe would have a vested interest in this team failing?"

"Army's team, probably." When the first one's eyebrows snapped together, he shrugged. "We're a boxing team. It's fun, it's a diversion, but we're not really out there solving world hunger or creating a crisis. So no, not really. I can't think of anyone who would want the team to fail."

"Anyone with a personal vendetta then, against you or a teammate?"

That was an interesting question. He considered for a moment, but came up empty. "Not that I can think of."

"Do you have a key to the gym?"

"No, I don't. And I have no clue who all does. I could guess, but that's all."

The first MP stood, nodding curtly by way of dismissal. Greg stood and gave the second MP a quick smile. "It's been a pleasure, gentlemen."

"Be careful, Marine. They might stop at pranks, or they might push further. It's not possible to tell."

The warning from the older MP chilled him, but he gave them both his best I'm-good grin. "Bunch of fighting Marines? Let 'em try."

LIKE a chicken with its head cut off.

The expression finally made sense to Reagan. She'd been running nonstop since four that morning. The bus had to be checked, then rechecked. She'd called the MPs out to do an inspection of the vehicle because, well, better safe than sorry. And she'd left Marianne's two interns in the bus in the parking lot as a deterrent against any mischief.

But making sure that was completed, along with the host of other issues that cropped up as you were about to leave for a three-day trip, was insane. She'd been putting out spot fires all over the damn place, and she felt like she hadn't even had a chance to breathe yet.

Now the Marines were loading on the bus, each standing there in his matching windbreaker outfit looking like a solemn troop ready to head off to war. Maybe that's how the coach wanted them. To her, it seemed unnecessarily tense.

Coach Cartwright walked up to stand with her as she ticked the Marines off the list. No man left behind. "How's the prep coming?"

"Fine, thank you. Do you have everything with you, Tressler? Okay, good. Is there something I can help you with, Coach?" she asked as she checked another Marine off the list.

"No, just making sure you're aware we can't afford any mistakes on this trip."

She looked at the tall, string bean of a man, and shot him her best I've-got-this smile. The one that said *I'm so professional and competent I won't even pretend to be offended you asked that*. "Everything is wonderful. Looking forward to getting to Paris Island."

"Not sure why," he grumbled as he walked off. "Hellhole of a place."

"Oh, goodie," she said under her breath. "Costa, got everything?"

"Yes, ma'am." Bradley gave her an encouraging smile as he walked onto the bus.

See? Not every man was out there, determined to make her look like an idiot. Just certain ones.

Greg was the last Marine to load, though she wasn't sure if that was by choice or by luck. He paused while she did a quick run-through on her clipboard. Then when she glanced up, she found him a tad too close. "Hello, Greg. Got everything?"

"Are you coming?"

"I am."

"Then I've got everything." He winked at her, and it was a wink designed to say something akin to *If we weren't in public, I'd have my mouth all over you.*

Winks could talk, you know.

She shivered, checked her list twice, then halted. "Where's Garrison?" The parking lot was empty. She climbed on the bus, which was like a noise explosion. She cleared her throat, but that did nothing. She shouted, "Hey!" but only two people turned around, decided she didn't mean it, and went back to talking.

With exasperation, she turned to Coach Willis. The man was basically half her size, but she'd heard his lungs before. The man could do some damage with those pipes. "Coach, could you please?"

He nodded, stood on his seat, and let out a deafening roar so loud it vibrated off the walls of the bus. Reagan covered her own ears just in time to be spared the worst of the blow-back. When all eyes were up front, she nodded. "Thank you, Coach. Gentlemen, I'm missing Garrison. Christopher Garrison. Is he in here?"

They all turned and twisted in their seats, but no Garrison popped up.

"Not here," said one Marine from the back.

Greg stood. "I saw him earlier. Probably still in the bathroom. I'll grab him."

"Thank you," she said, grateful she wouldn't have to go pull him out of there herself. Because, well, ew.

Five nerve-racking minutes later, Greg emerged from the gym with a slightly-green looking Garrison in tow. He said nothing, just pushed the man to the middle of the bus, got him settled in his seat, sat down and shot her the okay sign.

"Driver," she said, taking her own seat in the front, "let's roll!"

* * *

TRAVEL, Greg decided, was basically no different whether it was for a training operation or for a boxing match. Bunch of sweaty, smelly Marines on a bus, singing stupid songs or laughing about the same five jokes they'd been telling each other since the beginning of time. A few humble brags, a few not-so-humble brags. Some talk about friends everyone had in common, some gossip—oh yeah, Marines could outgossip a granny.

It wasn't that bad, all in all. But the worst was . . . he couldn't sit next to the one person he wanted to.

Reagan.

Reagan, who looked so proper in her business suit and neat ponytail. Who wore heels that were completely impractical for travel and a suit that had to be stifling and uncomfortable as she sat up there with the coaches and Marianne. Reagan, whose voice was so deep and husky while she was in her professional mode, it gave him the most untimely boner of his life.

Nothing said awkward like popping wood in the back of a bus with a dozen other guys.

"How's Garrison?" Sweeney leaned over the top of his seat, arms folded. "Was he booting in the head?"

"Oh, yeah." Greg wrinkled his nose. "Not cool. He's an okay guy, but man, his nerves aren't really where they should be."

"Or maybe he's just that bad outside of the ring, and once he's in the ropes, he's got nerves of steel."

Possible. Greg shrugged. "Either way, I think he'll be happy when it's all over."

They were silent a moment. "How's Reagan holding up?"

"She's holding." He wouldn't let her crack. "How'd baby-sitting go the other night?"

Sweeney grinned. "That kid's hilarious. Seriously. And

hey, did you know there are, like, fifteen different substitutes for peanut butter?"

"No . . ." Greg said slowly. "I don't suppose I did."

"Some aren't all that great in your regular PB and J, but are good for cooking. Others suck in the cooking department, but are better on bread." He held up his hands when Greg stared at him. "What? The kid's got allergies. We talked. I learned a few things. Have you read Kara's blog?"

"Can't say that I have."

"It's really interesting. And sort of awe inspiring, all the stuff she's had to go through because of his allergies."

"Well, she's a good mom." Anyone could see that after two minutes with her and the kid.

"She is." Graham was quiet for a minute. "Think she'd say yes to a date?"

That had Greg swiveling his head back around. "With you?"

"No, with Coach Willis," Graham said dryly.

They both looked forward, watching as Coach Willis leaned over his knees and discussed something with Coach Cartwright across the aisle. The man was like the Lorax come to life, with his shocking orange beard and short, stalky stature.

"I think she'd say no to Coach Willis. Just a hunch," Greg said, grinning. "But with you, I dunno."

"What's wrong with me?" his friend asked defensively.

"So much," Greg said with a grin, dodging his friend's joking punch. "So much."

"Cool it, or the coaches are going to come back here and separate you two." Brad leaned over from across the aisle. "We've got a match tomorrow. Don't be a bunch of assholes and ruin it for everyone."

"Speaking of ruining it for everyone . . ." Graham dug through his bag for a moment and pulled out the morning paper. "Anyone read about the protests? It's that guy again, the same guy who wrote the first article."

"It occurs to me," Brad said as he took the paper from

Graham, "that this guy is getting a lot of play off what looks to an outsider to be a bunch of harmless pranks. He's really pouring the gasoline on the fire."

"And why?" Greg asked, angling himself to read over Brad's shoulder. "There are more interesting things to write about."

"Maybe he's the one creating the story in the first place," Graham said, voice dark. When both the other men stared at him, he added, "What? It's a theory."

"And hardly that," Brad added, dryly. "He doesn't have base access most of the time. And he barely seemed interested at all in us until those paint balloons hit. That's when he saw gold."

"He's an asshole," was all Greg felt confident in adding to the mix. He was too close to the situation—okay, too close to Reagan—to be unbiased. He couldn't care less what people wrote about him, about the Marine Corps, about the team. But he knew it hit her so much harder than it hit any of them, and he hated that for her. "But I doubt it's him."

"So maybe it's someone who got cut." Graham stretched. "They'd have motive. That whole 'bitter ex' complex."

"But not opportunity." Brad folded the paper neatly, offered it to Greg. He shook his head, so Brad handed it back to Graham. "They all had to report back to their own commands after getting cut. It's not like they have the chance to run around here without getting noticed. We'd have heard if one of our guys went AWOL."

"Auxiliary staff," Greg said, stating his own opinion. "Someone who works in maintenance, or maybe one of Marianne's interns."

Brad mulled over that a moment. "Opportunity," he admitted, "but no motive."

"Motive is as simple or as complicated as someone wants it to be," Graham stated, sounding every inch the lawyer he normally was. "He cut me off in traffic, she stepped on my foot as she walked by and never said sorry." He shrugged. "It's not always a mortal wound that scars, boys."

"Point taken," Brad said, crossing his arms. "It's pissing me off, whatever it is."

"I have a feeling it's costing Reagan," Greg added. When both men looked interested and leaned forward, he added, "I think she's struggling with it. She's got to handle the fallout when something negative happens, and her superiors keep harping on her to make it stop."

"As if she has that power," Graham muttered. "How do you know all this?"

"We talk," Greg said defensively. "We talked last night."

"Just talked?" Brad asked with a teasing kick.

"You know as well as I do I was in my room last night. Alone," Greg emphasized. "Reagan had an early start so she wasn't going to hang out last night. She's freaking out about making sure everything lands in place and nothing is disturbed for this trip. So if you see something suspicious, stop that shit in its tracks before it gets to her. She might lose her mind otherwise."

"Yeah, of course." Brad sat up straighter.

"Whatever you need, man." Graham clapped a hand on his shoulder. "We want this team to be successful, and we don't want her to get fired. She's nice to look at."

Greg growled, and Graham chuckled and settled back in his own seat.

Brad leaned in closer. "You having any problems with the whole dating-someone-close-to-the-team thing?"

"No," Greg said with a laugh. "That was your problem, not mine. We're adults. She's already given it the okay, and we're good. But thanks anyway."

Brad scowled. When he and Marianne, the team's athletic trainer, had first started seeing each other, they'd hidden their romance, concerned it wouldn't look good to others. Instead, the romance itself hadn't been the problem, but the secrecy. "Yeah, well, shut up. Not all of us are perfect, Higgs."

"I know. Not everyone can be as lucky as me." He

grinned as Brad threw him a glaring look. "Get over it, Marine. You got the girl, so move on."

"I did, and I am. Just wanted to make sure you weren't walking into the same trap I was." His roommate shrugged. "But since you seem to have it all under control, mazel tov." Brad slipped earbuds in his ears and closed his eyes.

Brad thought he had it all together? Ha. Not even close. He was a ball of nerves around Reagan, not that he'd let her know that. She had enough on her plate without worrying about a nervous Marine. She'd make that her problem, too. No, he was nervous not because of the team, or boxing, but because of her.

He'd never held off this long from sex when he'd really liked a woman. Not that he'd been a man whore either, but when they'd both felt the urge, they'd taken the plunge.

He felt the urge with Reagan, in a big way. But it was what that urge combined with more than lust that had him holding back. He wasn't prepared to make a mistake with her. Normally, he was of the "live and learn" philosophy when it came to mistakes in life. But with Reagan, there was an extra layer of caution in their dealings. As if both were afraid that a single mistake, no matter how small, might shatter the tentative bond they'd been building.

The only bright spot was that she seemed as aware of it as he was. And was just as reluctant to make a misstep as he was.

That did not, however, solve the problem of when they would actually take the next step in their relationship. Would she be ready soon? Or not until after their season was over?

Please, God, not that.

He could be a patient man, but even his patience had limits.

He watched as Reagan stood to reach over the next seat and ask Marianne a question. Her laugh caught the ear of several Marines, and they all turned to watch her speak.

Yeah, look all you want. But she's mine at the end of the day, boys.

He'd just have to walk them past the point of fear and into certainty to make it happen.

CHAPTER

16

Reagan knocked on the final door, closing her eyes for a moment and praying the inhabitant answered while wearing pants.

The door cracked, and a young Marine poked his head out. "Hey, Ms. Robilard."

"Hi, Jonathan." She smiled. "Everything okay? You have everything you need for tomorrow?"

"Yes, ma'am." He grinned, but didn't open the door wider. For that, she was grateful. "You doing bed checks? Coach Ace was already by like half an hour ago."

She held up the clipboard. "Just part of the service here with the Marine Corps boxing team. I'm in 112 if you need anything."

He nodded, then closed the door quietly. She made a check mark next to his name, then started walking back down the hallway. Counting with her pen, moving down her list, she did her best to estimate how long it would take to do a wakeup visit to everyone in the morning. If they had to be up by six thirty, then she'd need to start at—

She didn't have time to shriek as an arm whipped out from seemingly nowhere and yanked her into a room before shutting the door. She gathered enough oxygen to gasp, but not shout. A hand covered her mouth and she started to bite down . . . until she recognized the scent. Then her eyes adjusted to the dark room, and she identified the outline of the man pressed against her.

"Meph?" she managed to get out.

The dark figure chuckled. "Sorry, sweetheart. Didn't want you to sound the alarm before you realized it was me." His hand dropped away, smoothed over her frazzled hair and down to cover her still-frantic heartbeat. "Easy now."

She took a deep breath in and out, then repeated the gesture until she felt confident she wouldn't vomit or pass out. When her arms felt strong enough, she punched Greg's biceps as hard as she could with her left hand.

Given how he laughed, it felt more like swatting at a fly to him. Damn the man.

"You suck so bad," she bit out, then tried to bend down to grab the clipboard she'd dropped. But he wouldn't let her budge. "Greg, stop. I have to get back to my room."

"You will . . . eventually."

"Greg," she protested, but stopped trying to fight when he kissed her. She couldn't think when he did things like that to her mouth. He played with her tongue, traced the edge of her teeth, swallowed her little moans and gasps of pleasure as his hands cruised up and down her body.

"Greg," she finally managed to gasp as his lips worked their way from her mouth to just below her earlobe. "Greg, we can't. We're here for work."

"I'm not working right now. Are you?"

She kicked at her clipboard, barely nudging it an inch. "I should be."

"You know what I love about you and your obsession with heels?" he asked, completely ignoring her protests. "They put you right at the best possible height to kiss."

"Which was my intention, of course," she said dryly, biting back a moan while he sucked on her earlobe. "Gre . . . oh God. Okay, you have to stop that."

"No," he said, then gripped her butt and pulled her to him. On instinct, she wrapped her legs around his hips and clung.

"Oh my God. Greg, you can't carry me like this. I'm too heavy!"

"Bullshit."

"Put me down," she hissed, then gasped when he dropped her. She bounced on the bed once and then was covered by his hard weight, pressing into her. She cradled him, her hips opening in welcome before she even realized what she was doing. "We can't."

"We can." He kissed her, while using his fingers to undo her suit jacket buttons.

"We shouldn't," she tried again.

"We should." He pushed the jacket off her shoulders, rotating her until he could peel it off and toss it aside.

"We could get fired," she whispered as he traced the lace of her camisole tank. Its neckline was high enough to be business appropriate, but when he dipped his finger down under the lace, it felt far less than decent. It felt decadent.

"We won't." He pressed a kiss in the center of her breast bone, moving the tank down with him. "Are you going to do a bedroom check on yourself?"

She thought about that for a second. Was it worth the risk that someone might need her? Was this man worth it?

Before she even knew she was doing it, she knocked on the nightstand twice. "Reagan? Are you in there? Yes, I'm here." She grinned. "All set."

"God, woman." He kissed her hard, ending with a playful smack. "You kill me."

GREG had realized, as he'd sat in his small private room that night waiting for Reagan to finish bed checks, that the problem had been him all along. He'd been pushing back the inevitable for so long, it built up to a bigger deal in his mind than it needed to be.

So the solution? Get back to the basics. Take back what they needed to begin with. What they needed . . . was each other. And they needed each other tonight.

He pushed her tank up to rest just above her breasts, then leaned over and kissed the spot between each rib. She squirmed, but he didn't relent until he'd driven her crazy.

"Greg," she whined. "Greg, don't tease. Please."

She ripped off her camisole and tossed it in a corner. He nearly chuckled at her impatience. But the sight of her gorgeous bra stopped him from laughing. As serious as the woman was with her shoes, she put equal dedication into her underwear choices.

The bra was like a cupcake, with how gorgeous and pretty it sat there. Black, like her suit, but with threads of silver highlighting a flowery pattern throughout the cups that molded over her generous breasts. And each side topped not with a cherry, but a sweet pink bow.

"Tell me," he said, pausing to swallow. "Tell me you are the kind of woman who matches her underwear sets."

Catching the hitch in his voice, she smiled like a woman who knows she has a man caught in her traps. "A woman like me, going out without matching underwear? Unheard of."

"Amen," he said, and reached under to unsnap her bra. The cups relaxed enough for him to remove the bra entirely, and he rubbed a thumb over each pink line over her creamy flesh. "Why do you wear it so tight it presses in on you? Seems like it hurts."

"Curse of the curvy girl." As he passed a thumb over one nipple, her eyes closed in bliss. "Gotta keep it tight enough so the girls don't escape."

"That's not very nice." He pressed his lips to one particularly dark pink line in apology. "Sorry, girls. I'd let you free way more often than she does."

"Are you talking to my boobs?" She laughed and swatted at his shoulders. "Weirdo."

"But you like it." He took one tip in his mouth, ran his tongue over it, and felt her sigh of agreement. Moving on to the second breast, he did the same, and placed the palm of one hand over her racing heart.

Her hips thrust up, grinding against his stomach with every suck, every tug of his mouth. He knew what she wanted, but she'd have to wait. He did, however, reach down and pull on the zipper to her skirt, giving her the chance to wriggle out of it. Her bottoms did, in fact, match the bra. Another confection waiting to be delved into.

She moaned, then lifted her legs to kick her heels off. He wanted to ask her to keep them on, but too late now. But when he leaned back to take in the entire picture she made in nothing but her panties, he realized he didn't miss the heels as much as he thought.

Quickly, before she lost that look in her eyes, he undressed and grabbed a condom from his bag. When he turned back around, he found she'd stripped her own panties off and had tossed them aside. Sheathing himself, he slid back on the bed and nudged his way between her thighs.

"We waited way too long for this," she breathed as he nudged the head of his penis against her opening.

"My bad." He pressed in, and she moaned. "Yeah, definitely my bad."

When he was fully inside her, he forced himself to stay very, very still. Absorb as much of the sensation of her surrounding him as he could. As she writhed beneath him, trying to get him to move, he watched. Her skin glowed in the weak light. It was pearly, the purest sort of alabaster that sun had barely touched. Marred only by the lines from her bra—*poor boobs, trapped in your prison day after day*—he couldn't absorb enough of her.

Then she rolled her hips, squeezed him deep inside, and he was screwed for waiting. He moved, and she found his rhythm perfectly, wrapping her legs around him, pressing her heels into the backs of his thighs as he pushed and pulled.

He nuzzled against her neck, inhaling her scent. Imprinting the moment when she smelled like jasmine, looked like heaven and felt like sin. Her hair, loose from its normal twist, tickled his nose and made him want to laugh.

Why? Why had he been denying them both this moment? *Because you wanted to make sure there were more to follow.*

He ground into her, pressed hard enough that his pelvic bone rubbed against her in a way that had her jolting, like she was coming out of a dream. "That, oh God, more of that."

"The lady asks, and I deliver." He did it again, and barely managed to bite back the smug grin when she moaned and her eyes rolled back with pleasure. That, right there, was the biggest compliment a man could receive. And getting it from the woman he wanted to impress more than anyone else? Priceless.

"Yes, please . . ." She gasped, and he kissed her, absorbing as much of her sexy sounds as he could. No telling how thin the walls were, and though he wouldn't give two hot damns who knew, he wouldn't have her embarrassed.

Before long, he knew he was a goner. The pulsing of her walls around him told him she was just as close. Balancing on one elbow, he maneuvered around enough to reach down one hand and caress her clit.

That touch was the catalyst she needed to explode. Head thrown back in exultation, she bared her throat to him. He kissed against the rapid pulse point, fighting to finish with her. Just as she tilted her head back down to capture his lips, he followed her into his own climax, muffling their groans together as they kissed and their bodies erupted.

GREG rolled so Reagan was splayed over the top of him. She was no lightweight thanks to her height, but her weight felt good pressed against him. He liked the reminder that she was with him, and not going to just fade away, as if their lovemaking were only a dream instead of a real event.

"I've got to be crushing you," she moaned, but didn't move. "I couldn't care less, though."

"Shut up," he said mildly, and kissed the top of her head.

"I suppose," Reagan said, tracing a hand over his shoulder, "I have to disclose our relationship now to my supervisor."

She said it with all the excitement of a woman walking in front of a firing squad. "You could skip that, but it wasn't the best idea when Marianne and Brad tried that."

"I know." She sighed again. "It's just my supervisor isn't really my biggest fan right now."

"Speaking of your biggest fan, that'd probably be me. How could I not be your fan after you did that thing with your hips where you—" He muffled a laugh as she kissed him to keep him quiet. "Sorry. Slipped out."

"Uh-huh." She glared at him, then snuggled into the crook of his neck. "I could just stay here for a day or two."

"Fine by me." His fingertips walked a path up and down her spine, starting at her neck and ending right above her butt. Each time he circled that little dimple of skin, she shivered. "So the real question is . . . are you going back to your room now, or in the morning?"

"Now." She started to push off his chest, but he held her flat against him. "Greg, I have to. I don't have clothes here."

"Sure you do. I'm positive I took some clothing off you at some point this evening."

"Any *fresh* clothes," she corrected, looking exasperated. "Men. Only they would think you could wear the exact same outfit two days in a row and nobody would notice."

"We do it every day," he pointed out. "Nobody says, 'But Greg, you wore those cammies *yesterday!*'"

"I'm going to ignore that." She sat up and ran fingers through her hair. She looked up, disgruntled, when they snagged in a snarl of hair. "I also don't have a brush, or anything else I need to get ready in the morning. And I refuse to do the walk of shame ten minutes before I'm doing wakeup rounds."

"Task master." He sat up himself and kissed her shoulder before hopping over to grab his boxers. "Fine. Get dressed and I'll walk you down to your room."

"You will not." Looking about as offended as possible while still buck-ass naked, she rose up on her knees and let her jaw unhinge itself. "You're not walking me back. I'm five rooms down. I can manage myself, and it's much less suspicious if I do it alone."

"But we're not hiding the fact that we're dating," he said reasonably. That, he knew, was his first mistake. Being reasonable with a naked female.

She glared, then started gathering up her clothes. She'd gotten as much as she could when she walked into the adjoining bathroom and closed the door sharply.

"Okay, then." He picked up his jeans, then changed his mind and turned the air up in his room. It had been comfortable . . . but that was before he'd gotten sweaty in the sheets. When the door opened a few seconds later, he turned and found a wet dream standing in the opening.

She wore her skirt, her bra, an unbuttoned suit jacket, and bedroom hair. Her feet were bare and she was scowling at him.

"Hold on. Don't move." He closed his eyes for a moment. "I need to commit this to memory, so when I'm ninety-two and I can't remember my birthday or my middle name, I can still remember what you looked like just after sex."

She slapped a hand into his gut and walked by. "Clearly, I forgot something when I went to the bathroom." She took the jacket off, slipped her tank back on and righted herself . . . dammit. After a few tugs, she pulled her hair into a haphazard ponytail. Minus the shoes, she passed for normal again. Not quite as starched up as she normally would be, but anyone giving her a passing glance wouldn't see a problem.

After he got one leg through his jeans, she bent down to kiss his forehead. "I'm going now."

"No, wait." He hopped, trying to catch his balance to slip the second leg into his jeans, but fell back on his ass. "Stop. I said I'd walk you."

"And I said I was going alone." She grinned as she opened his door just enough to slip through. "I win. Good night, Greg."

He narrowed his eyes at her retreating back just before she closed the door behind her. It was oh-two hundred, and he had about four more hours before he had to be up.

That meant he needed to get some sleep. So for tonight, he'd let her go. They'd hash out her hasty exit in the daylight.

CHAPTER

17

The next morning, Reagan began her true education on the sport of boxing. And while she'd paid attention during practices, what she'd witnessed paled in comparison to watching the real deal.

Though she had watched a few boxing matches online to prepare for the job, the actual match—unofficial though it was—took her breath away.

Tressler waited for his opponent to touch gloves before the bell rang. But the moment they had, it was on. Tressler came out swinging, which didn't shock Reagan. The young Marine had more cockiness than he could back up, from what she'd seen. His opponent, who she guessed to be closer to twenty-five or so, let him take a few swings at air before coming at him with several punches on his torso and shoulder. Tressler stumbled back, looking dazed and maybe a little shocked.

But training won out, and he pulled his head out of his butt enough to refocus and strategize on the fly. Reagan could almost see the wheels turning in his head while he ducked and dodged his opponent's attacks. After a few moments, he managed a more complex bob-slash-weave thing, then threw an upper cut while still half-ducked over that took the Paris Island Marine totally by surprise. Blood flew as the bell rang to signal the end of the first round.

Marianne, along with Coach Willis, assisted in the corner while the Paris Island Marine stumbled over to his own corner to be looked at by his coach. Sixty seconds sped by as the coach fought to keep the blood in check, and right at the bell, he ducked back under the rope to let the Marine fight round two with the energized Tressler.

Reagan sat beside Nikki the athletic training intern as Tressler fought his second round. With each punch, Nikki blanched a little more. She was definitely not used to a more physical sport. Maybe she'd been lulled into complacency by watching the guys fight in the practice gym, where they mostly tagged instead of threw hard punches.

No tagging here. It was full-out boxing, with flying fists and crunching knocks. The sounds alone made Reagan's stomach turn. But she swallowed it down, forced a smile on her face, and cheered their team on.

It helped, maybe, that they were winning. It wasn't a blowout—because Greg'd explained it, Reagan watched for signs of backing off, and saw them—but it was definitely a solid win.

But next up was Greg's round, and she wasn't at all sure she could swallow down the feelings that was going to evoke.

The crowd mixed and mingled while the referee and the maintenance switched things out for the next matchup. Coach Cartwright, the corner man for Greg, took his spot next to his boxer.

When Greg let his robe fall, Reagan nearly swallowed her tongue. Completely naked, the man was a specimen of all that was right and good in the world. But there was something special about seeing him in a pair of boxing shorts, with his hands stuffed in boxing gloves. Those little bits were hidden from the view of the normal public, and only she knew what they covered.

Nikki leaned over. "He's so hot, isn't he?"

"Hmm." Reagan wrote down a few notes—work-related, of course—about how the event was running to distract her from the sight in front of her.

"Nervous?"

She glanced at Nikki a moment. "No, why?"

"Your leg." Nikki bumped her knee against Reagan's, which was jingling rapidly. "I thought maybe you were nervous for the team. Or maybe you don't like the violence." She leaned in closer. "It sort of makes me feel sick to my stomach, honestly. The guys are all so freaking hot, but the blood . . ." She shuddered, then mimed gagging.

Lovely.

"No, I'm good. Just . . . anxious, I guess." *Anxious about watching my boyfriend get punched in the face.* He was a damn good boxer, she knew that. Faster than greased lightning, but even the fast ones got a few knocks from time to time.

And when that first bell sounded, and Greg and his opponent knocked gloves then started throwing the punches, she did suddenly feel a little ill. Damn Nikki for putting that in her head . . . Greg threw a combination, and she nearly jumped out of her seat cheering. He took one to the shoulder, then the torso, then a few more to his stomach and she wanted to groan. He evaded, dodged, weaved, and threw a few more punches his opponent didn't see coming until the bell sounded for round one. Greg retreated to the corner to sit on the small, almost child-sized stool Coach Cartwright had placed there. His back was to her so she couldn't see his face, which was probably a good thing.

She looked down and found she'd crumpled the notebook paper in her hand. Smoothing it out, Reagan fought hard to keep her breathing in check. "I'm sorry, I have to . . ." She stood and left a confused Nikki as she exited the gym and moved into the cool air of the hallway beyond.

Leaning against the tile wall, she hesitated, then took a few slow, deep breaths. How could she be so stupid? How could she think she could sleep with the man one minute, then watch him get punched the next and not let it affect her? She should have been more prepared. Should have read-ied herself for it.

How exactly did one ready oneself to watch one's boy-friend get beat up?

Must look that up online when she got home.

A tall, lanky man walked out of the gym and approached. "Feeling okay?"

She squinted, then barely took in the features of Levi, Marianne's other intern. He was quiet, usually, but a good student and followed directions well. And had a horrible crush on Nikki, bless his heart.

"I'm good, thanks." She took another cleansing breath. "Shouldn't you be in there?"

"Taking a break. This one was Nikki's to assist." He shrugged and leaned against the wall beside her. Not close enough to crowd, but there, nonetheless. A comforting pres-ence. "Saw you come out here, thought I'd make sure you were okay."

"Thank you." She hesitated. "How do you like your intern-ship?"

"Ms. Cook is a good teacher. She lets us get our hands dirty when we need to." He stuffed his hands in his pockets. "Not sure I would have chosen to work on a base, but it is what it is. I'm learning."

She wanted to ask more, but he seemed content to be quiet, so she let him. After another few minutes, she heard what she thought was the final bell of the last round, and a round of heavy cheering.

"He won," Levi murmured. "That's my guess, anyway. He was in the lead when I left."

"The violence of the sport doesn't bother you like it does Nikki?"

He smiled a little. "Nah. Nikki's smart, but she lets her gut get in the way."

More like her young heart. While Levi seemed content to quietly pine for Nikki, she flittered around the training room, offering her heart willingly to any Marine who would hold it for a moment.

Luckily for all involved, nobody had yet offered.

"Well, I guess that's my cue to get back in, then." She pushed away from the wall, waiting a moment for him to join. When he shrugged and settled in with his cell phone, she nodded. "Have a good break."

SHE entered the arena again, thankful that the ropes were empty and Greg was somewhere other than having his face punched. She didn't doubt he'd won. That was, in her mind, indisputable. But seeing him get hit, get *hurt*, no matter what the scoreboard said, hurt her, too.

And yes, she was being such a weenie about it. But how the hell was she supposed to feel? Contact sports were not really her thing. She'd been clinical about the rest of the team, but watching someone she looooooo—liked a great deal be hit was too much.

Whew. Close one, there.

She settled down behind the Marines who had already boxed or still had time to kill before they started getting ready for their own date with destiny. A few gave her small smiles as she eased in, but most either didn't notice or didn't acknowledge her. Fine stuff. She was there as a support, not to garner attention.

Unlike . . . Nikki. Reagan watched with a grimace as the young woman pouted because apparently, her seat had been taken while she'd been up doing her job. She joked, then mimed sitting on the young Marine's lap as a solution. And

Reagan had to bite her lip to keep from laughing when the smart Marine popped up and out of the seat like a Jack sprung from the box. With a slight scowl, Nikki sat.

Sorry, sweetie, but we're here to work.

Another minute or so passed, and she saw Levi tap Nikki on the shoulder, apparently relieving her to take her own break.

Over the roar of the crowd, Nikki cupped her hands and called out, "Does anyone need anything?"

There were a few shakes of the head, but most ignored her, again.

She put her fists on her hips. "Does anyone want to get some air with me?"

Even fewer head shakes; most kept their eyes forward and ignored.

Wise, wise men.

With an eye roll and a glare, she stormed past the team and up and out of the arena.

"She's not happy." Marianne sank down beside Reagan. "I'm not sure what to do with her."

"Give her a talk." Reagan was over the childishness. She wasn't even sure how Marianne put up with it daily. "It's sort of pathetic."

"No kidding." Her friend sighed and rubbed at her temples. Now here, Reagan thought, was a woman she could look up to. She dated a member of the team, but managed to hold herself together without running out the door at the first sign of contact. The team respected her—truly liked her—and nobody had a problem with them dating. And they could be in the same room together without doing that sick touchy-feely thing some couples resorted to.

Brad sat in a clump of younger Marines . . . his own little mini-platoon, Marianne had called them earlier. He doled out advice and encouragement when warranted. Greg did the same thing, as did Graham Sweeney.

It was nice, seeing them all get along. Reminded her of her brothers.

A momentary homesickness pinged against her heart, working its way like a pinball through her ribs until it embedded in her stomach to sink like a cold iceberg. She rubbed discretely at her stomach, hoping in vain to dislodge it. God, she missed her family. And wasn't that a joke . . . She'd all but run away from them, from home, to make a point to everyone she could do it alone. That she wouldn't get sucked into the poverty trap of her hometown. That she'd be better. She'd be more.

And yet, she missed them.

"You okay?" Marianne nudged her a little. "You look a little sick."

"Let's just say, boxing isn't my thing." She sent Marianne a wobbly smile. "How was Greg?"

"You didn't stay?" Marianne widened her eyes, then nodded slowly. "Okay, I can see that. Well, he did good. He won, obviously. Though I think the coach was pissed at him for dragging it out as long as he did."

"The rounds are timed. How could he drag it out?"

Marianne smiled a little and bumped her shoulder. "You need to watch more fights. He was unmatched, basically. Could have put the guy down at the end of round one, but he played with him instead. There was no point to it, he just wanted to get some extra swings in, I guess. More practice. It would have been over way faster if he'd wanted it to be."

"Oh." Reagan let that sink in. "Maybe he wanted to give the other guy a fighting chance."

"Nice pun," Marianne said, but shook her head. "Nah. He just wanted to stay in the ring as long as possible. It's not surprising. I think these guys are all pulling their punches a little, without trying to make it look obvious."

Reagan nodded, trying to look like it made sense. Past what Greg had told her about not making things a blowout, she just didn't know.

But then the lights dimmed for a moment, and the crowd started to pick up in intensity and she knew another match was coming. Picking up her camera from her bag, she scooted out to the aisle along with Marianne.

Here goes nothing.

GREG started to knock, then held off and pressed his ear to the door instead. He heard nothing. And judging by the lack of light under the door, she either wasn't in the room, or she was already asleep.

If it was the first, there was nothing he could do. If the second . . . he'd fix that.

He knocked, then waited. Nothing. He tried once more, waited, then sighed and leaned his back against her door. So she was out. It wasn't like they'd made plans or anything. He didn't have the right to feel left behind, just because he'd said no to plans with the guys to spend time with her.

One minute he was upright, and then the next, he wasn't.

Greg blinked and stared up at Reagan's shocked face, only upside down. Her mouth gaped open, and she slapped a hand over it to hide a laugh. "Sorry, I wanted to finish my sentence before I answered the door. Didn't realize you were using it to prop yourself up."

"I think this is the time," he said with a groan, "where I say something witty and Bond-like about how you knocked me off my feet. But I'm coming up empty."

"How about, 'I was hanging around, thought I'd *drop by*?'" She grinned when he moaned.

"Very punny." He rolled onto his stomach, kicking the door closed as he did. As he opened his eyes, he realized he was eye level with the sexiest pair of heels he'd seen yet. "Did you wear those to the matchup today?"

She tapped one peep-toed shoe at his nose while she flipped on the lights. "I did, though I'm not sure why my footwear has anything to do with it."

He wasn't sure he could take his eyes away from that little sexy peep of her toes, the way the leather hugged her instep, or how it crossed over her ankle. But he did a push up and stood anyway. She was still fully dressed, in another of her starched-up business suits. A skirt, this time, with matching jacket or blazer or whatever it was called. The hint of lace showed to cover her cleavage in what he thought she considered modesty, but he chose to see as her own wild side fighting for a turn. All in all, there was nothing about the outfit that screamed "Do me now!"

But he wanted to.

Except that his body had already been pummeled once, and he wasn't sure it would be wise to give it a second beating. Damn common sense . . .

"How are you feeling?" Reagan rocked toward him, as if wanting to melt into his body, but held back instead. *Shoulda gone with your instincts, sweetheart.* Now he'd have to do the moving. He stepped in, gripped her hips and pulled her into him for a gentle hug. As if understanding he needed tenderness, she wrapped her arms around him and smoothed them gently over his back.

The fact that they were eye to eye, thanks to the heels, made the hug that much easier on his abused body. No bending and scooping. He liked that they were evenly matched.

"Let's sit. You've gotta be hurting." She took his hand and led him to the bed. But when he sat on the edge, she took the chair at the table with her laptop. The screen glowed brightly with a white Word document. A few paragraphs had already been typed.

"Working with the lights off?"

"Keeps me focused." She shrugged one shoulder, then clicked a few buttons. Maybe to save the document, though he wasn't watching closely enough. "But really, how are you feeling now?"

"Feeling like I got knocked around a little. It's nothing," he said when she worried her bottom lip. "Seriously, it really wasn't. I've had way worse."

The second he said it, he knew it was the wrong thing to say. Reagan's eyes widened, and she snapped her laptop shut. "I couldn't even watch it. I had to leave."

That, he didn't like. "You didn't watch any of the matches?"

She glanced to the left for a second, hesitating. "I watched some."

"Some?"

"Most," she corrected.

"Most."

"All of them but yours," she said in a whisper, then covered her face in her hands. "I'm sorry. I just . . . couldn't. Not yours. I tried, and it freaked me out and rather than being that weirdo who rushed the ring yelling, 'Stop hitting him!' I just ducked out for some air." She peeked through her fingers. "But I was glad you won. Does that count?"

He growled, then—ignoring his protesting body—grabbed her wrist and pulled until she sprawled with him on the bed. They lay side by side, and he traced the lace of her top, dipping a finger in to brush against her breasts. Her breathing grew heavy, and her legs squirmed.

"I can't say that I'm pleased you didn't stay to watch. A guy likes to show off a little to the woman he's involved with."

She scowled. "Showing off is a completely pointless exercise."

"Says the female wearing sex for heels and walking around in this erotic little number." He undid one of her jacket buttons.

"'Erotic number.' It's a suit," she muttered. "How dare I . . ."

"And the way you always keep all this hair pulled back." He nuzzled against her neck, left completely open thanks to her basic ponytail. "It's just begging to be touched."

"I'm full of ulterior motives. It's a wonder I can get dressed in the morning, with all my nefarious plots." She sighed and angled her head so he had better access.

"But despite all your showing off and nefarious plots,"

he said, finishing the last button, "there's something I need you to do."

"Hmm," was all she could hum as he pushed the top sleeve off her arm.

"I need you to go over there, and strip all this professional armor off, one piece at a time," he began, sucking gently on her throat.

"And then?" she breathed.

"And then, put on your pajamas and come to bed."

She froze, then lifted her head. "What?"

He grinned at her confusion and kissed her nose. "Honey, I might have won that fight, and I might have been under-matched in the whole thing, but I still got handed a few knocks and I'm not up for tearing the sheets apart."

She blinked. "Oh." Then slithered off the bed and headed to her suitcase. She pulled her jacket off her other arm with economical motions he knew meant she was annoyed with him.

That was fine. She could be annoyed. But they both needed a night off from sexy times. Him, for the sheer purpose of recovery. Her, because her head was struggling to catch up. Even if she couldn't see it, he could.

In reality, he could have survived just fine having sex. Guys did it every day. The adrenaline of a good fight was a powerful drug to push past any pain or soreness. Hell, some-times the adrenaline was more potent than a shot of Viagra for some. If they didn't find a willing woman twenty minutes after leaving the ropes, they were crawling up the wall.

Fighting had never been his aphrodisiac. It had been sur-vival. Always survival. Foster homes with shitty bio kids or fellow fosters, the streets, even his earliest days in the Corps . . . his fists had been the one thing he could count on. Nothing sexual about survival.

As she slipped into her pajama bottoms, he grinned. "Penguins?"

She glanced down, then back up with an exasperated sigh. "I didn't bring these thinking you'd see them." Then, smoothing a hand down the short shorts with surfing birds all over them, she added in a defensive tone, "Penguins are cute."

"That they are." So was she, in her bare feet, cute penguin-themed shorts and practically see-through tank top. He held out a hand and, after a contrary moment of glaring at him, she relented and laid down with him.

"You suck," she mumbled as she snuggled against him. Lying down, she fit against him perfectly. With her head nestled against his shoulder, she wrapped one arm around his chest, slid her leg between his, and sighed. "You're still dressed."

"I've gotta keep the mystery alive, you know." When she chuckled quietly, he said, "I've got bruises. I don't want to freak you out."

There was a hesitation, but she said, "They won't." She tugged at the band of his polo shirt and slid it up until it caught under his arms. She traced one bruise on his ribs. "Did you get checked out?"

"We all did. They're completely anal about it, thanks to concussions and all that. I'm fine." He caught her hand and pressed it flat against his chest.

"Show me."

When he cracked open an eye, she sat up and motioned for him to do the same. With a reluctant groan, he did. She pushed his shirt up and over his head.

Not too much damage, thankfully. His left jaw took the worst of it, but a good-sized bruise was forming on his left shoulder as well. Raising his arms up to pull the shirt off wasn't what he'd call a fun day at the park.

After letting her fingertips trail over the discoloration, he closed his eyes. It felt so good, just to be touched lightly. As if the simple brush of her hands could release any pain and suffering the injuries contained, leaving them nothing but colorful reminders.

"How about down here?" She stuck one finger in the waistband of his jeans and tugged.

"Ever heard of the term 'below the belt'?" When she nodded, he winced. "It exists for a reason. Nothing's going on down there." Except for an erection, which was a damn inconvenience when he'd sworn he wouldn't push tonight.

"Hmm." She rotated him so his back faced her, then pressed so he laid down, face first. "Looks like you're okay back here, too."

"You really didn't watch the fight, did you?" He meant it as a joke, but when her hands halted in their exploration of his flesh, he knew she'd taken it personally. Reaching around blindly, he grabbed one hand and pulled it down to press a kiss to her palm. "Sorry. I know it was hard for you. I'm not offended or upset about it."

She let a heavy sigh go, but he wasn't sure what that meant. He almost asked, but then she started to massage his shoulders, and every good piece of conversation fled from his mind like a bird taking flight.

"Oh my God," he muttered as she found a particularly tense knot of muscles just at his right shoulder. "If you could just keep doing that forever, that'd be great."

She laughed. "No way. My hands will get too tired. But now that I think about it . . ." She went silent, and he could all but hear her making mental notes.

"Are you working?"

"No," she said, but the guilt in her voice said, *Of course I am.*

"Well, stop it. No work tonight."

"But I have to—"

"Have to spend time with one of your Marines. That's work, right?"

She snorted. "I doubt my boss would condone considering this work. But now that you mention it . . ." Her voice trailed off again, and he bit back a sigh. The woman wouldn't quit.

So, while she rubbed him down, then raised his flesh

with fleeting, light touches over his spine and shoulders, he let it go.

And an hour later, as she lay beside him, with a bag of microwave popcorn on his stomach, watching some movie from the eighties, he realized even without sex, it was easily the best night he'd had with a woman, ever.

CHAPTER

18

Reagan's fuzzy brain fought to keep track of the plot. "But why is he so interested in that boat?"

Greg placed one finger over her lips. "Shh, don't analyze. Enjoy."

"I know, but—"

"Shh." He pushed a piece of popcorn into her open mouth, causing her to bite down. "Watch."

She poked him in the ribs—the non-bruised ones, she wasn't a monster—and watched him squirm. "Jerk."

"That's me. It's on my business card." They were quiet another few moments, and she enjoyed the feeling of his hand smoothing over her hair, down her shoulder to her elbow. It was hypnotic, and made her eyelids feel heavy. Without thinking, she matched her breathing to his . . . slow and even, deep and relaxing. And felt herself start to drift.

"Tell me about your family."

"Hmm," she said, fighting the siren song of sleep. "Brothers. Lots of brothers."

He massaged her scalp lightly, and she all but wept.

Yummy. So yummy. "You mentioned them before. Older or younger?"

"Mix. I'm in the middle." Her fingertip traced through the hair that led down his chest and into the waistband of the jeans he still hadn't taken off. "You could get more comfortable, if you want."

"Trying to seduce me out of my clothes?" He tugged gently on a strand of her hair in mocking reprimand, and it felt good. "Not gonna work tonight."

"Darn." She sighed. "Two older, two younger."

"Smack in the middle. What was it like growing up like that?"

The term *hell* came to mind, but she swallowed that back. The growing up part, that wasn't true. "Loud, crazy, sometimes painful. They weren't always very nice and protective to their sweet princess of a sister." She batted her eyelashes up at him. "Gonna beat them up for me?"

"Oh, yeah. Just point the way." He paused. "Which way is that, exactly?"

She grinned. "Wisconsin. Just head toward nothing and keep on going, turn left at nada, and stop when you reach nowhere."

"Population: Your family, huh?"

"Give or take eight hundred." She could dance around it, but he seemed so intent on getting to know her. And she wanted to know him. Time to be a mature woman and step forward. "You know that term *dirt poor*?"

"Sure." He sifted his fingers through her hair again, and she nearly went comatose with the pleasure. But then he tugged—still felt good—and made her look at him. "Don't stop now, or I'll stop, too."

"No, don't." When he resumed his scratching and tracing of her upper arms and shoulders, she wriggled with pleasure. "That was us, literally dirt poor. As in, the floorboards of our ancient farm house were warped and had so many splinters my mom and oldest brother decided to rip them up, only to discover the ancient house we lived in didn't have a sub floor. Built straight on dirt. And since my mom didn't have the cash to fix it . . ." She shrugged. "It stayed, for about two years. Laid down tarps, some cardboard, switched that out every so often. For a few months, we had carpet . . . sort of." She smiled. "Another family had done their house in carpet, had a lot of leftover remnants, gave them to us for free. They weren't even nailed down. But they were warmer than tarp."

"That sounds rough." He stared at the TV, which he'd muted. "But with the right family, you can get through it."

"We got through it. What choice do you have?"

"Was it rough?"

Now he was starting to sound like a reporter. "What's with the third degree?" She playfully tugged at a few of his chest hairs, but he flattened her hand over his chest.

"I want to know you, all of you. It's not such an odd request, is it? Knowing the woman I'm involved with."

When he put it like that . . . "No."

"Was it hard, moving away from them?"

"No. Maybe that sounds bad, but it just wasn't. They were content with that life, all of them. Staying in that town was admitting to yourself you were fine being below the poverty line for the rest of your life. Nobody stayed there thinking they'd have anything more than government assistance, or barely above it." That sounded ugly, but it was just the truth. "So I left. They didn't."

"And you ended up here."

"When it takes you as long as it took me to graduate from college . . . you take the first job offered." She tried to smile, but it went a little sideways. "I was so scared about not making it, I leapt at the first job offer. I wasn't even really qualified for this. I lied through my teeth about liking sports and all that." She blew a raspberry. "Sports. We didn't even have a football team at my high school. Too small. We could barely field a basketball team with guys on the bench. I was a cheerleader during basketball season, because it was better than 4H. So, no, sports were not really my thing. But I feel almost no guilt, which probably sounds horrible now that I say it out loud."

"You make the choices you have to make in order to survive." His voice was so calm, so serious, she knew he wasn't talking about just her. But this was a man who had seen the ugly side of war. His idea of 'choices' were likely very much a matter of survival. She wouldn't push on that front. Smoothing a hand down his torso, she brushed lightly over his bruising.

"'Survive' is probably a little intense where I'm concerned. But I made choices I felt like I had to in order to make steps toward the life I wanted. So I took this job, moved here, live in the world's crappiest apartment so that I can actually afford to live without a roommate, and wonder every day how I got myself into this mess."

"'World's crappiest apartment,' huh?"

She bit back a groan. Apparently, the skeletons were just dancing out of the closet tonight. "Yeah, I, uh, don't live in a great place. Which is why . . ."

"Which is why you've yet to let me pick you up at your place."

"Maybe," she whispered, her cheeks heating from the embarrassment. She nuzzled into his shoulder, not wanting to look him in the eyes.

"Reagan, look at me."

She shook her head. No, thank you.

"Reagan," he said again, his voice commanding. "Look." He guided her chin up with one finger. "I don't give a shit where you live. I don't care if you live in your car." He thought about that for a second. "Well, I might care about that because it's not the safest thing in the world. But what I'm saying is, where you live doesn't matter to me. I respect that you're keeping your expenses down to keep your privacy. It's a personal choice, and one I can understand. Trust me, there are times I'm ready to crawl the walls having a roommate again, even though he's not there half the time."

She closed her eyes, feeling the relief roll down her body in waves. "So, yeah. There it is, I guess. My life story."

"Hardly that, but it's a nice outline. We can fill in more details later." He kissed her once, twice, then a third time, deeper still, until she was gripping his shoulders.

Then she let go with a shriek. "Oh my God, I'm sorry!"

"Huh?" He pulled back, confused. "What?"

"Your shoulder! I squeezed and—"

He burst out laughing, kissing her nose when she wrinkled it in confusion. "Reagan, sweetheart, you're not gonna hurt me. I promise." One more kiss to the forehead this time, which felt mildly patronizing and mocking. "But thanks for thinking of me."

"Starting to regret that," she muttered, pushing at him so he lay flat again.

"I have one question, though."

"Maybe I have one answer." She waited, but he twisted and got out of bed, stalking across the room and picking up one of her discarded heels. "Those won't fit you, you know. You'd probably need a wide."

"Smart-ass." He said it fondly, throwing her an arch look. "If you're broke as a joke—"

"Classy."

"Thanks. If you're so broke you're living in a crap apartment . . . what's with all these?" He held up the shoe by the heel, waving it as if it were evidence in a court case. *Your Honor, I present Exhibit B to the jury.*

"I really would rather live in my car than give up my shoes." When he gaped at her, she laughed. "No, silly. I buy them on auction sites for pennies on the dollar or at thrift stores or swap sites. Everything I have, I searched for hardcore and bought at a fraction of the retail price." She glanced at her now-wrinkled, discarded suit on the floor of her hotel room. "You wouldn't know it, but I usually take very good care of my things so they last."

He surprised her by picking up her suit and folding it

neatly, laying it across her suitcase. Then he made his way back to the bed, stretched out beside her, and curled them up under the comforter.

"Thanks," he said quietly after a moment, then turned the TV off. His hand drifted up and down her back, lifting her tank a little to scratch at her lower back. It felt heavenly.

Just as she drifted off, she realized she'd done all the talking, and he'd done all the listening.

GREG awoke to a pounding at his door. He cracked one eye open, glanced at the clock, and groaned. It wasn't even six yet, and they weren't supposed to muster until half past seven. What dumbass would take his life into his own hands and knock so early?

He grumbled, pulled the pillow over his ear, and prayed the asshole away.

But the pounding persisted. With a grumble, he levered out of bed and headed for the door, suddenly aware he was still wearing jeans and his running shoes. A half-second before he opened it, he heard a hissed, "No, stop!"

He froze, hand on the doorknob, and looked behind him. Reagan stood, darting one leg into a pair of skin-tight black pants. Her ass was bare, but he couldn't even concentrate on that when she looked so comical, hopping around the room.

Her room. Right. He was still in her room. They'd fallen asleep and he'd never made it back to his place. Shit. He'd nearly broadcast their sleeping together—literally sleeping—to whoever was on the other side of the door. Not that he cared . . . but she would.

"Who the hell is coming to your room at this hour?" he asked quietly as he sat back on the edge of the bed.

"I don't know," she whispered, then called out, "Who is it?" at the next set of knocks.

"It's Coach Willis, ma'am."

She rolled her eyes, though he wasn't sure if it was at the

coach—unlikely—or the *ma'am*—more plausible. "Can I help you, Coach?"

"Just need to speak with you a moment, if you don't mind."

She grabbed her black jacket from yesterday, buttoned it over her sleeping tank without putting on a bra, then wrapped her hair up with two quick flicks of her wrist and clipped it. "Just a moment." She waved him back, and he understood she wanted him out of the line of sight from the door. He scooted back toward the headboard and listened as she opened the door.

"Yes, Coach, how can I help you?"

The coach answered, but it was so low, Greg couldn't make it out. Her own answer was equally quiet, despite his strain to hear. After another two minutes, she closed the door quietly with a click. Then she walked to her suitcase and started tearing through it. "You've got to head back to your room. Get packed and ready to roll. I'll see you at the bus. Or . . ." She chewed on her bottom lip for a moment. "I'll think of something."

"Think of what?" He stood, caught her shoulders and forced her to look at him. Forced her to slow down a moment and breathe. "What's wrong with our own bus?"

She took a deep breath, then let it go again. Kara would have been proud of that. "I have to go check the damage for myself, but it appears as though someone has vandalized it."

Greg waited for more. "So, what? Someone spray paint the sides? Did they draw a penis or something? What's the real problem?"

"The real problem is the driver says he can't drive it in its current condition, and has already reported the damage to his own supervisor. He can't drive passengers on it due to liabilities. Which means I have to figure out how to get all of you, plus all your equipment, plus the support staff home." She stepped back, cleared her throat, and nodded toward the door. When she spoke, her voice had dropped into Professional Distance Reagan mode. "I think you should take care of that while I get dressed. We both have a lot to get done this morning."

"Yeah, sure." He glanced around and found his polo, pulling it on. He wouldn't make it weird, because it wasn't. She had a job to do, and he wouldn't be in her way. That was the mature, rational way to handle it, and he wasn't going to get butt hurt over it.

But damn, he thought as he closed her door and quietly walked the hallway back to his own room. Would it kill her to bend just a little before she snapped?

REAGAN sat in the driver's seat of the bus—ironically, the only seat not ripped to shreds—and did some quick Internet searching on her phone while she waited. The team was inside, having been woken up early to congregate and ask who had seen what. Marianne had her own little team and was doing the same.

She'd probably have to answer questions as well, to the base MPs as well as the MPs at Lejeune. There was no way this was coincidental. Not after so much else had happened to the team in such a short period of time.

But the scary part was . . . they were hours away from home. And unless you were a friend or family member of a teammate, most civilians wouldn't know the team had headed down for a simple scrimmage.

So the culprit had most likely traveled down with them on the very bus he then vandalized. Very comforting.

Another ten minutes later—including one short and not-so-sweet call to her supervisor—Reagan had secured travel for the team back home. She hopped down from the seat and walked through the broken front doors, and nearly screamed when she hit the pavement and saw a tall figure lurking to her right.

"Hey." Greg reached out and stroked a hand down her arm. "Sorry. You okay?"

She pressed the hand gripping her cell phone to her racing heart and took a deep breath. "Let me check my blood pressure and get back to you on that one." Then she realized . . . "Why aren't you inside with the rest of the team?"

"I told coach I wanted to stay with you. Just in case." He shoved his hands into the pockets of his team-issued jogging suit bottoms. In general, she thought windbreaker outfits were a little on the silly looking side. But he managed to make the parachute-like material sexy, anyway. She was in over her head. "He agreed. He thought it was best we kept eyes on everyone. Nobody is alone, battle buddy, that sort of thing."

He'd told the coach, not asked. As if he wasn't asking permission, but simply making the choice. Could have gotten him in serious trouble. It warmed her down in her still-chilled belly that he'd gone against the grain to make sure she was okay. "Well, thanks, but I'm fine. Just stressed."

"Understatement."

"No kidding." With one last glance at the torn-up bus, she sighed and headed back toward the BOQ main lobby. Greg fell in step with her. "I guess it could have been an opponent from last night? Someone with sour grapes over losing?" Even as she said it, her voice lacked conviction.

Greg lifted one shoulder in a "maybe" gesture, but he didn't appear convinced.

"But going inside like that . . ." She shuddered. "Just feels like more of a violation. Slashing a tire or keying your paint job sucks, but doesn't feel like this does."

"And that's what they wanted. Whoever is pulling this junk wants to get in our heads."

"What if he's one of you?" She said it quietly, and Greg was silent long enough that she thought he hadn't heard. She regretted asking the moment the question left her lips. There was no way he'd want to think about that. She shouldn't have asked. He had enough to worry about.

"Probably is," he said just as quietly. "Guess we'll find out."

CHAPTER

19

Greg played cards with Graham and two others while they waited for the replacement bus. The coaches had quizzed the team in groups of two or three, asking if they'd seen anything. Noticed anything. Heard anyone joking or whispering about damage to the bus. As far as he could tell, none had. Marianne had met with her interns, and Reagan was now in conference with the coaching staff herself.

The entire thing was a lame rodeo.

"So who was it?" one of the younger guys asked, playing a card. "One of the interns?"

"That chick was pissed when Hood wouldn't let her sit in his lap," the other confirmed. "Did you see the steam coming outta her ears when she stormed off?"

"Just the kind of female to pull shit like that," the first said, scooping up the cards to shuffle.

Graham and Greg exchanged a look, but both declined to say a word.

Yeah, maybe it was a vindictive female. Women were just as capable of tearing up a bus as a man. But it seemed rather impersonal, to his way of thinking. Nikki would probably prefer a more direct hit to whoever had insulted her. Cutting up that specific Marine's clothes, or slapping him in front of an audience.

Unless she considered a group punishment just desserts for the one Marine that had pissed her off . . .

He'd lose his mind heading down that path. This wasn't his investigation to worry about.

Twenty minutes later, he sat with Graham at the back of the new bus, bumping out of the parking lot. Reagan had seated herself in the front, her phone permanently attached to her ear. He'd mock her for working nonstop, but thanks to this new problem, she was pulling double duty. And there was nothing he could do to help her or bear some of the burden.

"So who was it?" Graham asked, keeping his voice low. There was no way even Brad, sitting in front of them, could have heard. "Any of your guys seem likely?"

"Not really, no. But why would any of them want to punish the team? They *made* the team."

"So maybe someone who got cut." Graham nodded slowly. "Yeah, okay, I could see that. But it started so early, before the team was finalized . . ."

"People were cut on the first or second day. Injuries and junk. If someone is willing to roll up a paint balloon in a banner, or slash tires, then he's not thinking straight. Plus, think about it." Warming to the idea now, Greg turned. "Whoever this is knew everyone's car who was at the barracks. They obviously know how to get into the gym, maybe because they've been in it recently. Maybe they know some door that gets left unlocked a lot. They know our schedule of travel because we were given all that info from the start. And the reason itself is clear. They didn't make the team; they're willing to punish those who did."

"Maybe." Unconvinced, Graham sighed and let his head fall against the window. "It's gonna be a long-ass ride home."

"No kidding."

"At least you have something worth coming back home to," Graham said with a snap, then sighed again. "Sorry. Getting tired of being the fifth wheel these days."

"So ask her out."

"She's not ready." Graham grumbled, "She might never be ready."

"A woman like Kara's gonna be ready. You might just have to nudge a little."

"Nudge," Graham said in a low voice. "Something tells me she's going to appreciate that."

"All the more reason." Greg grinned as he thought back to his own nudging with Reagan. "Sometimes the ones that need a nudge are the ones that are the most ready to jump. They just don't know it."

"Speaking from experience, grasshopper?" Brad popped his head over the seat with a smug smile.

Apparently they'd been louder than he'd realized. Greg attempted to shove his roommate's head back down, Whac-A-Mole style. But he was stuck with the grumpy guy.

"Yeah, how are things anyway, on the Love Boat?" Graham crooned, making Brad snicker and causing Greg to punch him in the shoulder. "What? It was appropriate."

"Hardly. And things are . . ." *Fantastic. Amazing. Better than I've ever hoped for.* "Good. Things are good."

"Somebody's in loooooove," Graham sang again, which made Greg honor-bound to do his best to kick his ass without anyone on the coaching staff noticing. Rough work, but he gave it his best. After a few minutes of grappling and playing around, Brad reached in and thrust an arm between them.

"Knock it off, you two. People are looking back here. You want the coach to assign seats like we're in freaking kindergarten?"

"Might not be a bad idea," said a new voice.

All three jerked their heads to the other side of the bus,

where Tressler sat, earbuds in, eyes shut, head back as if asleep or zoned out to the music. But apparently he'd been listening the whole time.

"Butt out, Tressler," Brad said easily. The younger Marine had been in Brad's imaginary platoon during tryouts, and though those had naturally dissolved as the final team had been announced, each of them had felt a little more responsible for those who they'd been in charge of. Greg had breathed a serious sigh of relief when he'd missed the Tressler trap.

"Just saying," the younger man said, ignoring the warning. He never opened his eyes, just swayed slightly with the bus. "The odds are, someone on here slashed the seats of the old bus. Maybe they weren't alone. Maybe it's a duo, or a trio."

The three looked at each other. He saw surprise register in his friends' faces as well. None of them had considered that.

"Maybe breaking up cliques would be for the best." Opened his eyes now, he turned and shot them a shit-eating smile. "Starting with you three."

Graham vibrated beside him, but Greg knew guys like Tressler. They lived to stir the shit pot, and were usually well out of range when the entire thing exploded. Annoying little gnats who were irritating to listen to, but harmless in the grand scheme of things. And definitely not worth blowing up over.

Greg smiled back. "You know, quality attracts quality. Might be why you're sitting alone."

Tressler flushed. Brad thumped back down into his seat, but Greg could hear the man swallowing a laugh. Graham coughed and turned to the window, his shoulders shaking.

And Greg settled back in his own seat, satisfied when Tressler turned his back to them to look out his own window in a childish pout.

Greg leaned into the aisle to watch Reagan again as she walked down the rows doing another headcount like an RA on a dorm floor. When her eyes met his, he winked. She didn't acknowledge his wink, except to flush and turn her head back around. She wobbled a little on those damn impractical heels of hers when the bus listed to the left. Someone—he couldn't see his face—reached up to steady her by gripping her elbow. And when she bestowed a grateful smile on them, Greg's hands fisted so hard the knuckles cracked.

"The Love Boat," Graham sang under his breath. "Soon will be making another run . . ."

"Eat me."

"OKAY." Reagan took a deep breath, then stepped out of the car and met Greg on the sidewalk in front of her apartment building. Her palms were sweating. "So, don't judge the outside. It's not as bad as it looks."

Greg glanced down at what appeared to be an ashtray full of blunts dumped on the small, patchy lawn leading up to the main door, and raised his brow.

"Fine, it sucks. Just don't judge it until you get inside." She opened the door, walked up to the second story, and unlocked her three locks.

"Three?"

"There were only two, but I added one after getting approval." The door stuck, swollen by the heat, and she muscled her way in.

"You know how to add a deadbolt to a door?"

"I've got brothers. They like tools. I paid attention." She shrugged a shoulder. "Home sweet home."

He did a quick circle—that's all it took, really, to see her entire apartment—and stayed quiet. She swallowed back the "what do you think?" question because it was just too damn needy for her to even admit thinking, let alone actually ask. It sucked, but it was hers. And embarrassing as it was for her to bring a man back to her place, she knew going forward they needed privacy to keep connecting. They wouldn't get it at the BOQ. So, here they were.

"Well, you're clean," he said finally.

How did one admit that she was scared if she didn't bleach everything twice a day, there would be roaches? Not that she'd seen one . . . yet. Or at least, not the crawling kind.

"I can see you in here." He sat on the small, secondhand couch she'd searched for for a week before picking out. She could have settled for something ugly and blah-brown immediately and been fine, but she was holding out for pretty. She'd found it. The charcoal gray didn't look like much at first, but the piping of bright, cheerful yellow around the edges had sold her. And the gray-and-yellow throw pillows were fantastic. She'd found a coordinating throw blanket to drape along the back, and two end tables she'd stenciled the tops of to coordinate.

"It's not much," she started, hating her defensive tone.

"It's great." He held out a hand, and she sank down beside him. "I know what you're trying to accomplish here, and I respect that. Stop worrying that I'm judging you."

Resting her head against his shoulder, she did her best to mentally shake off the day. "Today sucked."

"Yes, it did." He sifted his hands through her hair, disrupting her French twist and making a mess of the strands at the edge of her neck. But who cared? She wasn't leaving again tonight. "Any news?"

"None. No leads from the MPs down there. I guess there's no security cameras in that parking lot. And people were in and out all night. Combine that with the fact that nobody saw the inside of the bus after about four that afternoon until the early morning next morning, and there was a disgusting amount of time available for whoever to make their move."

He was quiet awhile. "Could have been one of their boxers."

She snorted.

"Probably not," he agreed. "Figured out how to spin it yet?"

"Since it happened so far out from here, I'm hoping we can all just play the It Didn't Happen game and move on." She snuggled tighter into his embrace. "Tell me something."

"Like what?" His voice was thick, as if fighting off sleep.

"About you. Your family. You know about mine, so tell me about yours."

He didn't respond, and for the longest while she wondered if he'd fallen asleep. Then he murmured. "I didn't have any brothers to show me how to put in a deadbolt." Then he sighed, and she knew he was gone for the night.

"SON of a bitch!"

Greg came awake with a start, and promptly rolled off the bed and landed with a thud on the floor. His legs flailed and he found himself completely trapped in a pile of bedding. "What the . . . Reagan? Did you set a trap or something? What the hell is going on here?"

She stormed in, sexy with a short robe on, her hair in a messy bun and no makeup. Her legs were tanned and long under the robe and she was barefoot. She tapped one foot next to his head. "No, I did not set a trap, Gregory. Get up."

He struggled, fought and finally waited for her to help him untangle his legs from the girly bedding. Seriously, who needed this much lace on anything? Once he was free from captivity, he sat on the floor, arms locked around his knees and his back to the bed. "What's wrong?"

"This." She handed him the morning paper she'd tossed on the bed before assisting him, then slid down to sit beside him. "How do they already know?"

"This," Greg quickly found out, was an article—more like opinion piece—about the ruined bus from the day before. The newspaper had taken the vandalized bus story and run with it, adding in some color commentary about the previous "tragedies" that had befallen the Marine Corps boxing team thus

far. Was this an indication of what was expected when someone put that many trained killers—WTF?—together and
encouraged them to beat each other bloody? Was this inevitable? Or maybe the violence and horrifying nature of the sport
had spawned a vigilante of sorts out to right the wrongs created
by this bloodthirsty pairing of military and "sport."

It was signed by their all-time favorite asshole journalist,
David Cruise.

"This guy," Greg said with a sneer, "needs a new hobby."

"This guy," Reagan said, taking the paper back as he
started to wad it up, "is making my job impossible." She
smoothed the paper down. "We have a leak."

"I know." That hit him right in the gut. He'd wanted, so
very badly wanted, for this to be unconnected. For the acts
in the gym to be the work of a crazy pack of unruly teens.
For the whole thing to blow over so they could focus on the
team, on the sport, on the challenge ahead. And he wanted
to delude himself into believing the bus was vengeance from
the team from Paris Island, completely unrelated.

But this sealed the deal. The asshole was one of them.

"Maybe," he said, grasping at straws, "someone from the
MPs here leaked. When you called them, maybe someone
talked and—"

"They don't know yet." She sighed and pushed some hair
behind her ear, staring at her primer-painted wall blankly.
"I never called them. I had planned to stop in today and give
them the rundown in person but . . ." She let her hands lift
and fall again in a helpless gesture that looked so very wrong
on his strong, independent Reagan.

"We'll figure it out." He pulled her close, let her rest her
head on his shoulder for a moment. "We'll get there."

She sighed and burrowed in a little tighter. "Can I tell
you a secret?"

He kissed her temple. "Always."

"I'm afraid of getting fired," she whispered.

The way her breath hitched at the end, as if she were

swallowing back tears, gutted him. "No, baby, you won't get fired."

"You can't know that."

"I can, because I won't let it happen." He had no clue how, but the promise sort of just spilled out, and he knew in that moment he'd do almost anything to keep it. "First we—"

"Stop," she said quietly. "Please, just for a minute . . . can you not fix it? For a minute, just let me be scared and hold me and not do or say anything logical for sixty seconds?"

Wrapping his arms tighter around her, he murmured, "Yeah, sure," and let her cry for a minute. After the tears slowed, he waited until her breathing had caught up to his, mimicking the rhythm of his chest rising and falling. And he knew the storm was past.

"Better?" he asked against her hair.

"Thank you." She nuzzled his neck. "You can fix it now."

He chuckled. "Oh, can I?"

"I know you can . . . but it's mine to fix, I guess." She sighed and sat up straight. He instantly hated the distance between them. She grabbed the paper behind her and stared at it a moment. "What's this guy's deal, anyway? He's got a personal vendetta against the team."

"Maybe that's for you to find out." He stroked her hair once more, then stood. "I need to get dressed for practice."

"Oh, right. Of course." Following his lead, she started picking out her clothes for the day. "I've got to grab a shower first. Will you be here when I get out?"

"Nah, I've gotta hit up my place for clothes. I'll take off." He kissed her briefly, then longer until she melted against him. One bare foot rubbed against his calf, and he was half-tempted to toss her on the bed and work out their frustrations together.

But they both had work. Work centered them, and he knew she'd feel worse if he made her late. So off to work they both went.

With his promise echoing in his head.

*   *   *

REAGAN sat in the lobby of the reserved, surprisingly small office of the Jacksonville newspaper. It wasn't a large publication, and online media had eaten up a great deal of its readership as she'd come to find out. Each year, the paper seemed to shrink in terms of staffers. Perhaps their rabid reporter was working on a sensationalistic angle because of fear of being let go.

Not that she excused his choices. No way. But she could definitely understand the flames of failure licking at your heels.

"Ms. Robilard?" David Cruise stepped out from a hallway and looked surprised. He wore a pair of perfectly pressed pants, shiny shoes, and—to her surprise—a T-shirt instead of collared shirt or suit jacket like he had when at the gym interviewing the team. "I hear you're here to see me?"

"Yes, I . . ." She blinked, then picked up her bag. "Is there somewhere we can speak privately?"

His eyes darkened, and she could see his mouth twitching behind his beard. But he led the way through a general work area with cubicles to what she assumed was a generic conference room. The lack of noise was disconcerting. Where were the staffers running around with coffee or the journalists barking into phones demanding quotes for articles? It was nothing like what she'd expected, based off movies and television. The few individuals who were there seemed very relaxed, and it was mostly empty.

"Everyone's out on assignment," he said, as if reading her mind, before shutting the door. "I only have a few minutes. I have a meeting soon."

"I won't take much of your time." She put her bag on the table and pulled out a file folder. Laying it down, she opened it and pulled out a few sheets to slide across the table toward him. "A year ago, you were writing home and garden pieces. You had nothing to do with sports, or base activity. Those were the work of other journalists at the paper. Those journalists are still here. Why did you get the assignment to interview the boxing team?"

He glanced down quickly at the old articles of his she'd printed from online, then back at her. "I'm given assignments, same as everyone else. It's how the paper works. Sometimes, you have to fill in."

"Did you always want to cover sports?" she asked idly, looking through the three articles he'd written thus far on the team. "Is this a step up for you? In the right direction?"

The reporter crossed his arms and scowled. "I have no clue where this is going, Ms. Robilard, but I'm the reporter here. I don't get interrogated."

"I think," she went on, "that you thought you had a story and you ran with it. I think maybe, just maybe, someone has been feeding you information on the goings-on in the gym, with the team, et cetera. And that's why you asked for the assignment, well out of your comfort zone."

"I think you've got a lot of nerve. I don't have to tell you a goddamn thing."

"Fine." She stood. "Just tell me who leaked you the info about the bus being vandalized and I can leave you be." When he raised a brow, she shrugged. "I can be accommodating. I have better ways to spend my time than being here, so let's all move on."

He laughed. Actually laughed, so hard and so loudly that even with the door closed, several people from the main room turned to stare. Reagan felt the heat creep up her neck and burn her cheeks. So maybe this wasn't the best idea. Actually, now that she thought it through, it was a horrible, stupid idea.

Oh, God. How dumb could she be?

"You think . . ." He gasped and grabbed his big belly, huffing a little with the laugh. "You think I'd just give you a source? For what? No, wait, let me guess." He laughed so wide he looked like a deranged jack-o'-lantern. "Because you're so pretty and people just hand you things. Ha!"

Do. Not. Cry. Don't you dare cry.

"Apparently not." Mustering up every single ounce of dignity she could find—which sadly, was very little—she stood, putting the file back in her bag and slinging it over her shoulder. "Have a good day, Mr. Cruise."

He was still laughing as she left the room, and his stupid laugh echoed through the hall until she left the building. But she managed to not cry until she was in her car.

CHAPTER

20

"So you're saying it didn't go well," Marianne said later that afternoon at Back Gate.

"I'm saying, if Satan had opened a portal right there, crooked his finger and said, 'Come on in, the water's fine,' I would have jumped willingly." Reagan took a sip of her water, wishing it were something stronger. So, so much stronger. But the bar was crowded and they'd be waiting a few minutes for their ordered drinks. "You didn't cancel any plans with Brad to meet tonight, did you?"

Marianne made a face that said, *Come on, really?* "Hell no. He's a big boy and can keep himself entertained for a few hours while I have a healthy bitch session. Plus," she added as the server put down their drinks, "I think he and the guys were having a late-night practice or something."

Reagan paused with the drink halfway to her lips. "How are they getting into the gym?"

"At Graham's house," Marianne clarified, just as Kara sat in the third seat. "I ordered for you. I figured bottle was your choice."

"Read my mind," Kara said fervently. "Mmm. I have approximately two hours before I have to pick up Zach, so I can have exactly one more before I'm back to water."

"Babysitter?" Reagan asked, grateful to avoid the topic of her crying like a wuss on the way back from her meeting with Mr. Journalist.

"Uh, no. I mean yes, but no." Flustered, which was unusual for her, Kara set her drink down and looked through her purse a moment. Reagan knew that routine. It was the I'm-avoiding-eye-contact-by-pretending-to-search-for-my-lip-balm routine.

"Spill!" Marianne poked her friend in the arm. "What's going on with the babysitter?"

"I couldn't get one. So I texted you, but you didn't answer."

Marianne's brow crinkled, and she dug in her back pocket for her phone. When she glanced, she winced. "Sorry, it was on silent. Oh, hey, look." She showed her phone to Reagan. "Kara can't make it, no babysitter."

Reagan sipped her drink and smiled. "Shame."

"Anyway," Kara said more forcefully. "When you didn't answer, I tried texting Brad, because I figured maybe you two were still together and you hadn't left yet. So he could pass on the message." Kara smiled at Reagan smugly and added in a side voice, "Brad answers his phone in a timely manner."

Marianne blew a raspberry.

"Moving along." Kara took another sip, closed her eyes in reverence, and continued, "He informed me you had already left, but to hold tight and he would come get Zach himself, because he didn't want me to miss out on the fun."

"Aww," Reagan said, her heart lifting a little. When she glanced at Marianne, her friend simply had a small, knowing smile on her face.

"But then ten minutes later, the person knocking on my door wasn't Brad. It was Graham Sweeney," she finished in a whisper.

Reagan glanced around, then leaned in. "Why are we whispering?"

"Because." Kara threw her a dirty look. "It's . . . he's . . . I don't know."

"Cute," Reagan supplied.

"Sexy," was Marianne's contribution.

"Pointless," Kara finished. "The whole thing is pointless. I know he's hitting on me. And I think he had a good time with Zach the other night. I'm not one of those people trying to use my kid to shelter me from life." She paused after sipping, glancing to Marianne for confirmation.

Marianne shrugged one shoulder and nodded.

"So while I appreciate the interest, it's just pointless. And for completely legit reasons."

Reagan waited a moment, wracking her brain. "Because he eats small children for breakfast?"

Kara scowled at her. "Be serious."

Finally, Reagan admitted, "I don't get it. What are the reasons?"

"Baby daddy drama," Marianne said, grinning when Kara pushed at her.

"You know I hate that phrase. *Baby daddy*," she said in a mocking tone. But she sighed. "But she's not wrong. Or not entirely. Graham's in the military. He'll eventually leave. I can't. I'm here until Zach graduates, at least. What's the point of starting something with someone if you can't move with them when they go?"

"Oh." That hadn't occurred to Reagan. "But kids move all the time. Zach could adjust to a new location. He's a smart, good kid."

"I can't leave the state," Kara explained.

"So his dad is involved in his life?"

"Only as much as he can get away with, which is very little. It's his way of controlling him—me—us." Kara's fingers tightened around her glass, then she set it down with a delicate clink. "Moving on . . . how was your day and why are we here sucking down drinks that don't taste nearly as good as they look?"

"Because I screwed up at my job. I'm screwing up all over the place. I confronted that reporter, trying to get a name for the source." She laughed, but it was humorless, and covered her face with her hands. Delayed embarrassment—wave two—hit her like a tsunami. "God, how stupid am I? What person waltzes into a newspaper and just expects to be handed a source because they asked nicely?"

"A really kind one?" Kara offered, rubbing a soothing hand up and down Reagan's back. "You didn't know, that's not your fault."

"I didn't know. But that *is* my fault. It's my problem. This might have ended if I'd been more forceful. If I'd been more take-charge." She sighed and finished her drink in one swift gulp. "Or if I'd just known what the hell I was doing. How naïve am I?"

She didn't miss the looks Kara and Marianne exchanged as they waited for her to continue. But what more was there to say?

"So let me get this straight." Marianne waved her hand for the waitress, indicated they wanted another round, waved thank-you, then settled back in her chair, fingers twirling her empty glass. "You're responsible for all the vandalism happening around the team."

"No, I didn't say that."

"But you did say it wouldn't have happened if you'd been better at your job," Kara pointed out.

Thanks for the backup . . .

"What I meant was—"

Marianne cut her off. "You did something proactive, albeit a bit naïve, to attempt to shake loose the culprit, and you're beating yourself up for it because it didn't work."

"I'm not beating myself up, I'm—"

"Having a pity party, which is totally logical," Kara said kindly. "But can't last forever. I've only got one more drink in me."

"So I get exactly two cocktails' worth of pity, and then I have to . . . what?" Reagan frowned at her empty glass, which apparently represented exactly half the amount of pity she was allotted.

"Put on your big girl panties and try something new."

"And if I fail?"

"Then you did your best."

She closed her eyes a moment. "Then I have to head back to Wisconsin, the loser who thought she was better than her friends and family, and failed miserably. Not to mention leaving Greg behind."

The three women were silent while their replacement drinks were laid down.

"Which part of that is bothering you more?" Marianne waited a half second. "I'm guessing the second part. The part about leaving Greg behind if you get fired."

"Which you won't be," Kara added firmly.

"You can't know that." God, she was being so damn sulky. But it felt just a little good . . .

"I can be positive. It costs nothing and is scientifically proven to jump-start your metabolism and creativity. What's wrong with that?"

"Nothing, I'm just adding *bitchy* to my pity party attitude. I have one more drink to shake it off, apparently, so I'm going hog wild."

"Go for it." Marianne tapped her glass with Reagan's in a 'cheers' gesture and sipped. "My mom is fantastic at pity parties. I remember when I got my first period, and I felt like shit."

Both Kara and Reagan groaned in remembered pain.

"So while I was taking a nap with a heating pad, she decorated the kitchen table with pads and tampons—did you know tampons can make a pretty impressive garland?—and when I woke up she had made red Kool-Aid and cookies with strawberry jam on them for snacks."

Kara grinned.

Reagan recoiled. "That sounds horrifying."

"It was, for about seven seconds. Then I laughed. What the hell else was I gonna do? I still had my period, but I could laugh about it." Marianne nodded. "Moral of the story . . . be able to laugh. It really cuts the party short and helps you move on with life with a better outlook."

"I wasn't done with my second drink," Reagan said, but she felt her lips curve in a ghost of a smile. "But thanks."

"Are we ignoring that you bypassed the whole 'How I Feel About Greg' essay? Because I, for one, have not." Kara waved her hand in a come-on 'gesture. "Let's hear it."

"So . . . I'm in love." When the other two women sighed, she added, "Don't get all gooey on me. I'm not even sure if I like it."

"You'll love it," Marianne said with confidence. "And if you don't, then just wait five minutes. Kind of like the weather in the Midwest, I hear. Love constantly changes at the drop of a hat. One minute you're ready to tackle the guy because you can't keep your hands off him and you want to kiss him all the time, and then the next you're ready to beat him with a sock of oranges until he apologizes for implying you suck at cooking."

"But you do suck at cooking," Kara said.

"He's not supposed to *say* that, though." Marianne rolled her eyes. "The point is, if you're in love, it's a good thing, even if it doesn't feel like it at the moment. Give it a few minutes and you'll have a new perspective on the whole thing. It's ever-changing."

"That sounds like the world's worst roller coaster," Reagan grumbled.

"It is," both Kara and Marianne said in unison.

"SO, men, what's first on the list of videos?" Greg settled into the couch and propped his feet up on Graham's coffee table, a beer in his hand and a plate of finger foods on his stomach.

Zach eyed him warily. "You're not supposed to do that."

"What?" Greg looked around, found nothing wrong.

"Put your feet on the coffee table. It scuffs the wood."

"Zach, my man." Graham handed him a water and a bag of unopened Oreos. "You're in a man's house now. We scratch, we belch, we fart, and we put our feet on the furniture."

"It's as God intended," Greg agreed.

"Don't listen to these idiots." Brad settled himself in the corner of the couch, his beer on a coaster and his feet firmly on the floor. "If your mom says to keep your feet off the furniture, do it."

"Fun vampire," Greg muttered. Then he watched as Zach tore the Oreo package open. "Are you supposed to have those? Should we call your mom first?"

Zach glared at him and popped one in his mouth, as if to show him exactly what he thought of Greg's plan to tattle.

"It's all good." Graham smiled and toasted their young guest with his own bottle of water. "I got them because I saw them in Kara's pantry. She wouldn't stock anything he couldn't eat or drink."

"Except the alcohol. She's got a lot of wine," Zach said, so easily and with the ringing endorsement of innocence behind it. Greg nearly spit his beer out laughing. "What? She does. But I couldn't have that even without my allergies."

"Good call," Brad said easily. "First video, we've got some video from our scrimmage at Paris Island. I really want to pick up some additional notes on . . ."

Greg tuned him out. He just wanted to watch some damn good boxing, eat some good food, drink a beer or two and bask in being with friends outside of practice.

As they watched, Brad asked casually, "So how's Reagan doing?"

"Stressed." Without taking his eyes off the screen, he reached for his beer. "Why?"

"Just thought maybe you two were taking it up a notch,

what with you two spending the night together the last few nights."

Greg did choke on his beer this time, and he reached for a paper towel from the roll Graham had set on the coffee table. "What the . . . how did you know that?"

"You weren't in our room last night."

"But on the road, we were in separate rooms." He had a sinking suspicion. "Does everyone know?"

"No." Brad shook his head. "I knocked on your door to ask you a question the other night and you were conveniently missing. Then you and Reagan showed up within minutes of each other at the bus the next morning and . . ." He lifted one shoulder. "I put two and two together."

"Guys." Graham motioned to Zach, who was staring at them with wide-eyed fascination. "Maybe we could leave the girlfriend chatter for when the runt is home?"

"I'm fine," he said quickly. "I know adults hang out and stuff."

"Oh, really?" Smiling now, Greg settled back. "We hang out?"

Graham shot him a look that warned him not to take it too far. As if Greg were that big of an asshole. He knew when something was over a ten-year-old's head.

"Yeah." Zach nodded wisely. "Grown up guys and girls hang out. It's just what they do."

"But not ten-year-old guys and girls," Greg teased, and watched Zach blush and stare intensely at his Oreo.

"The video is still on," Brad said mildly. "In case any of you actually care."

Graham and Greg looked at each other, grinned and said, "Nah."

REAGAN opened her door, relieved to find Greg there. As much as she had needed the girl time to drink cocktails, bitch, complain and generally get the worst of the day out of her system, there was something about having Greg nearby that settled and soothed her more than an entire vat of cocktails could.

Greg's large hand cupped the back of her neck and he pulled her in for a seriously heated kiss. One that melted her memory and erased the day's stresses.

So he could settle and soothe, but he could also frazzle and ignite. Point made.

"Missed you today," he breathed as he pulled back and rested his forehead against hers. "Practice wasn't the same without you clacking around the gym in those heels of yours. Where were you all day?"

She started to answer honestly then closed her mouth. It wasn't something she wanted to relive again, for the third time.

She swatted at his arm and closed the door behind him. "I wasn't expecting you tonight." Which explained why she was wearing a pair of ripped sweatpants and a loose, see-through ribbed cotton tank. She could have done a little better with some advance warning.

"Missed you," he reiterated, toeing off his running shoes. "Hanging with the guys is nice, even with a half-sized man-cub in the mix, but this is where I want to end the evening."

The simple statement, made effortlessly as he moved to her kitchen to get a bottle of water, warmed her even more than that kiss had. "How was hanging with Zach?"

"Interesting. I don't have much experience with little kids, so that was different. Sweeney guarded him like a hawk. Seriously, he had his pantry stocked with enough Oreos to feed a platoon. He's crazy about that kid."

"Aww." She debated for a moment sharing what Kara had said about there being no chance with Graham, but she figured that was Kara's battle to fight. Or not fight. Personally, as much as she respected and admired Kara's independence and willingness to make it on her own, Reagan was secretly pulling for Graham on this one.

"But he's ten, and smart, so not completely green." Greg grinned as he sat on her couch. "I got quite the lesson in dating."

"Oh, really?" Reagan straddled his legs and settled herself on his lap. Thanks to their near-identical height, her face was a few inches above his, and she had to look down to smile at him. "Share the wealth, please."

"Well . . ." Greg set the bottle down on her side table, careful to use the coaster she'd placed there, and ran his hands up from her hips under her shirt to press against her back. She leaned against him. "I've learned that guys and girls 'hang out.' That's what we're doing. Hanging out. Adults, of course. Kids don't do this sort of thing."

"Naturally." She breathed in the comforting scent of his skin and nuzzled against his neck.

"Ah, woman. Your nose is freezing." He pulled away a little, but she pressed harder into him.

"Tell me about your family."

He stiffened under her, but she pressed a kiss to his jaw. It hadn't escaped her that he'd fought off questions about his past before. But things were different now. It wasn't like she needed him to spill all his deep, dark secrets. She just needed something—anything—to tell her she was important enough to open up to, even if it was crack by crack.

He said nothing, and she felt his hands start to drift from her back. "You said you don't have experience with kids . . . no nieces and nephews?"

"Why are we talking about kids when I've got my hands on your skin?" he growled, kissing her hard.

But she couldn't let him get away with it this time. It was too important to her now. "Just something. Anything."

His hands gripped her hips, thumbs sweeping down below the waistband of her ratty sweats. "My life started at seventeen, the day I stepped onto that bus on the way to boot camp. Can you accept that?"

She could have pushed. Probably should have. Relationship

experts would have said she was a pushover. But the desperation in his voice, hidden under a thin layer of steel meant to armor, squeezed at her heart the way no amount of deflection could have.

She smoothed a hand down his cheek, cupping his face with her palms. "Sounds like we both ran from something."

"So let's start running *to* something." He captured her lips with his.

CHAPTER

21

His initial instinct had been to avoid. Distract, duck, evade and maneuver his way out of the conversation that led to him confessing his entire ugly childhood. He didn't want to go there willingly.

But as Reagan deepened the kiss, pressing into him, his motive turned from distraction to . . . oh, who the hell cared what his motives were? There was a smoking hot woman on his lap and she was kissing him senseless. Motives be damned.

"God, you do the best things to my body," she said, gasping when he nipped at her ear. And when she started to pull the tank up and over her head, she was grinning. She threw the fabric to the armchair and arched her back as he took one nipple into his mouth. His hands rubbed down her bare back, loving the feel of her soft, smooth skin. The arc of her body was almost artistic as she rested her hands on his knees behind her.

He was crazy for this woman.

Slipping one hand inside the waistband of her sweats, he

squeezed her ass. No panties. Perfect. She wriggled, but made no move to help him out with the sweatpants like she had the tank. So, he'd just do it himself. He walked that hand, those fingers, around to the front, where she giggled as he pressed into her stomach momentarily before finding her center. Parting her, he found the exact spot he wanted by touch alone and rubbed at her clit.

"Oh . . ." She rubbed against his hand. "Yes, please yes."

"Like I'd say no to you," he growled, moving to pay attention to her other breast. Her hands squeezed hard on his knees in response. She was still arched back, offering herself to him in every way possible.

After just a few flicks, a couple of caresses, she exploded against his hand. Her body raised up and then over him, pressing him deeper into the couch as he helped extend her orgasm as long as he could. Thighs pressed against thighs, skin against skin, and he was ready to throw her down, rip her pants off and plunge into her with all the grace and elegance of a water buffalo.

But she finally stilled, gripped his wrist to pull his hand from the waistband of her sweats, and climbed off with a secret smile. "Come to bed."

"What's wrong with the couch?" he protested, following along easily. He liked a bed as much as anyone else, but there were other ways to make love. Creativity and variety added a dash of something else to the mix.

"It's a nice couch, and I paid good money for it, that's why." She grinned as she entered her bedroom, then hopped out of her bottoms. "The bed's more comfortable, and less likely to be wrecked when I attack you."

"Attack me, eh?" He pulled his own shirt over his head and tossed it, working on the buckle of his belt before she could say more. "Sounds exciting."

"Hopefully." She chewed on her bottom lip a moment, and he immediately dropped what he was doing and walked to her.

"Whatever you're thinking, stop. I can't wait to have you again. Whether it's slow and sweet or fast and sweaty, I'm going to be inside you in the next two minutes, and it's going to be damn good. Because it's with you, and there's no other way for it to be."

Her eyes closed briefly, and he wasn't sure if she were composing herself or convincing herself. But either way, when her eyelids lifted, it was determination and anticipation he saw in those beautiful brown depths, not trepidation.

Picking her up with a squeal, he tossed her on the bed and jumped on top of her. He reached into her nightstand and fished around for one of the condoms they'd thrown in there the evening before. Then he stood, shucked his jeans and donned the protection. He slithered back on bed and rolled them so she was on top, straddling him.

"Off you go."

She glared at him. "Off I go? What, like I'm a racehorse now?"

"No," he said slowly, enjoying himself more than he could ever remember before. "But I'd been ready for some girl-on-top sex on the couch, and you deprived me of it. I think it's only fair you make up for it now."

Her scowl was adorable, and totally unbelievable. "Make up for it, hmm?" Grasping him with her hand, she squeezed once, and he swore he saw stars behind his eyelids. "You want me on top, riding you, like we were on the couch? You want me to do all the work, so you can watch me bounce around?"

"Yes, please." He grinned when her annoyed look only darkened further. "Bounce away!"

She positioned herself over him, slid down his length, taking him entirely. He moaned, knowing she liked the sound of reassurance. "There we go. God, that's good. You're amazing, Reagan."

She huffed.

"A goddess. Temptress." She pulsed around him without moving a muscle. "Ah . . . siren. Pick a noun, it's yours."

She rocked, just a little. "Let's try *tease*."

His eyes flew open. "No, please. Back to goddess. That was a good one." When she simply stared at him, unmoving, he added, "Reagan, please move."

"I'm not in a very bouncing mood currently. But maybe just a little . . ." She squeezed and rolled an inch. The smile she shot him was sharp. "You did say you wanted me to do all the work. Me on top, riding you. I get to pick the pace. Girl on Top's prerogative."

"Dammit!" He swore, then reached up and pulled her down for a kiss. She complied easily, meeting his thrusting tongue. But her hips stayed irritatingly still, minus little pulses just random enough in tempo to keep him guessing.

"C'mon baby," he whispered as he worked down her jaw to her neck. "You can pick the speed—" He gritted his teeth when she pulsed around him, rolling forward and back quickly before stopping with a cheeky grin. "You can pick the motion, anything." His hands glided over the smoothness of her spine, around her hips, to where they were joined. She sucked in a breath, but stayed stubborn. "Maybe this will help?"

He fought for his most contrite look when she reared back and glared at him. But as his fingers played through her intimate curls, then found and played with her folds, her eyes closed as if in unbelievable pleasure. He removed his hand, and her hips rocked forward to find his fingers once more. He did it again, playing for a moment then removing, and she moved without thinking, seeking his touch. Then her eyes popped open, aware of the game he played.

"You suck," she bit out, thrusting again. "You suck so bad."

"But you like it." He grasped her hips, pulled her hip a bit, then let her naturally slide back down. Their twin groans were in harmony. "Let's do this, Reagan."

As if those words unlocked her willingness, she started to move. Slow at first, then gradually picking up steam. Relief at finally having a pace he could match, could anticipate was quickly covered by the realization he was going to come way faster than her.

Those little pulses and quick thrusts, frustrating as they were, had done a number on him.

"Not so fast," he muttered, finding her clit once more with his thumb.

"You wanted fast. You begged for fast." She let the motion of their hips rock her, and she arched back, face tilted to the ceiling. She was a goddess. "Now you want me to slow down?"

"No, I . . . forget it." He pinched her between two fingers. From the way she tightened around him, he'd found what she wanted. "You do whatever you want, baby. Your show."

"You say that now, after you manipulated me to—oh!" She shot up straight as an arrow, looking down at him. "Do that again."

With a grin, he did. She fell forward until her hands landed beside his shoulders. "I'll pay you a million dollars to never stop . . . never stop . . . that."

"For you, Reagan, I'll do it for free." He didn't stop, until neither of them could slow down the inevitable climax that gripped them both.

Spent, she draped over him, their sweat causing a suction of skin to skin along their bellies.

"Bouncing," she grumbled, biting his collarbone. He yelped, because she wanted him to, and smacked a hand over her ass playfully.

"You do wonderful work in that department, baby."

GREG was currently hogging the shower—and all the hot water for the day. Reagan debated a moment fighting him for it—ha! like she'd win that one—then gave up. Let him have the hot water. She'd go surf online for a bit. Maybe dig up some dirt on Mr. David Cruise that would have him begging forgiveness.

Probably not. But it was a nice thought, at least for the moment.

She sat down at her computer, tapped a finger to the mouse pad to illuminate the screen, then just stared at it for a moment. There was nothing pressing, at least not yet. But it wouldn't hurt to get started on another round of positive campaign ideas. Maybe something about the yoga lessons. She could work that into making the boxing team sound more gentle and nurturing . . . you know, when they weren't beating the crap out of others inside the ring.

Her phone vibrated beside the laptop, and she glanced at the readout. Mom. Before she could even think twice, she sent the call straight to voicemail.

Two minutes later, she received a text from her younger brother, Dale, who was three years behind her.

Dale: Answer mom's call. I'm sick of listening to her bitch about it.

A few moments later, the phone vibrated with another call from her mother. She hesitated, checked to make sure Greg was still in the shower, then answered.

"Mom? Everything okay?"

"Well, you answered this time." Huffing out a breath, her mother sounded like a wheezing chew toy that had the squeaker ripped out. "Figured you'd send me to your answering machine again."

She recognized that tone. No, there was no problem. Just her own mother's impatience and belief that there was nothing more important in this world than your mama's call. "It's a cell phone, Mom. No answering machine, just voice mail."

Reagan could actually visualize the eye roll her mother was now performing in Wisconsin.

"Never mind that. Tell me how things are going."

"Going good. Everything's good. I'm . . . good," she finished, then winced. That wasn't even remotely believable.

And her mother, using the maternal intuition that must be created along with the hormones in pregnancy, caught on immediately. "Reagan Marie Robilard, tell me right now what's going on."

She could lie. It wasn't as if her mother were going to know the difference. If she lied and said all was fine, or hedged and gave half-truths, she could make it out of the phone conversation without bleeding.

That's wrong. You just mentally scolded Greg for not being up front with you. Start taking your own advice. Don't hide from your own mother. Maybe this time, she'll surprise you.

"Well," she said, fingers nervously tapping on the desktop, "I've had some trouble with my job recently."

"Trouble?" Her mother's voice sharpened. "What kind of trouble?"

"Just . . . stuff. Vandalism issues with the team, which aren't my fault of course. But I'm struggling to keep everyone and everything together, and keep the PR spun the right way. There's a reporter who can smell blood, and my supervisor won't get off my ass about it and . . ." She bit her lip, and the feeling of helplessness swarmed her once more. Which only served to piss her off. "I'm not sure how much longer I can hold on."

"Good."

Reagan blinked. "What?"

"Good. Then you can come home."

Some children might think that was a loving thought. That their parents wanted them to come back and be a part of the family unit. That they missed their daughter. That they missed their sister. That it was love that gently tugged her back.

She knew better.

"Mom, I'm not coming back."

"You just said you're failing out there. You know you shouldn't have taken that job. But you got all high-and-mighty about that degree of yours, and thought you could do anything you wanted to do. Everyone knows that's a crock."

"Gee, Mom, you should put that on a motivational poster for elementary school classrooms. 'That's a crock.'" Reagan focused her eyes on a spot on the wall above the laptop screen. If she stared hard enough, she wouldn't cry.

"Don't you start that. You know you were meant to be here. Your brothers didn't hightail it out of here when they graduated."

Only two had actually graduated high school to begin with.

"And they stay around here and help me out around the house. Your brother is getting close to marrying the Casper girl. And where are they gonna live?"

"In your basement?"

"Three blocks over," her mother said, as if she hadn't spoken. "Because they know where they belong. Never could impress on you that a degree was pointless. You'll just end up back here anyway. Nothing in this town needs a degree. You spent all that money, *still paying* all that money, and for what?"

So I could get yelled at once a week by you for my stupid choices, Mom. Obviously.

"Hey, Mom, I'm ahead of you time-wise so I'm getting pretty tired." She faked a yawn, though after it was finished, she realized she truly was exhausted. "I'll have to call you another time to catch up. Say hi to the boys . . . and that Casper girl, whoever she is."

"Doreen," her mother snapped.

"Sure. Add her to the list. Love you, bye!" She hung up before her mother could argue and demand she stay on the line. Then she blinked as hard as she could to clear the tears.

"Family sucks sometimes, doesn't it?"

She gasped, dropped her phone and turned to find Greg leaning against the door from the bedroom. "How long were you there?"

"Long enough." He walked to her, wrapped her in a hug where she sat, and just held her awhile. Reagan wrapped her arms around his waist and pressed her face to his stomach, which was at face-level. "I'd apologize for listening in, but I'm not all that sorry."

She laughed a little, then sighed and bit his stomach lightly. Or what she could get of his stomach. Not much there to sink her teeth into. "Eavesdropping is rude."

"Let's call it a recon mission. Nobody has to apologize for missions." He tilted her back enough that she could look up at him. Swiping his thumbs over her cheekbones, he nodded. "No tears, so it couldn't have been that bad."

"Not that bad. Just that expected. You're not supposed to be embarrassed by your family." She paused. "Are you?"

He gave her a pained look, then shrugged. "I don't think there's any 'supposed to' when it comes to family. You just . . . do or don't." He wiped a hand down his face. "I'm not Dr. Phil over here, Reagan. I don't have the answers."

"Okay." She sighed and pressed against him. "I'm a mess."

"Do you want to"—she could feel him swallow hard—"talk about it?"

"Let's not, for tonight. I just want to feel you."

She swore the sigh he released came with its own whispered *thank God*. But he merely stroked her hair and let them both breathe.

It wasn't everything she needed, but for the moment, it was enough.

THE next morning, Greg watched with a grin as Reagan sauntered—no other word for it—into the gym about fifteen minutes into practice. She wore a tight pinstripe skirt and matching jacket with a deep purple shirt underneath. Her long legs ended with heels that matched the navy of her suit, and her hair was up in its normal elegant twist that left her gorgeous neck bare.

The team was still in cardio warm-ups, about to be divided into weightlifting and shadowboxing groups. But at the sound of her heels, the entire group looked up from their stretching and watched as she approached Coach Ace. The burly, barrel-chested man had his arms crossed, watching his team for any sign of weakness or incompetence.

Most of which he found daily, and let them know it.

Someone gave a low wolf whistle, and Greg fought against the urge to stand up out of his hamstring stretch, find the asshole and kick him.

But Reagan seemed to take the unexpected attention in stride. "Good morning, gentlemen." She clacked up to the coach, whispered something in his ear that had him dropping his arms, then walked toward his office. Coach Ace followed, barking for Coach Cartwright to finish the warm-ups.

They stood, and Tressler leaned in from behind him. "Jealous?"

"Don't be an ass," Greg replied in an easy voice. "If you can manage that, I mean."

"Just wondering if it matters much that your current mattress partner is constantly spending time alone with other guys. Coach Ace looked pretty excited to meet with her. Wonder if that's how she's keeping her job after all those fuckups."

Greg pushed him back a step. "Shut up."

The younger man held up his hands. "Hey, it's no biggie to me if she keeps her job by 'servicing' others. The longer she stays, the longer I get to admire that ass walking around the gym. Just don't be shocked if you find out you're not the only fuck in town for her."

Greg realized then that the color of rage wasn't red. Everything he'd heard before said when you went into a rage-induced bender, the world was covered with a red mist.

He realized, three minutes later, it was black. Pitch black, like his memory of the past three minutes. He came to, half-sitting on the mat, half-lounging with his back against Graham's front, his arms locked behind him. Tressler was likewise trussed up, with another teammate holding him back and Brad crouched by his face, speaking quietly into Tressler's ear.

Whatever Brad was saying wasn't going over well with the younger Marine, because he flung a fuck-you at him and kicked out as if to make contact.

Marianne hustled over, her two interns following behind. Nikki stayed back, eyes wide with fascination, while Levi looked disgusted at the whole thing.

Angry with himself, Greg struggled out of the hold and stood, turning his back on Tressler. Graham stood beside him, half-angled in front, as if to be able to grab him in case he went after the asshole again.

Greg shook out his arms, realizing then that his knuckles burned. He wasn't ready to turn around and see the handiwork on Tressler's face yet. Please, God, let him not have done damage.

"What. The. Hell. Is. Going. On."

In the nearly silent gym, the deep words, spoken low, were like a gunshot. They all turned in unison and saw Coach Ace, hands fisted by his side, standing beside a horrified-looking Reagan.

Damn. Damn, damn, damn.

"I wanna know what the *hell* is going on in my gym."

CHAPTER

22

Nobody moved. Nobody spoke. Greg wasn't sure anyone even breathed. He glanced across from him at Tressler, who stared steely-eyed at the wall to the left, mouth pulled into a mulish line of silence.

After thirty seconds of complete silence, Coach Ace stepped forward. "You," he said, pointing at Tressler, "let Cook look at you, then get back to work. And you," he added, pointing to Greg, "get in my office." When nobody moved, Coach added a bellowing *now!* that had them all scrambling.

He walked with stiff joints toward the coach's office. As he passed Reagan, he saw her reach out, just a fraction of an inch, then pull back.

Probably for the best. He wasn't in a good place to be coddled or soothed. He needed to burn the anger right out of him.

He stood, in parade rest, facing Coach Ace's empty desk, waiting his punishment. Would he get thrown off the team? Sent back with a black mark for his service record?

A month ago, he would have shrugged and not given a

hot damn. He was there for fun, not because he had anything to prove. If he got cut, so be it. If he made the team, so be it.

That was a month ago. Now he knew his leaving would put the team in jeopardy. He'd miss his friends. He'd miss the competition, the new way of pushing his body, the camaraderie that came from a different type of family outside of his company back at home base.

He'd miss Reagan.

God, that struck the hardest. His impulsive, stupid actions could have cost him the chance to stay and be with her as long as possible. The longer he boxed, the more time he had with her.

Even if they kept him, she might have seen more than enough of his behavior to be done with him. Couldn't blame her if she was. In those moments, he'd ceased being a human, a man, a Marine, and become something more base. An animal whose pride and position had been challenged.

More like a freaking whiny bear with a thorn in his paw. So the idiot kid made a few sexual jokes, who cared? He should have shrugged it off. He should have been the bigger person about it.

Instead, he'd shown his true nature. His upbringing.

Nature or nurture, he was screwed either way.

He heard the door swing open all the way behind him, though he didn't look. Coach Ace walked into view, slammed his massive, muscular body into his desk chair and gripped the edge of the desk to keep from rolling away. "God damn it, Higgs."

He waited quietly, eyes faced straight ahead.

"What the hell are you doing pulling shit like that in my gym? You're old enough to know better. You've been around longer. He's just a damn kid." After a moment, he added, "Answer."

"Yes, sir. I apologize for my lack of temper and control, sir."

"Coach."

"Coach. I apologize. I let some comments get into my

head and it affected me more than it should. I apologize for disrespecting your gym and the team, sir. Coach."

He watched as Coach ran a large hand down his face, scrubbing hard before settling back in the rickety chair. "You put me in a shitty position. What the hell did he say to you to make you go off like that?"

Greg debated a moment. This was what they called a no-win situation. "Personal insults, nothing more. I should have ignored them, Coach."

"You should have. But you didn't, and now we're here." At the soft knock, which Greg didn't turn around for, Coach Ace waved an arm. "Come on in, Ms. Robilard."

Greg's entire body tightened until his neck hurt from the strain. He waited while she brushed by him to take a seat. The soft push of her breasts against his shoulder nearly had him groaning. He wanted to look at her, study her face, see exactly what was going on in that beautiful mind of hers. Was she as horrified at him as she'd looked out there? Disgusted? Scared?

Please, God, don't be scared of me.

"Ms. Robilard, is there a policy in place for fighting amongst the team members?"

"Not that I know of," she said quietly. "I believe this is at your discretion on how to handle it. But before you do," she said quickly, rushing on when it looked like Coach Ace was about to speak, "you should know that Gregory and I are seeing each other. I've already submitted the paperwork to my supervisor, but was going to tell you today after practice."

He had to bite back a sigh of relief. She wouldn't have confided that if she'd been ready to dump him, would she? Probably not.

"Lovebirds," Coach Ace groaned, his dark face contorting into agony. He let his head hit the desk. "I'm surrounded by lovebirds. What did I do in a previous life to deserve this?"

"Just lucky, I suppose," Reagan said, and this time Greg

bit his cheek to keep from grinning. God love his smart-ass woman. "It has nothing to do with the situation, but I needed to disclose it anyway and hadn't gotten around to doing so yet. So . . . disclosed."

"You have a way with timing." After raising his head again, Coach glanced between them. "You're still capable of doing the duties assigned to you."

"I am," she said confidently. He wanted to give her a quick kiss for sounding so calm and smooth, with her deeper business voice.

"And you're going to keep yourself from pounding every little shit who says something about your mama or God knows what else Tressler insulted, got it? You show that kind of temper in the ring and an opponent is gonna wipe the mat with your impulsive ass."

"Yes, Coach." He squeezed his fists tight, praying this was the end.

"You'll be spending the rest of practice . . . nah, rest of the day, with Coach Willis, doing some conditioning exercises." His grim smile creased the coach's dark face. "You've clearly got enough energy for it, so let's burn some off."

"Yes, sir." He waited for the coach's nod of dismissal, and left without looking Reagan's way. It killed him to leave her there, but he did it.

And while he was puking two hours later, after having run more than he could remember running in his life, he still thanked God he was there rather than on a plane heading home, away from her.

"I didn't want to say anything while he was here," Coach Ace said as soon as the door closed behind Greg, "but some stuff's missing."

Reagan blinked, focusing her rioting mind back on the moment. "What kind of stuff?"

"Pads, other equipment. It was all locked in the cage in the storage room, but it's gone now."

She thought for a few seconds. "Well, maybe the maintenance staff moved it to clean the cage? Or another coach came and borrowed it. There are a dozen explanations for that which have nothing to do with our vandal."

"I've spoken to maintenance, and they've got nothing. Same with the other coaches I know, nobody took it. I guess there are a few other options but . . ." He sighed and let his ham-sized fists hit the desk hard enough to make her jump. "This is getting damn old, pardon the language."

"Yes, it is." She thought for a moment, then decided to go for it. "Security cameras would solve a majority of our problems."

He looked amused, as if catching on to her act. "I'm sure your supervisor already told you the reason why that's not going to happen. No budget." He said the last sentence as if it were a curse. "We're lucky they didn't stop hosting teams, period. The entire Corps—entire military—is cutting back. And if we keep making a nuisance of ourselves with vandalism and crime, we're very likely going to be next. We already have a target on our backs thanks to the violence of the sport."

It was the exact thing Reagan feared. "That's not going to happen," she said through stiff lips. "I won't let it happen."

"Good luck then." With a weary sigh, Coach Ace nodded and dismissed her.

"Stubborn group of Marines." She walked out to the practice area, and noticed most of the team attempting to give her a sidelong glance. Tressler, Greg's opponent in their ill-advised bare-knuckles brawl, was nowhere to be seen. Probably in the weight room, then. But she noticed Greg almost immediately. He was running laps around the catwalk. His gray shirt was soaked through, and his face was screwed up in intense concentration.

She hustled to Marianne's training room to avoid catching his eye. She didn't want to cause even a moment's distraction. Walking in, she stopped when she found Marianne giving an impromptu lesson on something at her laptop. The two interns were hunched over her shoulders, watching. Taking a moment, she got herself a cup of water and sat. Being off her feet felt good, but in general, just being away from the gym was good for her. The tension was triple its normal level, and she knew it was due to the scuffle Tressler and Greg had had . . . though she still had no clue what it had been about.

Marianne finished up and sent her interns on their way, then rolled over to a filing cabinet while still in her chair. "I bought you something."

Reagan smiled a little at that. "Is it chocolate?"

"No, but it's better for you, on several different fronts." She pulled out what looked like a shoe box from the bottom drawer and shut it again. Then, wheeling over, Marianne handed the box to Reagan. "You recall that in my training room, I make the rules."

"Uh-huh." She nodded, but was paying more attention to the box than to her friend. Just because it was a shoe box didn't meant it had shoes in it. She shook lightly, but the weight and movement gave nothing away.

"And so what I say goes?"

"Sure."

"You'll wear these, then, when you come in here." Looking pleased with herself, Marianne crossed her arms and nodded. "Open up."

Suddenly wary, Reagan lifted the lid and found herself staring at a very fuzzy pair of slippers in a vibrant blue. She pulled one out. "What the . . ."

"They're better for you than heels. Plus," her friend added, taking the slipper from her and turning it upside down, "look. Grips. Good for walking on the tile. Now you won't be risking your neck in my training room with those icepick heels you insist on wearing."

"Oh, but I can't . . ." She glanced at Marianne, and the very firm line her mouth formed. "You're serious."

"Serious as a broken ankle. Put them on."

Reagan watched her friend for another moment, praying to see a glint of amusement in her eyes.

Nada.

With a sigh, she slid her heels off—being careful not to sigh in relief in front of the traitorous trainer—and slid the slippers on. She extended one foot, then the other, then tapped the toes together and watched the fuzzy shoes quiver. They were actually kind of cute, if you ignored all normal fashion sense and just went with what made you smile. They looked ridiculous, though, with her suit.

"I guess they're better than borrowing your Stewie-and-Brian slippers."

"Keep them by the door, slip into them when you get in here, and back out when you leave. You know I'd rather you wear flats all the time in the gym, but it's better than nothing. It's something I can control." Nodding in approval, she took the box, placed Reagan's heels in it and slid it by the door. "So how goes it?"

Reagan lifted a brow at that. "You're not serious, are you?"

Marianne sighed. "How can I keep on top of the gossip if my own friend won't give it to me? What were they fighting over?"

"No clue."

"Who took the first punch?"

"Didn't see."

"Did Tressler deserve the beat down?"

"Couldn't say."

Marianne blew at a strand of hair that fell over her forehead. "You suck, you know that? Your boyfriend is in a fight—"

"They always fight. It's what they're doing now," Reagan pointed out, mostly to annoy her friend. It worked.

"You know what I mean."

"Was Tressler okay?" Reagan asked quietly after a moment. "I didn't . . . I couldn't . . ." She winced. "I couldn't look."

"He's fine. His left eye's going to be swollen, but he'll survive. The real problem with that one is his ego, followed swiftly by his pride. They're both oversized, with the ego leading the pack at three times too large."

"They're Marines. Aren't they all egotistical, prideful patriots?"

Marianne laughed at that. "Probably. Add some crazy in there and you've got your basic definition. God bless them, every one."

That made Reagan smile, just a little. "I hate that I can't solve any of the problems around here. I feel like they're only getting worse."

"What if someone donated some surveillance equipment? You know, like got a sponsorship for the team?" Working up steam now, Marianne went on, "If the equipment was free, then there's no cost. If there's no cost, then why would they say no?"

"Liability." Reagan shook her head, sorry to see the excitement in her friend dampen. "Sorry, already tried that with my supervisor." And about a dozen other ideas.

"Oh. Right. Of course you did." She scooted her chair back to her desk and closed her laptop. "Make sure Greg puts ice on his knuckles tonight. And the way he's working . . ." Marianne leaned forward to peek out of the door from her seat. Reagan followed her eye line and noticed Greg running past on the catwalk above the gym. "He might need an ice bath. You got a bathtub at your place?"

"No." She barely had what constituted as a shower, with the water pressure that was somewhere between someone squeezing a sponge over your head and someone shooting an old Super Soaker at you. "Maybe he's got access to one there."

"Just bring him back to the gym tonight. You've got keys, right?"

Reagan lifted her shoulder in a shrug. "Yes, but why . . . oh, right. You've got the tubs and the ice machine. Of course."

"I'm here almost every other night, but not tonight, so you'll have to let him in." Marianne stood, grabbing the fanny pack she kept her supplies in when she was out in the gym or on location. "Bring him back by, let him soak, then help him heat back up again." She ended with a wink and headed for the door.

"Will do." Reagan followed her friend out of the temperature-controlled athletic training room and into the sweltering gym. "Nice fanny pack, by the way. Really brings out the color of your eyes."

Marianne smirked as they walked toward the middle of the gym to where the water jug sat on a rolling cart. "Nice slippers."

Reagan gasped, looked down, then shuffled back to change her shoes.

"YOU got the okay to do this, right?" Greg held open the door for Reagan to walk through, then let it close behind them. He'd never been in the gym when it was so empty and lifeless before. Shadows tossed around the walls via the emergency lights and the echo of their own footsteps created an other-worldly atmosphere that had the hairs on his arms rising up.

"Marianne said it was fine. She mentioned she's opened the gym several times before for Marines to work out. Besides," she added, holding up her own key ring, "it's my keys, and I work here, too. So I can't see why not. Now." She opened Marianne's training room door, swinging it wide and flipping the lights on. "Let's get you into some ice."

"You sound way too sadistic and happy when you say that." But it was cute how concerned she was about him after the hellacious day he'd had. Greg was fast—probably the fastest one on the team. But it was Brad who had the endurance to keep going for hours like he'd been forced to. Brad who could have made the whole workout without puking in the trash can.

But he'd have done it again, just to see the look on Tressler's face when he'd walked beside him on the way out of the gym that night. The kid had wisely kept his eyes down and his mouth shut. For the first time, showing a little sense. Maybe it'd stick this time. He'd have a shiner tomorrow as a reminder, in case he forgot at some point.

That shouldn't have pleased him. It was too animalistic, too rough. He'd smoothed down those edges years ago. Hadn't he?

Maybe not.

Reagan, still dressed in her work outfit, pointed to the tub in the corner. "You know what to do? Where everything is?"

"Yes, ma'am." He gave her a smart salute, turned on the cold water, and immediately felt his balls shrink up in anticipation. Nobody ever enjoyed an ice bath. If they did, they were just as sadistic as his girlfriend. But he knew he'd pay for it tomorrow if he didn't. He'd rather pay tonight.

Bonus, maybe Reagan would baby him a bit afterward.

"Need help with the ice?"

He dumped in the first shovelful. "Nah. Do you have stuff to keep you busy while I'm in there?"

"You keep me busy." When he glanced over his shoulder, she blushed. "I mean, talking to you. You know, keeping you entertained with . . . words," she finished, color deepening. She turned away without a word when he laughed. The water was about right, so he added the last scoop of ice and shut off the valve. Then, stripping down to the board shorts he'd worn, he slid in and hissed through his teeth.

When he turned back, he found Reagan shuffling from the entrance. Shuffling, because instead of the heels she'd worn in, she had fluffy blue slippers on her feet. He stared at them while she made her way over to sit in a chair beside the tub.

"Did you skin the Cookie Monster to make those?"

She pinched his shoulder. "They were a gift. Marianne hates when I wear heels in her training room, so I am abiding by her wishes."

He glanced at the four corners of the ceiling. "You know she can't see you, right? The place isn't bugged."

"I'm abiding by her wishes," Reagan said firmly. Then she let her hand drift to his hair. Fingernails scratched lightly against his scalp, and he could almost—almost—forget he was submerged up to his nipples in ice-cold water. His head drifted back to the edge of the tub, he let his eyes close, and he sighed.

Still scratching, she used her other hand to pick up one of his. Her thumb ran over the abrasions on his knuckles. "These need some ice time, too."

He let his fist drop into the water, though he'd already iced it once when he'd run back to the BOQ for his swim trunks.

"What happened?" she asked quietly. "I'm sorry, I know you probably don't want to talk about it but I had to at least try."

He sighed. She'd held off longer than he thought she would. "He pissed me off."

"I imagine a lot of people piss you off. You don't often use your fists to solve it."

There had been a day when fists had been all he'd known. His, someone else's . . .

"He said some rude stuff, and I overreacted. I was in a bad mood, I made a bad choice . . ." *Yadda yadda yadda* ". . . and that's it. It's over. I served penance, I won't be making the mistake again. I was stupid, but I'm not an idiot."

Her fingers paused then, but resumed their delicious path through his hair. "That's an interesting way of putting it."

"You can always be stupid in the moment. But an idiot . . . that's a permanent address. I'll have stupid moments all the time. But I'm not an idiot."

"Never said you were. Far from." She sat back, her fingers trailing down his neck, his shoulder, his arm until they fell away completely. He missed the touch. "I'll let you soak now."

It was caught in his throat, to tell her what Tressler had said. It wouldn't have changed anything between them. He knew she wouldn't be offended. She might have even laughed. But for some reason, he couldn't make the words come out.

CHAPTER

23

Greg waited until Reagan unlocked her apartment door before giving her the truth. "I'm gonna leave it here tonight."

She turned, raising a brow at him in the weak light of the single exposed bulb that served as a security feature in this piece of shit building.

"I'm tired, you know. Rough day." When she said nothing, he felt an unexplained urge to fill the silence. "Because of all the running. Not my thing, the distance part." When she just stared, he felt his irritation rise. "Say something."

"You done?" she asked quietly.

"Done what?"

"Making shitty excuses."

He blinked at that. "They weren't excuses, they were—"

"Excuses. If you don't want to come in, then just say you don't want to come in." She walked through the door, but left it open. Talk about irresponsible. In an apartment complex like this, an unopened door was an invitation for serious trouble. He quickly followed her in.

"You can't leave your door open in this place. It's like asking Satan in for tea." He closed it firmly behind him, locking all three deadbolts.

"Got you in here, didn't it?" She walked in from the kitchen, holding two bottles of water. She handed him one with a smile, uncapped hers and drank. "Sucker. I also do card tricks and make balloon animals." She took one last sip and put the bottle back in the fridge before walking into the bedroom.

"You do?" He uncapped his water, downed half of it in one swallow, then put it in the fridge next to hers and followed her into the bedroom. She'd already removed her suit jacket and was kicking her heels off. He knew she'd put them away properly in a moment so they would stay nice. He loved watching her get undressed. It was about as economical as anything he'd seen before. So methodical, how she folded this, hung that, straightened everything perfectly on the hangers so she saved on dry cleaner bills. All her shoes lined up perfectly in little rows like good soldiers in the closet and along one wall because, well, she'd run out of room in the closet for them.

And he loved that she didn't give him crap about leaving his own clothing in a pile on the floor. Oh, he wasn't an asshole. If it was dripping with sweat, he draped it over the shower rod to dry. But for the most part, he was a strip-and-dump kind of guy, and she never hassled him for it.

He loved this part of the day, just decompressing with her. The little nuances of her personality and his meshing in their own private cocoon.

And that was beyond mushy and there was no way he would ever admit to thinking it. God.

When he'd changed into dry boxers, board shorts hung to dry, he found her already in bed, rubbing lotion on her hands. He slid in beside her, waited for her to turn the light off, and let her curl up beside him.

"Your skin is still cold," she said, running her hand from

his shoulder down to his wrist, then back up and over his chest. Her fingers inadvertently—or maybe purposefully— flicked over his nipple, and it tightened in response.

"Ever taken an ice bath before?"

She shook her head, lips brushing against his arm.

"Here's a secret . . . it's fucking cold. I might still be cold next week."

She chuckled quietly, pressing a kiss to his side. "Poor baby." Her hand skimmed lower, until it dipped into the waistband of his boxers. "We should probably warm you up a bit."

He squirmed, giving her time to feel and explore his cock with her hands. Her fingers brushed over his balls—which were still indignant about their dunking earlier—and they twitched. She cupped them, rubbing her thumb over them, and the heat of her hand spoke a language they knew well. They grew heavy under her fondling.

"Poor Greg," she said in a whisper, kissing over his chest. "I bet your lower half wasn't all that happy about the temperature of your bath tonight, was it?"

"Hell no." She worked her way down, pushing the covers to the side as she did. Her lips were warm, so warm, but they left a path of goosebumps in their wake.

She pushed down his boxers, and then—before he could ask, because he was damn near close to begging—she wrapped her lips around him and pulled hard.

One hand cupped his balls, the other wrapped tightly at the base of his shaft. And there was no longer an inch of his skin that felt the chill anymore. He was burning up, burning for her. She did a little sucky-swirl thing with her tongue, and his hips pumped up on instinct.

He was on the brink, so close, when she pulled away completely.

"Wait, no . . ." He bit back a moan. "Reagan, honey . . ."

"Stop your whining." She grabbed a condom from the bedside drawer, rolled it down him herself, then lifted up her simple cotton nightgown. It was like the curtains going up on a stage, and he had the most gorgeous, sexy seat in the house.

"No jokes about riding this time," she whispered. "Just make love to me."

He rolled her under him in one quick flash. "Not a problem, baby."

GREG lay spent, Reagan's body draped over his like a cloak. Her breathing had returned to normal, and his was nearing the same pace. Her breath was hot on his neck.

"Tell me something."

He waited for her to finish the question. When she didn't he thought she'd fallen asleep midsentence. "Hmm?" he prompted quietly.

"Tell me something," she repeated. "Anything about you. Just . . ." She fisted one hand over his heart, then spread it flat. He felt his heartbeat quicken again, as if it wanted to pound harder just for her. So she could feel the physical way she affected him. So she would know what she made him feel just by touch.

"I need something, Greg. Please."

He debated throwing out something pithy, just to answer the question. But he had a feeling "I secretly like lima beans" wasn't what she wanted. He ran fingertips up her bare back, tracing her spine until he reached the soft, baby-fine hairs of the nape of her neck.

"I'm jealous of your family."

He felt her eyelashes blink several times against his shoulder. He'd surprised her. "You've never met them. And I . . . they're . . . I don't know."

He knew. Despite the fact that she felt like they held her back, wanted less for her, he understood. They didn't know any more than what they knew. And they wanted the best for her of what they knew. He could see her side, and didn't blame her for her feelings of guilt and embarrassment. She was entitled to them. But at the end of the day, even if they were horrendous at showing it, they loved her. She had brothers who would show her how to use a power tool, a mom who called to check in on her and make sure she had a place to land if she stumbled.

It wasn't conventional, and it wasn't what Reagan had hoped for, but it was a family Greg would have killed for as a child.

She was quiet so long, and her breathing evened out enough he knew she'd thought herself to sleep. He'd have to answer more questions later, there was no avoiding it. He'd opened a can of worms, and they weren't going to be stuffed back in again.

He just prayed when she finally got a good look at what she'd been after, she still wanted him.

"HEY."

Reagan batted at the thing—whatever it was—that was attempting to shake her awake. "No," she mumbled.

"Reagan," the intolerable thing whispered again.

"Go away," she whimpered and rolled onto her stomach, pressing her face into her pillow.

"I just wanted to let you know I was taking off."

That had her raising her head. It was still pitch black in the bedroom, and she had to blink several times before the bleariness cleared enough to see her bedside clock. "It's not even three in the morning yet."

"I know, but I didn't bring anything over, and I've got a hella early workout with Coach Cartwright this morning."

She rolled onto her back, draping one arm over her eyes. "Why are you telling me this?"

"Because I didn't want you to wake up and wonder why I'd split in the middle of the night." Greg kissed her lips, and she let him because biting him in retaliation would have taken too much effort. "Now go back to sleep, and I'll see your sexy ass in the gym."

She grumbled, but he just chuckled and left, closing the door quietly behind him.

She woke several hours later, not feeling nearly as refreshed as usual, and cool. Though the temperature wasn't all that chilly in her apartment, she knew it was because she'd grown used to a furnace lying beside her in bed. When her feet grew cold, she'd been able to slide them under his legs, relish his momentary gasp of breath, and warm right up.

"Men," she said, sitting up. "And now I'm talking to myself. I should get a cat so this is less weird."

She thought about that a moment.

"Nope, it would still be weird."

There were still benefits to waking without a man, she realized as she trudged to the bathroom to heed nature's morning call. She wouldn't be sharing the bathroom with anyone who had to have the world's closest shave. Wouldn't find his stuff lying around everywhere and trip over his ginormous shoes. Wouldn't be making a breakfast for two— one of which was a nasty protein shake that smelled like dirt and tasted worse. And she could take her time this morning, since she wasn't in a rush to get to the gym with him. There was time to really read the newspaper, not just skim, with a cup of coffee. Maybe even do some Internet surfing before getting ready for work.

Throwing on her bath robe, she started the coffee, pulled a bagel out of the fridge to toast, and went to her front door to grab the paper. She really should just pay for the subscription online, but she wasn't prepared to give up the actual physical words just yet.

She flipped through the first section—crime, death and taxes, as usual—and set it aside to get to the sports section. Now there was a shocker. A year ago, she would have bet a quarter of her shoe collection she would never hustle to get to the sports pages first. Now, it was all she could think of. If they didn't mention her team or any other base teams, she still read, because she wanted to see what the media was focusing on these days.

Same with blogs. Her blog roll used to be nothing but fashion blogs that featured the Look For Less and other ways to spiff up her wardrobe on the cheap. Now she had more sports newscasts than anything.

She was on her second cup of coffee when her phone rang. She sighed, seeing Marianne's number. She answered the call, crossing one leg over the other. "If you're calling to wake me up, you're late. If you're calling to demand I bring you breakfast, you're early."

"I'm calling to demand you get here now."

Reagan froze on her stool. "What happened?"

"Stuff's missing. Remember the video equipment the coaches had last week?"

"Sure," she said slowly, getting up and moving to the bedroom. Her leisurely morning before work had been cut short.

"Missing. All of it. It had been locked in the storage cage, but it's gone now. Along with some other training equipment, but only the more expensive stuff. They left the grimy, daily use junk alone."

Coach Ace had told her about some missing gear, but the video equipment was news to her. "Have they called the MPs yet?"

"No. They asked me to call you. I think the coaches are fed up with the lack of progress." She lowered her voice, to the point Reagan could barely hear her. "Something else is going on. I can feel it. But nobody will say anything. Get here fast."

"Sure, right." She hesitated as she picked out a cami top from her dresser. "Why are you there so early? Practice doesn't start for another hour."

"Brad wanted to get in a quick workout with the bags. I wanted to get some paperwork done. We came in early, and found the coaches setting up, except for Cartwright, who's running Greg ragged. They realized the equipment was gone when they went to watch some practice tape and asked me to call you." She sighed. "Sorry for the crappy morning."

"It is what it is. Let me call my supervisor and then I'll be over. Tell them not to mention anything to the team. Just keep going with the day. Kara's running yoga this morning, so focus on that."

"You got it, dude."

"Uh-huh," Reagan said, and hung up. Two minutes later, she had her supervisor on the phone.

"Robilard, you need to come in."

"Yes, sir, but first I'd like to run by the gym and—"

"This is about that . . . sort of." Her supervisor made a gruff sound that she couldn't decipher over the phone. "Just come in to the offices first."

"Sure thing." She hung up the phone, dread creeping through her veins, along with the feeling that everything was about to change, and not for the better.

SITTING in her supervisor's office, waiting for him to come in, Reagan thought back to her final interview. She'd been down to her last fifteen dollars, and ready to promise the world to land the job. It hadn't come to that . . . just close enough.

"Robilard." Andrew Calvant, her supervisor, a trim man in his late forties, came in and tossed a file folder on his desk. The papers beneath fluttered, then lay still, as if they didn't dare fly off for fear of his wrath. "We've got a problem."

"We've *had* a problem for several weeks now, sir." She saw his eyebrow wing up in silent question. *That's right. I have the job now. I'm going to act like I'm here to stay, even if you're seconds away from firing my ass. Fake it.* "I'm not sure what changed today that you needed me in here. I understand this is an expensive hit to take, but—"

"It's more than that. We might have a suspect."

She blinked at that, and had to remind herself to breathe. "Thank God."

Andrew opened the folder, let out a deep breath and passed it over to her. It took her a full ten seconds to understand what she was looking at. Greg, but a younger version, staring at her from a mug shot.

A mug shot.

She looked up, saw her supervisor's grim face, and held up the file. "What is this?"

"I thought you would be telling me." Andrew swiveled in his chair, as if giving her a moment to answer. When she just stared, dumbfounded, he continued. "A couple of days ago, you were in here signing a form disclosing your relationship. You're telling me you had no clue about this?"

"I . . ." She looked down again, reading the text that came with the heartbreaking photo. Words jumped out at her, like popcorn from the oil. Foster homes. Fighting. Petty theft. Criminal mischief. Juvenile detention.

"Where did you get this?" When he didn't answer, she held it up. "Where? Where did this come from? If these are juvenile records, they should be sealed. This isn't stuff you can just search online for."

She would know. She'd searched all her Marines' names, most especially Greg's. She'd uncovered none of this.

"It was dropped off anonymously." Andrew lifted a hand, let it fall heavily to the desk. "Someone is concerned that he's our man. Our vandal. The thief," he added with a grimace. Then he motioned for the file folder back. "Can't say I don't blame them, with this history."

Her head hurt, which was nothing to say of her heart. He'd kept this from her. Made her look like a fool in front of her boss, probably in front of more than just him. And yet, she knew in the heart that was breaking, he had nothing to do with the vandalism and theft.

"He was a kid. He's not our guy." She fought for

something—anything—to make this go away. "He couldn't have done some of those pranks. I was with him for some."

"See, there's the problem. You're connected emotionally. I have to take everything you say with a grain of salt. Plus, he had access to your keys. Can you tell me, without a doubt, he never made a copy of your key?"

She couldn't, not when put like that. But she wouldn't have ever assumed it possible.

"People will be breathing down my neck, saying you're lying for your boyfriend." He muttered something into his hand then unbuttoned the top collar button of his polo shirt. "Why are all my Marines just falling ass over boots for my employees? Why am I cursed with this? Couldn't have been the women's volleyball team. No . . . gotta be the boxers with a stalker."

She took a few deep breaths. "You realize whoever sent this to you is probably our guy, right? I mean, who would send this besides someone trying to cause trouble and focus your attention elsewhere?"

"I'm not an idiot," Andrew said with a sneer. "I understand that's very likely. But what do you think will happen when this hits the newspapers?" When she sucked in a breath, he nodded. "You think David Cruise is going to bypass the chance to say something about the 'thugs' we have on our boxing team?"

"He's not a thug." She stood, realizing her knees were shaking but doing it anyway. "Don't ever say that. Whatever this is, it's not him." She snatched the folder off his desk. "I'll handle it."

"Robilard, I don't think—"

"I'll handle it," she snapped. "It's my job."

Or it was, for now.

CHAPTER

24

Kara led the team through a series of stretches she swore were a great prematch ritual. Something about loosening certain muscles while keeping the tension necessary to box. Greg didn't listen, just followed along. When she moved, he moved. When she stopped, he stopped. He figured she was the expert for a reason.

Beside him, Graham panted. Greg looked over to see his friend's head in the wrong position for what they were doing, making it more difficult for him to breathe. "Head down, Sweeney."

Graham tore his eyes away from Kara, narrowed them at Greg, then resumed watching his crush as she flowed to the next position.

"So bad," Greg sighed as he adjusted. "You've got it so damn bad."

"Bite me."

"We're not to that position yet."

"Gentlemen," Kara said softly, her voice carrying over

the sound of ocean waves on the CD she'd brought. "Focus, please."

He did his best to clear his mind, find his chi, locate his center, levitate his spirit, whatever. But his center was probably still in bed, warm and sleepy and a little mad at him for waking her so early to say good-bye.

His balance . . . that he'd lost an hour ago when Coach Cartwright had finally let him finish his sprint drills. His penance for the fight with Tressler was complete, as long as there were no repeats. Since Tressler had walked in that morning and immediately picked a spot as far away from Greg as possible, he doubted it would be a problem.

He finally felt his heart rate slow, and started to feel some of that peace Kara was always harping on, when he heard the click of Reagan's heels approaching. His body tightened in response, undoing all the hard work Kara had put into their relaxation breathing before their yoga class. He could barely see her legs as she approached Coach Ace, doing paperwork on the side by the folded-in bleachers. Heels, of course, in royal blue this time, with a skirt he assumed, as her legs were bare to the knees. That's where his peripheral vision cut off.

"Higgs!" Coach Ace bellowed.

He snapped up straight. "Yes, Coach."

"Ms. Robilard needs to speak with you privately." He paused. "For professional reasons."

Greg heard Graham snicker, but he ignored it. "Yes, sir." After rolling up his mat, he weaved his way through the Marines in downward dog, grabbed his shoes and socks, and followed her to Coach Ace's office across the gym.

"Good timing," he said as she opened the door and gestured him in. He sat and pulled on his socks, already tying one shoe when she sat in the coach's chair behind the desk. "I like Kara and all, but I'm really not sure about this yoga stuff. It's a nice break from practice, but—"

"Greg." Her tone firm but soft, Reagan cut him off. He

glanced up and realized her face wasn't one of contentment or happiness, or even morning grouchiness, but one of frustration and hurt.

"What? What happened?" He leaned forward, reaching for her hand across the desk. She moved it out of the way. His heart skipped. They'd been fine when he'd left. Was she pissed about his leaving in the middle of the night? "What's wrong?"

She blinked a few times, staring over his shoulder, then sighed. "My supervisor called me in this morning, before I could head here." Reaching in her bag, she pulled out a manila file folder. "He said this was sent to his office anonymously."

She handed it over with trembling fingers.

Greg stared at the folder, a feeling of dull knowing creeping through his body. After a minute of thick silence, he opened the folder and found his past staring up at him. He couldn't meet her eyes, just stared at the word "delinquent" and wanted to throw up.

"I'm so sorry," she whispered.

At that, he met her gaze. Why was she apologizing?

"I don't know why . . ." She swallowed hard, and he saw tears swimming in her eyes. "I don't know why they fixated on you, but someone seems to think you make a great fall guy for the vandalism and theft."

"Of course they do," he said, voice hollow.

"I need to know if all this is true." Her voice was wobbly, but her face was set in stone. Cold. So cold. And he deserved it. "If there are any mistakes in there, if there are any errors, if this was another kid with the exact same name who looks eerily similar to you . . ."

She was grasping at straws, and he couldn't blame her. But unfortunately . . . "It's me." He scanned the list of acts once more. "It's true."

Her breath sighed out, uneven. She held out a hand for the folder. "Thank you for your time."

He blinked, but she'd already bent her head over the desk, writing, as if she'd dismissed him. *From the meeting, or from her life?* "That's all?"

"For now. Go practice." She shooed him, like an annoying fly, without looking up.

It should have pissed him off. Would have, if he hadn't figured out she was upset, hurting, in a bad place. He deserved to be shoved out the door, and he couldn't blame her.

"So I'll see you later?"

"I have work to do." She laughed, and it sounded like nails on a chalkboard. "Understatement. Just be available by phone please, in case I have further questions."

He opened the coach's door, ready to escape the frigid temperatures of the office, but he had to know . . . "I didn't do it, you know. The pranks on the gym, the stolen equipment, all that."

"I know." Her tone was firm, no question to it. And though she refused to look at him, that unwavering belief in him had him leaving a few degrees warmer than he had been.

"SO you were in juvie."

Greg watched Graham flip a steak on the grill. "Yup."

"What was it like?"

"Better than some of the foster homes I'd been in up to that point. Worse than others."

Brad set his own bottle of water on the patio table in Sweeney's backyard. "How the hell are you just now sharing this with us? We've been a team for months now."

"Why did you keep your relationship with the hottie athletic trainer a secret for so long? Or that your knee was hurt?" Greg watched the tips of his roommate's ears turn beet red. "Yeah. Sometimes, we just want to keep stuff to ourselves." He rotated his beer, but didn't pick it up. "And that guy isn't me. I'm not that guy. He was a shit-for-brains heading nowhere faster than anyone could catch him."

"Well, you are fast," Sweeney said, grabbing a plate and pulling the steaks off the grill. When Brad made a noise, he sighed and put one back on. "Forgot, you like yours completely dead and burned to a crisp."

"Just so that it's not still looking at me when you put it on my plate."

"For those of us who like them the way God and all fine dining establishments meant them, we eat." He set the plate down, tossed a steak on Greg's plate, and one on his own. "Potatoes should be done in a minute."

"So what happened?" Brad waited while Greg chewed. "I mean, clearly you cleaned yourself up, but why? Nobody could catch you, you said so yourself."

"Nobody could catch me. But I ran into a brick wall. A kid I couldn't beat in a fight. We'd been friends, before." If one could call a partner in crime a friend. Now, he wouldn't. Back then, it was the closest thing he'd had to anything resembling friendship. "He stole a stereo, I hid it until we could hock it. He decided he wanted to sell it in secret for all the profits, we fought, he kicked my ass." Greg grimaced, taking a sip of beer while Sweeney grabbed the potatoes and Brad's fully cooked steak. "He left me with the merchandise, so I got hit for that, too. When I came to, I was cuffed to a hospital bed."

"How old?" Graham asked quietly.

"Almost seventeen. I could have been tried as an adult."

Graham nodded. "I probably would have pushed for it."

"Thanks." Greg gave his friend a slap on the back. "Helps to know who you can count on."

"He's consistent," Brad said in a helpful tone. "Back to the story."

"Not much of one. Someone saw something in me. Not sure if it was the judge, or the attorney that pushed for it. All I know is, I'm standing there, wearing orange—"

"Not your color," Graham added.

"Thanks, Fashion Police. I'm standing there with bracelets

that connect and this judge is reading me the riot act. I've got my tough guy face on, the one that says I don't care, doesn't matter, who gives a shit. And somehow, he just decides to cut straight through the BS. He notices I've got good grades . . . when I actually attend school. I guess he put two and two together on the foster-family round robin I'd been playing, and decided to give me an option."

"Military or juvie," Graham cut in.

Brad shushed him. "Let the man tell his story."

"Yeah." Greg sipped his beer, pushed a piece of steak around on his plate. Despite the fantastic cut of beef, he just wasn't in the mood to appreciate it. "Let the man relive the most embarrassing, horrifying time in his life."

His friends sat in silence, waiting.

"Military or juvie. I guess he assumed there was enough time for real jail—or prison—later on if it came to that. The way I was heading, it would have been inevitable. So I picked the military. Figured it was just a different kind of jail, but at least the uniform impressed the ladies. Plus, after four years, my record would be expunged. So technically, I don't have a record. Someone had to do some serious digging to find that stuff."

"Ah, a true patriot. In it for the chicks and the clean record." Sweeney toasted him with his beer. Brad scowled, as if unimpressed.

"So you went into the military at seventeen?"

"I was just shy of my birthday when I got busted. I spent the last remaining weeks under my probation officer's thumb. That lady was on me like barnacles on a schooner. I didn't have the chance to screw it up. The day after I turned seventeen, the judge signed me over to the military, and emancipated me. Off I went like a good boy. Found out the military wasn't that bad after all. Got a degree, moved to the officer side of life, kept clicking the yes button when they'd ask if I wanted another few years. Why not? Decent money, decent health care, and it wasn't the life I led before. Why fix what isn't broken?"

"You fixed it already." Brad settled back in his chair, fingers laced over his stomach. He watched Greg with an intensity that would have had him squirming if he hadn't known that would satisfy his friend. "You straightened your shit out yourself. The military gave you the opportunity, but you made the choice. So, good work."

"Aw, thanks, Dad."

Brad held up a middle finger.

"Not to be a sap, but he's not wrong." With a mouth full of potato, Graham grinned. "Nice work, asshole."

"Aw, my adoring fans." He fell silent, pondering the next step from here. His friends seemed to accept the reason for his sketchy past without much trouble. But his friends weren't the woman he loved and lied to for weeks. "I didn't steal anything from the gym."

Both friends made disgusted noises, with Graham throwing a piece of potato skin at him.

"Shut up," he said, annoyance clear in his tone.

"Just stop," Brad encouraged. "Nobody who has three brain cells to juggle thinks you did jack shit. Obviously, it was a setup. You just happened to have a pretty decent backstory to make people think twice."

"But you probably have an alibi for most of it. I mean, you were with Reagan, right? Either at practice, or with one of us hanging out, or with her. That's pretty solid."

Greg gave the JAG officer a raised brow. "This isn't a court case. There's no trial, so I don't need an alibi. She knows I didn't do it. Pretty sure almost everyone does. My past getting out would be embarrassing, but I doubt it will really move the needle on people assuming I'm guilty."

His friends looked at each other for so long, Greg growled, "What?"

"What's the problem then?" Brad asked.

"Reagan's pissed, that's the problem."

"Pissed at whoever dug that junk up? Hell yeah, she should be pissed. We're all pissed." Sweeney gave him a confused look. "So?"

"She's pissed because I never told her. Now she's playing clean up when she's already behind on the story." He rubbed at the back of his neck. "Sort of fucked that one up."

"Ya think?" Graham asked.

"Ho, boy," Brad muttered. "Word of advice from someone who just went through this shit . . . get your ass over there now and talk to her. Put your foot in the door and don't let her shut it until you've said what you need to. She's smart, and she can make up her own mind from there."

Greg picked at a corner of the label of his beer with a thumbnail. "And if she closes her door for good?"

Neither of his friends spoke for a while. He started to feel sweat gather down his spine, along his upper lip and at his temples. "You're not going to tell me to walk away quietly, are you? Do the noble thing or whatever and give her up for her own good?"

"Hell no," Graham said, looking offended. "I'm sorry, are we or are we not Marines? When was the last time you heard a CO say, 'Men, sit here and let everything we worked for walk away. Don't fight. Don't bother being proactive. Just sit here and piss and whine your life away. 'Murica.'"

Greg gave a watery laugh, then swallowed hard. "Very inspiring."

"What our theatrical brother over there is saying," Brad added quietly, "is if she closes the door, you wait until she moves off to the side, kick it down and keep fighting."

"And if she gives me a hard slap for it?"

"Marine," Brad reminded him. "You're not in the Air Force. You can take a slap and keep on moving."

"Oo-rah," Graham added, toasting them.

"Somehow, I doubt Reagan will be impressed with the caveman act."

"Then you're doing it wrong." Graham put his feet up on his coffee table.

"Or it's not something that appeals to her." Greg surged to his feet, setting the bottle down with a clink. "But you're right about busting down the wall. Charge the front lines. Take no prisoners. Leave no stone unturned."

"Leave no cliché untouched," Brad added dryly. "Just go. Fix this with your lady friend, be careful, and stop moping around."

"Aye, aye, Lieutenant Cranky Pants." With a salute that had Brad throwing a pillow at his back, he darted for the door. He halted when Graham yelled his name. "What?"

"You okay to drive?"

Greg looked at his still half-full beer. "That's all I had. You wanna insult me some more?"

"Look, I'm not in the mood to disrupt my training to stand up with any of you jack wagons in court on a DUI charge, so sue me for checking."

He gave another salute and closed the door behind him.

That was the last closed door he hoped to see for a while.

CHAPTER

25

If the carpet hadn't already shown several worn spots, Reagan was sure it would now.

She'd been pacing her apartment for two hours now, and there was only one conclusion she'd managed to make in that whole time.

She did absolutely no good thinking while pacing.

Huffing, she dropped down onto the sofa and rubbed at one aching calf muscle. Maybe other people relied on the blood flow they got from the cardio workout of walking in a circle, but she preferred to do her thinking in a more civilized manner: in bed, lying on her back, with a spoonful of peanut butter.

Five minutes later, that's exactly where she was. She used the spoon to trace the water marks on the ceiling, one eye closed. It was sort of like picking images out of clouds. "That one looks like a bunny, that one's a train . . ."

"I've lost it," Reagan said to nobody. "I'm talking to myself, picking shapes out of water marks and eating peanut butter from the jar. I'm seven cats away from being the crazy cat lady."

The apartment didn't answer.

After speaking to her supervisor one more time, she knew what she had to do. She needed to get ahead of the story before whoever found Greg's records went public. She just wasn't sure how much of a fan of the plan he would be. He hadn't even told his girlfriend about his childhood.

And what a knife to the heart that was. She'd bared her own shame about her background. Growing up poor, being ashamed of their financial status, being ashamed of her shame, the guilt she felt . . . the ugliness of herself, she'd shared that with him. And he hadn't reciprocated. Hadn't even tried.

The kinder, gentler side of her debated, maybe he would have, eventually, given more time.

When? After a year? On their wedding night? On their twentieth anniversary? He'd had weeks, and ample opportunity. It wasn't a stretch to think he'd hoped he could get away with keeping that part of himself quiet forever. He'd started fresh the day he jumped on the bus to basic. He'd said so himself. He wanted everyone else to believe so, too.

And that list of charges . . . She shuddered. Reagan was a mature enough woman to be able to pick out her own flaws. She knew, without a doubt, it was a horrible thing to feel, but it didn't change the instant recoil she'd done when she thought about who Greg had been as a teen.

What led a man like Greg into those situations? Into those actions?

She might have known . . . except he wouldn't freaking tell her.

The pounding on her door almost had her dropping her peanut butter spoon on the sheets. That would have just been the endcap to a delightfully shitty day. Sticking the spoon in her mouth, she shuffled in her bare feet toward the door.

As whoever it was pounded again, she yelled out a garbled, "I'm coming!" around the spoon and sticky peanut butter. Whoever it was could just damn well slow their roll and give her five freaking seconds to get to the door.

But when she opened it, spoon still lodged in her mouth, she fought against the urge to slam it shut again.

That wouldn't be the mature thing to do. And she was Mature Reagan. Professional Reagan. Can Handle Anything Reagan.

He looked her up and down, then raised a brow. "Nice outfit."

She slammed the door in his face.

Not so mature or professional, but she could call a mulligan on today and try again tomorrow. Looking down, she had to admit he was right on the clothing. She was still wearing her skirt, but the jacket had long been ditched in favor of her favorite University of Wisconsin hoodie that was a size too big. And her hair, she knew, was a tangled mess from lying down on the bed. Her makeup was either smeared or long gone, most likely, and her eyes were red from the crying jag she'd indulged in on the way home from the gym.

So yeah, she'd looked better. But as his own moral ground was damn shaky, he could have ignored that.

She leaned against the door, and heard him sigh on the other side.

"Reagan, come on. Open up."

She shook her head—despite the fact that he couldn't see her—and had another spoonful of deliciousness.

"Reagan, please." His voice sounded more hoarse.

She simply waited.

"Reagan." It sounded almost like a plea. "Please. Baby . . . we need to talk."

It was the "baby" and his tone—defeated—that had her opening up again. The look he gave her was so bleak, it almost broke the few pieces of her heart left. "I'm not sharing my peanut butter."

He looked surprised a moment, then shrugged. "Fine. Just let me talk and I'll get out of your way."

She motioned for him to come in, debated running to her room for a minute to change and pull her hair into something less manic-looking and wash her face clean. In the end, she did wash her face, because it felt good on her puffy eyes and seemed like a clean slate, and brushed her hair to pull it into a no-fuss ponytail. But she'd be damned if she changed in her own house just to listen to a five-minute story.

He sat on her couch—in the middle, of course—and waited for her to sit. So she did . . . in the computer chair. With one eyebrow raised, he silently called her on it, but she simply crossed her legs as calmly as she could, like she was fully dressed in a meeting instead of in her apartment about to have her heart shoveled out, dressed like a loon.

"Reagan . . ." Greg stopped, sighed and ran a hand through his short hair. "Can you come over here, please?"

"You wanted to talk. You can talk from there." If he wanted a pushover, he picked the wrong woman to start a relationship with.

No, not relationship. That word implied a give-and-take. A mutual sharing. Not a give-and-give-and-get-nothing-back.

He watched her, probably considering his odds, then just ran his hand over his hair once more before sighing and settling back. "My mom didn't want me."

She blinked. Didn't want him . . . to come visit? To join the military?

"Didn't want me, period. She gave me up. Dumped me, actually. I guess the reason I'm as lucky as I have been is because she gave me up to begin with, instead of trying to raise me with no help, no resources, and no real desire to bother with a kid." The corner of his lips tilted up, and her breath caught at that hint of vulnerability. "So, thanks, Mom."

"Greg," Reagan breathed, but he didn't hear her.

"Bounced around to a few foster homes. People seem to have stages they prefer when it comes to the temp kids. They like the infants, but when they start crawling, they're done. Or they like the toddlers, but when they start getting mouthy, they pass them on." His chest moved in an imitation of a laugh. "You can guess how many families want to deal with surly teenagers, especially the ones who already have a rep for being uncooperative and, well, sort of douchebags."

Suddenly, her stubbornness to sit alone in the chair seemed so stupid, so petty. But to move now might have broken the moment, and she knew he was finally ready to purge.

"Some were okay, none were great. Some were downright shitty. More than once, I ran away. I would have been better on my own."

No, never on your own.

"So when people, a few guys around the city, some from school and some not, started paying attention, I fell for it. Hook, line and sinker. I was their lackey. 'We're your family, Greg, do it for your family.'" He sighed and closed his eyes. "Such an idiot."

That unlocked whatever hold she'd had on her own control. She ran the three steps toward the couch, jumping to his side. He let out a big "oof!" as she landed against him, holding tight. Her legs wrapped around his waist, her breasts smashed against his ribs and her nose pressed into his shoulder.

"Hey," he said in a shaky voice, wrapping an arm around her. "What's this?"

"I hate this story." She could barely choke out the words, because she knew she couldn't cry and make it through the rest of the talk. And they had to talk. Now that the dam had been torn down, the rest had to be purged. But if she cried . . . game over. "And I just . . . I need this."

He didn't say anything for a while, just rubbed her back. "I thought you'd hate me because of it."

"No. I'm still pissed at you. Seriously, numbingly pissed. But I'm not going to hate you. I know who you are now, and whatever was behind you will stay there."

"Except it won't. Clearly, someone's out to get me."

She pinched his arm, and he yelped.

"Damn, woman, what was that for?"

"Just finish your story. We'll talk later."

He settled back against the couch, Reagan still wrapped around him like a barnacle. And she had no intention of leaving him.

HER belief in him filled him with awe. Even knowing what he'd done, seeing it in black-and-white, along with that horrible mug shot, she was willing to sit here like this with him. She didn't think he was tainting her presence, her life, her career. She was giving him the chance to stay. He'd damn well earn it.

"I was mostly the lookout," he began again, "a few times I was a distraction or a diversion. But my hands were largely clean of the major lifting when it came to any crime. Petty stuff, more than anything. The kind of stuff a judge would slap you on the wrist for as a kid, maybe do some community service. I got caught a few times, which you saw on the sheet. But other than moving to a new foster home each time, the penalty wasn't too severe. Never enough to make me quit. Because each time I moved, my crew found me. The foster families were never consistent . . . the crew was. It just reinforced in me I was making the right choice to stick with them. Follow in their footsteps. Screw the man," he said, feeling an ironic sort of humor in the whole thing.

"Screw the man," Reagan whispered as she absorbed it all. "So if it was mostly petty kid stuff, what happened?"

He reached up and undid her ponytail—what was left of it—and let the tangled strands float down around her shoulders. Chestnut, mahogany, some streaks of redwood in there . . . she was so damn beautiful it made him have to swallow. As he worked on a few tangles with his fingers, he told her the rest just as he'd told his friends. How he'd been sucked in higher, about getting in a fight, being caught, and a judge finally realizing where he was headed and wanting to give him an out.

"It was my choice to join the Marines," he said resolutely. "I had the choice, and I took what I thought was the easy way out. Play military hero for a few years and get a clean slate. Not a bad trade."

"It was right after 9/11," she argued. "Not exactly a peace-time service record. You've deployed. You've seen combat time. That's not a simple choice to make, especially not as a seventeen-year-old."

"Opposite . . . it's exactly what a seventeen-year-old would do. At seventeen, you're invincible. Nothing can touch you. Hell, you think you can respawn." When she looked up at him, confusion in her beautiful brown eyes, he added, "Video game term for restarting. Basically, once your character dies, you just start all over. There's no real death."

"Boys are weird," she muttered, burying her nose against his shoulder again.

"We are, yeah." Smoothing his hand over her now-untangled hair, he bent down and took in a deep breath of her calming scent. It filled him, his senses, with a moment of peace in what was now a very tumultuous moment. "I joined a boxing league after basic because clearly fighting was something I did well, and decent exercise. I stood out. I'm not big, but I'm fast."

"I've noticed. You kick everyone's ass in sprint drills."

"Long distance, Costa nails my ass every time. Don't tell him that," he added automatically, then smiled when she laughed. When she quieted, he sobered. "I did everything in that packet you read. All of it. And then some. I was a horrible kid, and I would have been a pretty shitty adult."

"You got out. You had the chance to make a change and you did. You haven't repeated those offenses once, have you?"

"Until I nailed Tressler, I haven't been in a fight outside the ropes since I joined the Marines. Haven't taken a dime, haven't done anything that would leave anyone with doubts about my character. The Corps is my family now. My crew. I'm not shaming it. I'm honoring it."

She patted his chest, and he realized he was breathing heavily. Her hand rested over his heart, and he fought to slow his breathing again. "Not sure why I keep getting worked up about it."

"You're defensive because it's hard to have something like this flung at you when you've spent the last ten years being a model citizen."

He ruffled her hair a moment, wondering how he'd gotten so lucky. It certainly hadn't been because of the sum total of his life to date. Karma, as he thought of it, still had some balancing to do before it fell in his favor. He pressed a kiss to her temple. "Does this mean you won't lock me out again?"

"Someone has to keep an eye on you."

He laughed and squeezed her to him. "You say that now, but if you feel differently later . . ."

Reagan looked up, her eyes clear and bright, and carrying a hint of mad. "I'm perfectly capable of making my own decisions. Don't patronize me."

There was the independent spitfire he loved. "And you're not just feeling some pity for me?"

"Stop patronizing yourself." One finger poked him in the belly, and he gave an exaggerated groan for effect. "You're hardly someone to pity. You had a shitty childhood. You were still a child when you had to make a very adult decision. You made the right one, because that's who you were meant to be all along. A good man. So there's nothing to pity about you. Unless you mean I pity you because you have to share the tiny bed in my room."

That made him grin, then roll them until she was pinned beneath him on the couch. "Since all that does is force you to plaster this sexy body against mine all night, that's hardly something to worry about."

"Then no pity." Her hands cupped his face, fingers tracing

his eyebrows a moment. "We still have a lot of work to do. Namely, figuring out how to address this before that horrible reporter Cruise gets wind of it and makes it another notch in his proverbial belt."

"I love it when you talk PR to me." Nuzzling her neck, he whispered, "Tell me more."

"I'm not sure," she said softly, gasping when he sucked at a spot just under her ear. "Gregory Higgs, don't you dare give me a hickey. It's too warm to wear a scarf."

His tongue soothed the spot. "Guess you'll have to wear your hair down for a few days." He grinned at her annoyed, pinched expression. "Oops."

"Oops, my ass."

"If you insist," he said, then gripping the aforementioned body part, stood, taking her with him, and walked them back to the bedroom with her shrieks and laughter soothing over his healing heart.

CHAPTER

26

Reagan traced over the contours of Greg's chest. His breathing was even, deep, indicating he was truly asleep. After the performance he gave her an hour ago, the man deserved some rest. But something had been missing.

More like something *had* been present that wasn't welcome in her bed. Penance. He'd loved her with the same skill as he had all the times before, but she could see in his eyes, as he'd hovered over her, stroking in and out, that it wasn't about his pleasure, but about hers and making her feel safe. Making her forget his mistakes. Saying he was sorry with his body.

That was all well and good in theory, but as far as Reagan was concerned, *I'm sorry* had no place in her bed. When they came together, it should be because of passion, carnal lust and love, if she were so lucky. Apologies and balancing the scales ran too close to power games and she wasn't interested.

It was time to remind him just what loving each other in bed meant. Reaching down, she smoothed her palm toward his abdomen, watching as the muscles tightened in reflex when she touched. Dipping below the sheet, she traced over his hip bones and the tops of his thighs, smiling as she tickled the rough hair there. Greg murmured in sleep, but barely moved. She grinned and placed her head on his shoulder for support. Walking her fingers up his thigh, she grazed the length of his soft penis with a gentle fingertip, tracing the thick head before running it back down again to cup his balls.

His cock hardened gradually, with just the barest breezy touches. Her man was insatiable, and she loved it. She sat up carefully, watching as he readjusted to slide into the warm spot she'd vacated. His arm made a few futile sweeping gestures, as if searching for her even in sleep. The thought made her want to cry, but a good cry.

She bent over and carefully folded the sheet down, keeping an eye on his face for any changes. But he was all but dead to the world. There was no point in worrying about it. The instant she took his growing erection in her mouth, though, he shifted, lifting his hips in search of more. The length hardened further, reaching its max potential as she carefully lavished it with attention, stroking, licking and sucking on the shaft.

When he hissed, she peeked up, but found his eyes still closed, though his face was now scrunched as if in concentration.

As she gripped the base and squeezed, he shifted a bit more. Grabbing the condom was a feat of acrobatic proportions, but she managed. Rolling it on in the dark was a trial and error moment. But the first inch as she sank down on his length . . . that was all worth it.

His hips moved up instinctively, and she grinned. Even in sleep, he was able to find the rhythm and move.

She closed her eyes, rocked over him, and then muffled a shriek when his hands grabbed her hips in a tight grip. Glancing down, his eyes met hers in the darkened room.

"How long have you been awake?"

He tilted up, into her, and grinned. "Long enough to feel all the good parts."

"And you let me crawl all over and contort myself to grab a condom for nothing?"

"Not for nothing." He moved his thumb so he stroked over her clit once. "I sure as hell enjoyed it."

She wanted to grumble, but couldn't. Instead, taking advantage of his consciousness, she leaned over his body and kissed him. The rough hair on his chest abraded her nipples, making her gasp into his mouth. She moved her shoulders side to side to feel it again.

"You've got a bit of the kink in there, huh?" Greg asked.

"This isn't about kink. This is about something more." She flexed, pushed against him, ground herself down against the hardness of his pelvic bone and reveled in the power she seemed to hold. Watched his eyes glaze over in passion, watch his hands claw the sheets until he couldn't hold off anymore and grab her hips.

And as he pumped into her, losing control, foregoing all need for apology or scale balancing, she smiled softly. This was what their lovemaking should be about.

She collapsed against him, felt his heart beating as hard as hers and sighed in relief. After a moment, he shifted them so that he spooned her back, arms wrapped around her.

"Not that I'm complaining, but can I ask what spurred on that wakeup call from heaven?" Greg tightened his grip around her for a moment to press a kiss to her sweat-dampened temple. "And believe me, you're welcome to try again, anytime."

"I wanted a do-over from the time before. I wanted to catch you when you weren't thinking, where you were just reacting." She stroked a hand down his forearm as it held her tight. "The time before bothered me."

She heard him breathe deeply, felt his chest move behind her back. "What'd I miss? You've gotta tell me if I'm too rough, or if—"

"That's not it at all." She wriggled and scooted until she was facing him, then pressed a kiss to his nose. He was so precious, with those worried eyes and the slight scrunch between his brows. "It's that I felt like you were trying to apologize with the sex."

He said nothing, but the lines between his brows deepened.

"I don't want apology sex. I know it's a running joke with anyone over eighteen, but when we have sex, it's not . . ."

"It's not just sex," he said quietly, and she was grateful he understood. Or at least, seemed to.

"I'd rather what we've got here be about something besides regrets." She pressed one hand to his chest, felt his reassuring heartbeat, and sighed. "And now we've both earned some sleep."

"Damn right." He cuddled her against him once more, and she felt like finally, they were walking into the light together.

"I have an idea." Reagan stroked over Greg's back, scratching lightly, and he fought the urge to purr in response. "You might not like it, but I have an idea."

"If I won't like it, let's keep thinking of something else." His eyes were so heavy, so very heavy . . .

"I·pull the rug out from under whatever jackass sent that letter and write an article on you myself."

"Sounds nice," he said on a yawn. "Keep doing that, please. Shoulder blades."

She shifted her scratching fingers up higher. "I'll frame it like a comeback story . . . only not that cheesy. Talk about how the Corps gave you the family you needed, like you said. How boxing gave you structure, how you left that old life behind."

He blinked, forcing his tired, wrung-out brain to stay present and not give in to the dark, welcoming call of sleep. "Run that by me again."

"An article." She said it so simply, as if it were obvious.

"It's a basic PR move. Get ahead of the story. Spin it our way first so if they try to come back and—"

"No." The idea made him clammy, and he rolled off the bed to hit the head, leaving Reagan behind. He gripped the bathroom sink and let his head hang while he breathed.

Jesus. It had taken everything he had to tell his two closest friends out here, and the woman he loved, and she wanted to make his past another human interest story.

Greg looked up at himself, nearly grimacing when he saw the tired, beaten expression on his own face. Was he stupid to trust her? His gut said no, but the survival part of his brain said you didn't trust anyone. Ever. Never show them your back.

A soft knock startled him enough to make him suck in a breath.

"Greg? You okay?"

He reached over and flushed the toilet, counted to five and turned on the water. "Yeah, be out in a sec."

There was a long pause, so long he thought she'd gone back to bed. Then, "Okay."

Her answer was so soft, he almost didn't hear it. But he could hear the hurt buried in there.

When he finally left the bathroom, she was gone, in the kitchen already making breakfast. He dressed quietly and headed to where she pushed scrambled eggs around in a pan. Her hair was in a messy bun, her feet were bare, and he wanted nothing more than to forget everything on the other side of the apartment door, carry her back to bed and not leave for a week.

Instead, he pressed a kiss to her temple. "I'm gonna get going."

She straightened and turned. "No breakfast?"

"I'll grab a power bar in my room before practice. I still have to shower and change."

"Oh." She turned the heat off, stared at the stove a moment, then turned. "I don't like this. It's weird."

His own shoulders sagged with relief. "I know. Look—"

"I'm not going to do it." She held up a hand to stop him from speaking, then wiped them on a dish towel. "I get this is still a fresh thing for you to deal with as an adult, and I'm glad you confided in me. But just know, I can't stop it from coming out another way. So you have to be aware of the realities that come with that."

He sighed and leaned against the door jamb. "I know. I just would rather hope for the best, I guess."

"That's . . ." She braced herself against the kitchen counter and he could actually see the internal war she was fighting. "That's your choice, I suppose."

He wanted to say more, wanted to stay and work it out. But if he didn't leave now . . . "I'll see you at the gym, okay?"

When she merely nodded, he knew they weren't leaving things the way they should. The way he wanted to. He walked back over and pressed a kiss to her mouth, pulling her tight against him. And he kept kissing her until she wound her arms around his neck and responded the way he knew she could.

It wasn't the perfect place to end things, but for now, it would work.

SWEATING like a whore in church, Greg sat down and scooted on his butt over to where the guys were changing out their shoes for lunch break. "That . . . was brutal."

"You're telling me." Brad removed his knee brace and stretched. "Thank God I don't have PT today, or I'd be done."

"Babies . . . both of you." Graham thumped down, heaving in breaths like a guppy on land. "Stop . . . complaining."

"Right," Greg drawled. "We're the babies. And that's why you're the one whose lips are turning blue."

"Shut up." He reached into his bag and dragged out a towel, running it over his head and neck. "I was . . . in the last . . .

conditioning group." He sucked in a long breath, then let it out slowly, muttering, "Fuck you," as he finished.

"We've got three hours to relax." Greg stood, looping his gym bag's strap over his shoulder. "Let's make 'em count, boys."

"I'm grabbing lunch with Marianne. Do you want to call Reagan and come with?" Brad asked as they headed out to the parking lot.

"Sure, yeah." A few weeks ago, an invitation like that would have been nonexistent from his I-work-alone roommate. The guy had definitely come a long way.

The thought of a lunch date with Reagan warmed him, and did a great deal to revive his exhausted spirit. She hadn't been around all morning, though he knew that wasn't unusual. She had other work to get done. But the gym was almost more vast without her, as if her presence took up more space than he realized. He tossed his bag in the backseat of the car he and Brad had shared over, then grabbed his cell. "I'll call first. Hold on." He dialed her number, waited, then heard her pick up. But she never said a word.

"Hello?" He raised a brow, then looked at Brad, who was watching him. "Reagan?"

He heard her voice then, but it sounded muffled. He grinned. She'd butt-answered. Likely reached in her pocket or bag and thought she'd hit one button to silence the ringer, but had hit the answer call button instead. Hoping she would hear him, he yelled, "Reagan!"

Brad moved closer to him, but Greg smiled and shook his head, mouthing, "Butt-answer." Brad huffed out a laugh and shook his head, climbing in the passenger seat. Greg sat behind the driver seat, waiting another moment to see if she'd realize what she'd done or not.

But when her voice, that was so distant, raised higher, he sat forward in the car.

". . . can't fire me."

Greg's body tightened. No.

Something was said, though the voice was so garbled he didn't even know if it was a man or a woman speaking. Then Reagan's answering, "I'm doing all I can with what I have. You can't fire me because some jerk is making a target of the boxing team."

"Damn it," Greg muttered, straining to hear more.

"Just hang up and text her," Brad said, tapping the dashboard. "Let's go, I'm starving."

"Shut up," he snapped. Luckily, his friend seemed to understand quickly that things had changed, and waited.

"No, I'm not going to . . ."

Not going to what? Greg strained, but he couldn't make out any more.

"I'm not giving you that information . . . but you're wrong . . . done my best."

"Shit," he said when he realized there was nothing more coming. He hung up, hand shaking a little.

"What? Is she okay?" Brad sat forward and gripped Greg's shoulder. "Does she need help? Talk, dude."

"I think she's getting fired," he said hoarsely. "I can't be sure but that's what it sounds like."

Brad scoffed. "No way. She's done great with all this shit she's had thrown at her. They're not letting her go. Who else would step in halfway through and pick up where she left off?"

"I doubt that matters. She's refusing . . ." He swallowed. "She had a plan, and I said no, and now . . ." He closed his eyes. "Can you have Marianne come get you? Lunch isn't happening."

Brad was quiet a minute. "You want me to hang with you?"

"No. I appreciate the offer but no. I've just got to figure something out." He let one side of his mouth tilt up, trying to reassure his friend. "Alone, you know. Just need to get stuff squared away in my mind before next practice."

"Sure, yeah." Looking unconvinced, but without anything to back him up, Brad stepped out of the car, opening the back door to grab his bag. "I'll just run in and wait for her. But call me if you need me."

"Thanks." The offer meant a great deal to Greg, so he did his best to show Brad a full smile before Brad walked back into the gym to catch Marianne in her work room.

He stared at his phone for a moment, then let his forehead drop to the steering wheel. What the hell was he going to do now?

REAGAN sat in her car, watching the minutes tick by on the clock at the top right of her laptop computer screen. Sometimes, her eyes would drift to the blinking cursor on the blank document. The document that should be titled "How I'm About to Lose a Boyfriend."

Or, more likely, "How I Lost My First Big Girl Job."

Maybe she should go with something more catchy and pithy, like "Mom Was Right: the Reagan Robilard Story."

Time was winding down before she had to go in and speak to her supervisor. And honestly, she still had no clue what the hell she was going to do about Greg. Her gut knew what was right, but her head—and maybe, if she were being honest, her mother—were shouting she was falling on her sword for nothing.

No, that's not true. Love wasn't nothing when it came to reasons for actions. That was too much her mother and not enough her.

Snapping the laptop closed, she shoved it in her oversized, Target clearance bag and got out of the car. For reasons she didn't want to examine, she felt like there should be somber music playing.

Your fate hasn't been decided yet. He hasn't fired you. Stop acting like he has, and go in with confidence.

She walked into the main building for the Marine Corps athletics and took a sharp left, heading for her direct supervisor's office. Just as her hand hit the door to knock, the phone in her pocket rang. She slipped her hand inside and hit the silence button right as she heard, "Come in."

"Mr. Calvant," she said, setting her bag on one chair and sitting in the other. "Good to see you."

He grunted, barely looking up from his computer. "What's the solution, Robilard?"

Yes, nice to see you, too. How's the family? Good, great, small talk is wonderful.

"The solution is . . ." She rubbed her forehead. "There is no solution. Yet," she added hastily when he looked at her, brows furrowed. "But I'm working on it."

"I warned you there would be repercussions. It's been nothing but babysitting you and your performance since you started. I clearly need someone with more experience." With a sigh, as if that were the end of it, he turned back to his computer.

Funny . . . in her wildest imagination, Reagan would never have pictured the worst moment of her life being so . . . benign. Almost no ripple at all.

"Sir, you can't fire me."

"Can." He hit the space bar hard as punctuation to his words. "Did. See security on your way out to give up your pass for base."

"No," she said, feeling her heart start to race. "I'm not going to just take this lying down. There are other options."

"Other options?" He leaned forward now. "What, exactly, are those? Do you have some sort of information that would make this work to our advantage?"

She immediately flushed, and it was like sending up a flare. He immediately called her on it. "What do you have? Let's run through it together. Maybe we can salvage this."

"I'm not giving you that information." When he rolled his eyes, she said, "It's not my information to share. I know you think I'm a huge screwup, but you're wrong. I've done my best."

"Never have I had this much trouble with a team before."

"Obviously, that's my fault," she snapped, realizing she was losing the thin restraint she had on her own temper. "I'm the one who invited some stalker to fixate on the boxing team. I'm the one who asked him to vandalize the place, to steal things, to follow us to another state and ruin our bus. My fault."

"Your job is to be a liaison. What exactly does that mean? It means," he went on, ignoring her, "that your job is to make everyone's lives easier. It's not hard. You're just not doing that. And I went on instinct to hire you. You were young, with less than zero experience. But hey," he said, throwing his hands up, "I told myself, 'She's got spirit, this one. She's hungry for it. She'll do anything asked of her. She'll be fine.' I was wrong." He shot her a truly angry look. "I hate being wrong."

She stood, swallowing back tears. "Then you should know, you're wrong now. I might not have experience, but experience wasn't going to make this vandalism stop. That's the MP's job. I can't be out fighting crime, making hotel arrangements and PR choices. Nobody handed me a cape when I signed my employment papers." If she didn't leave, she was going to lose it. "You weren't wrong to hire me, but you're wrong to let me go before I find a way to fix this. That's on you."

With what she considered to be the best parting shot she had in her arsenal—which was pretty low to begin with on verbal banter—she turned and left, ignoring his shouting her last name at her back. She passed the receptionist's desk, asked where she had to turn in her credentials, and got directions to the main MP office building.

Which she managed to get lost finding anyway.

CHAPTER

27

G reg spent his entire break looking for Reagan. It would
have been nice if she'd just answered her damn phone
and talked to him, but no. It was either on silent, or she was
completely ignoring just his calls. Either way, not helpful.
When he showed up for evening practice praying she'd be
there, he was met with both Brad and Graham shaking their
heads. They hadn't seen her, either. He poked his head in
to Marianne's training room, asking her to send Reagan
straight to him if she came in. Marianne gave him a sad
smile.

"Yeah, sure thing." She paused a moment, studying him.
"You wanna sit down and talk? I can tell the coaches I was
icing your knuckles or something."

So Brad had told her. "No." He needed to be active, needed
to burn out the worry against a heavy bag or doing footwork
drills. "Just . . . if you see her, send her over, please?"

"Absolutely."

Greg took his time tying his shoes, knowing he might
very well not need any stretching time. At this rate, he might

have already seen his last practice. But if that was what it took, then so be it.

Once everyone was stretching on the mat, he approached Coach Ace. "Hey, Coach . . . can I say a few words to the guys before we start practice?"

He looked annoyed, but Coach nodded. "Keep it brief."

"Sure thing." Not a chance. Greg nodded and approached. "Hey, guys, I just needed to say a few things, clear the air a bit."

He glanced down at Graham and Brad for support, saw their nods of encouragement, and took a breath. "I joined the Marines when I was seventeen, not really because it was a dream of mine or anything, but because I was given the ultimatum from a judge. Military or jail."

He saw a few guys raise their brows. His gaze clashed with Tressler's, but the young man's face hadn't changed. He just watched in silence, giving nothing away.

"So, uh . . ." Focus, Marine. "You don't need the whole long, drawn-out story—though you can ask me later if you want—but suffice it to say my childhood sucked, I made a series of really stupid choices and landed myself in front of the judge. I would have done probably anything to avoid jail time, so that's how I ended up in the military. But you know," he added slowly, looking around at the faces of his teammates, "once I was in, I found the family I'd been looking for that whole time. And boxing . . . boxing was that one way to channel my energy productively. The Marines are my family, you guys are becoming like my little nucleus."

A few guys chuckled at that, including Coach Cartwright.

"I would never do anything to hurt this team. You guys are all awesome, you're great athletes, damn good guys. So if my past makes problems, I'll step aside and we can bring up someone else to take my spot. The last thing I want is to be an issue for anyone I care about."

"We love you, man," one of the guys said from the back, causing them all to laugh.

"Yeah, yeah." Greg smirked and shook his head. "Sappy time is over. I just wanted to get that out of the way. I know we're coming up on some tough shit with whoever is bothering us, targeting our team. I needed you to know that despite the stupid mistakes from when I was a kid, I would do anything to stop the hurt from happening."

There was silence, and then several heads turned to the right. Greg followed their eye line and found Reagan standing off to the side, leaning against a wall. How had he totally missed her coming in?

Ah, she wasn't wearing heels, so no clacking across the floor. Wait . . . she wasn't wearing heels. That had to mean something.

"Uh . . . let's get to work," Greg ended with, pretending to shake pom-poms for a little comedic relief. The guys laughed, then stood and started jogging their laps. Greg caught Coach Ace's eye, who motioned for him to go talk to Reagan. He waved and headed over. "Hey. I looked all over for you during break."

She nodded. "I heard my voice mails."

"So . . ." He looked down pointedly at the flats she wore. "What's going on?"

"Wasn't in the mood for heels. Grabbed my emergency pair of flats from the trunk."

The thought made him want to smile. Only his Reagan would consider wearing flats to constitute an emergency situation. "Can we talk after practice? Maybe meet up and grab something at the Exchange food court and—"

"I can't." Her eyes drifted closed, and her crossed arms said *Don't touch*. Despite that, he wanted to grab her and pull her in. "I lost my security clearance. No tooling around base for me anymore."

"No," he breathed. "We can fix this. Maybe if we—"

"You were great." She smiled, though he saw her lips tremble just a little. "Really. I hope you just did that for you, though."

He hadn't. But now that she said it, he admitted it felt good to have the air fully cleared. "Not initially. I need you to stay."

"I needed to do my job. I chose not to. So I have to start looking for something else." She sighed and rubbed one temple. God, why did they have to be in the gym right now? He needed to hold her. "I have to pack."

"What? No." Fuck being at the gym. He leaned closer, bracing one hand on the wall beside her head. She was so short, it felt, without her heels, even though she was still only a few inches shorter than him. Looking down to converse with her felt wrong. Felt like defeat on her end. "Why would you need to pack?"

"Because I don't have a job. I can't afford my apartment without a job. I have to immediately start hunting, and let me tell you," she added with a huff of unamused laughter, "with only one piece of job experience under my belt—which I was fired from—I'm not optimistic."

He watched her eyes water, watched her blink the tears back, and felt like bashing his fist through a wall. "Don't give up. You got fired because of me. Let me fix it."

"That's not how this works." Her ponytail swished around her shoulders as she shook her head. "I just have to . . ." She raised her hands, let them fall to her sides, bouncing lightly off the wall at her back. "Start fresh, or something. Since I don't know where that will be, I need to be ready to go."

"Higgs!" Coach Ace boomed behind him. "This isn't Snuggle Hour, it's practice. Get a move on!"

He saw her ready to bolt. Saw she was done. And hated—so much hated—that he'd been a part of that. "We're not done." He meant it in more ways than one, and by the way her eyes widened, he knew she caught his double meaning.

THIS is it?

Reagan stared at the contents in the box she'd packed,

and wanted to cry. She'd spent months here, and had about one box of things—minus her furniture, shoes and clothes, of course—to show for it. She hadn't been sightseeing. She hadn't tried local restaurants. Hell, the beach was ten minutes away and she hadn't put one toe in the sand.

Because she'd been working. Her job, this job she'd considered the most important thing, had consumed her.

No, not true.

Gregory Higgs. He'd broken her shell, made her look at what she'd thought her life would be like. Made her want to consider something besides making it on her own. She didn't want to *be* on her own anymore. She wanted Greg with her.

The corner of something caught her eye. She found a book under her couch she'd forgotten and placed it in the still-not-full box.

At the knock on her door, she praised God she wouldn't have to stare at the pathetic contents of her independent adult life another minute. Marianne had promised to bring by a few boxes from deliveries to her training room. Which beat the hell out of buying the boxes out of her now finite funds. She'd need about five just for her shoes alone.

"Thank you, God," she said, unlocking the last latch and swinging the door open. "I so needed . . . Greg." She froze, blinking. "Uh, hi."

"Needed me, huh?" He grinned, then leaned down and kissed her. "That's always good to hear." Then he skirted by her and into the apartment.

"Come in," she said with an eye roll and shut the door behind him. After securing the last latch, she leaned her back against the door. "Practice is already over?"

"Had a quick word with Coach Ace and he let me out early." Greg peered into her one box. "Special circumstance. What's this box for?"

"Packing. Greg, you can't just come in and start distracting me. I have stuff to do."

"Is this for donation, or what's going on here?" He looked

around, but she knew he was likely wondering exactly what was different. Almost nothing, really. The place had had zero personality this morning, and it still had zero personality, even after removing almost all her personal items.

"It's for me to be ready to go. I have to talk to my landlord in the morning"—*if I can find him*—"but I should be able to be out by the end of the month with no penalty."

"Good. This place sucks anyway."

She started to argue, purely as a defense mechanism, but he stopped her by coming over and gripping her shoulders.

"I want you to move into something safer. I want to move my stuff in there with you. I want to spend every single night in the same bed with you, and not have to run back and forth between my bunk and your bed. And I want to know when you're here alone, you're safe."

"Fantastic. I'll just reach into my bag of magic cash and make that happen." Hurt, she shook his hands off. "I'm really not in the best mood tonight, so you should probably go."

"Can't do that. Don't cut me off," he warned. "I've got important things to say and I really only want to say them once."

Resigned, and knowing if she just gave in, he could leave faster, she sat on the couch. "Fine. What?"

"First off, you were right."

She held up her hands and wiggled her fingers. "Yay, me. Right about what?"

"We should get in front of it. It's . . . hard." Greg swallowed, but this time she wouldn't go to him to make it easier. "But I took the first step today, and I'm ready."

"Are you?" She waited a beat, but he didn't answer, or look at her. "I thought not. Don't do this because I got fired. Don't do this because you want to save me. I don't want saving. I've got to figure this out myself."

"I'm not saving you," he bit back. "I'm . . . I don't know. Every time I go over it in my head, it sounds stupid."

"Say it anyway. Whatever it is. I'm not going to laugh."

"Maybe . . ." He sighed. "Maybe I'm saving me. Or the old me. I don't know. It's like . . . this sixteen-year-old version of me is standing on the other side of some glass, wanting to know life turns out okay even though he's had shit up to then. Like, that promise that life is better is gonna keep him from making the bad choices later. And me being honest and putting it out there is my way of telling that kid it gets better."

Okay, that worked. Reagan pushed the heels of her hands into her eyes to keep from bursting into tears. "Why did I have to find you? I wasn't ready for you."

She jerked when she felt hands touch her knees, but she didn't look. Couldn't look, or the tears would flow freely.

"I don't think you have to be ready to meet the person you will love. But it happens anyway, and you have to be willing. And I love you."

She choked on a laugh. It was too much.

"I love that you wear these uptight clothes and those weird bun things in your hair to look all prim and business-like, but you still wear your sexy heels. I love that you wear those blue slippers Marianne bought you, even when she's not around, because you promised to. I love that you threw your all into your job, and it broke your heart to lose it, because that meant you were all in."

She felt his fingers push a strand of hair behind her ear. "You believed it wasn't me, even after hearing my past. So I'm guessing, even though you might not like me very much right now, you love me, too."

"You suck," she whispered. "I was supposed to say it."

He gently pried her hands away from her eyes. She probably looked like a red-eyed wreck, but he smiled and pretended not to notice. "I'm all ears."

"I love you," she whispered. He kissed her softly, and she said it again, though there was no way he could have heard her. She let her fingers roam up his jawline, across his brows, through his short hair, back down to the back of his neck to pull him in tighter.

After another minute of nerve-firing kisses, Reagan pulled away. "This is great, but it doesn't solve the problem of me being fired. I mean, knowing you love me is fantastic, but I've gotta have rent money."

"You and your shoes will have plenty of space, I promise." Greg sat back on his heels and reached into his pocket, pulling out a folded sheet of paper. "I wrote down as much as I could, from my side of things. If you want to go ahead and use this for quotes or whatever you need, feel free. I figured you'd want to make it more newsy though."

"'Newsy'?" she said, raising one brow and unfolding the paper.

"Hey, it could be a word."

She quickly scanned the sheet. "This is all the stuff you told me. The whole . . . oh, Greg." Her eyes watered. "Are you sure?"

"I'm sure. It's good for you, but it's definitely the right thing for me."

She sighed and refolded it. "I'm not sure this is the right job for me, honestly. Maybe I shouldn't even fight to keep it. I could . . ." She raised a shoulder. "I don't know, get a job as a cashier at the Piggly Wiggly."

"Reagan Robilard." His voice had some snap to it, and she looked at him in surprise. "You did not come three thousand miles to be a cashier. Maybe this isn't your dream job after all. Most people don't find it the first time out. But you're not giving up. You're not walking away from this job having been fired. Get your job back, and we can talk about the rest as it comes." He started to smile, slowly. "Besides, after the season's over, I'm hoping you'll come back with me, anyway."

"Come back . . . to California?" She blinked. "Seriously?"

"Hell yeah." He kissed her again. "I don't want to be away from you. Just think about it."

He left to head to the kitchen for some water, and her mind started to dance.

TWO days later, Greg pulled open the door to Back Gate, letting Reagan in ahead of him. From the back, he heard their friends let out a wild greeting, all raising a glass.

Marianne and Kara jumped up and ran to hug Reagan. "Sit down! Sit, sit, sit," Kara said, dragging Reagan with them to their table. "We ordered you a drink, we weren't going to wait."

"That's fine." Flushed and grinning, he watched Reagan sit and lean into her friend's side hug. He loved seeing her so damn happy.

"So?" Marianne leaned forward, arms crossed over the table. "How'd the meeting go?"

Reagan glanced between her friends, then Brad and Graham, before landing her gaze on him. "Do you want to tell it?"

"Hell no, it's your story. You tell it."

"Someone tell it!" Kara said, throwing her hands up in exasperation. "I told the babysitter I'd only be gone two hours."

Graham opened his mouth to speak, then seemed to think better of the idea and shut it again.

"Well, I . . . oh, thank you." Reagan paused to smile at the waitress, who set her drink down on a napkin.

The group groaned.

She took a small sip of the light beer and closed her eyes in bliss. "Mmm, good choice, ladies."

Brad growled. "How the hell do you put up with this?" he asked.

Greg just smiled and shook his head.

"So, I showed up, my article in hand, at the office. My supervisor didn't want to see me at first."

"Asshole," Graham muttered. Kara nodded in agreement.

"But I convinced him it was worth his time. He got all

excited I'd 'pried' the story out of Greg." She grinned at
that. "Pried. Right. Anyway, so I say that it's a good one,
and I'd love to let him have it, since it would help the team.
And I'm a team player," she added seriously.

"Of course. Go on," Greg encouraged.

"But when he just held out his hand, and I didn't give it
over, he got all flustered. I said it was conditional on having
my job back. And he got frustrated and said this wasn't how
team players worked. And when I reminded him I got kicked
off the 'team,' he got angry."

"Nice," Brad murmured.

"So after some negotiating, he agreed I would come back,
just for the rest of the boxing season. Once that's over, he
can find someone else for the next season. He's right, this
isn't where I belong in the long haul." She looked at Greg
then, and his heart swelled. "I'm not sure exactly where I do
belong, geographically, but I think I'm not on the right coast."

"Right coast," Kara repeated, confused a moment. "You
mean, east versus west coast? Oh," she added, looking between
him and Reagan. "Oh!"

"I might end up seeing what my prospects are like in
California." She shrugged, as if no big deal, and took another
sip. "This really is tasty."

"And that's her version of a mic drop, ladies and gentlemen." Graham clapped, startling a few patrons at surrounding
tables, causing them all to laugh. "Well played, Ms. Athlete
Liaison."

"Thank you, thank you." Reagan nodded her head regally
at the congratulations. "So for my first job out of school . . .
I wouldn't call it an unqualified success, but I definitely got
more out of it than I anticipated."

"Experience?" Mariane asked, eyes twinkling. Brad nuzzled at her temple.

"Oh, definitely." Reagan nodded quickly.

"New and exciting opportunities," Kara added, and Graham stared at her so intently—not that Kara noticed—that

Greg felt a little drop in his own belly for his friend's intense longing.

"No doubt." Reagan squeezed Greg's knee under the table. She turned to look at him. "And a new appreciation for what the word 'independent' looks like in practice, not just theory."

"They're gonna kiss now," Graham anticipated. "Let's talk amongst ourselves while they're over there being gross."

"Ignore them," Greg said under his breath, pulling her chair closer to his so he could give her a long, slow kiss. Without breaking contact with Reagan, he flipped off his groaning friends.

"Love you," Reagan whispered as they pulled an inch apart. His heart clenched, and he prayed he never learned to take those words for granted. "Now, how long before we can get out of here? I have a lot of shoes to pack."

He laughed, pulled her close, and mentally sent another mental message to his sixteen-year-old self.

Yeah. It really does get better. The best is coming up. Just hang on.

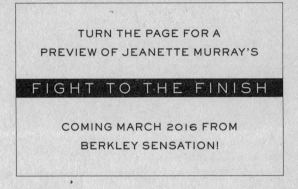

TURN THE PAGE FOR A
PREVIEW OF JEANETTE MURRAY'S

FIGHT TO THE FINISH

COMING MARCH 2016 FROM
BERKLEY SENSATION!

H ow did someone just knock on the door of the sexiest man ever? One who sent your pulse racing, your blood pounding, your knees weakening, and one who you could never actually be with?

Kara breathed in, then out. In one more time through the nose, and out, two, three, four . . .

"Mom!"

She jerked from her yoga breathing and looked down at her son. Not as much "down" as "over." In the last three months he'd grown nearly three inches. Her little boy was no longer so little. "What?"

Zach indicated the door with both hands, which were still gripping the three bags of allergy-approved potato chips she'd brought so he didn't feel bad being left out of potato salad. "Are you going to open the door? My hands are losing their grip here."

"Be glad you aren't one of those animals whose mothers eat their young. I'd be tempted." With a sigh, she knocked on the door. There. That sounded like a normal knock. "Where'd a ten year old get such a smart mouth, anyway?"

"I come by it naturally," he said with a grin that had her flashing an identical one back at him. The kid was incorrigible. It was one of the things she loved about him.

The door opened a moment later with her best friend, Marianne, standing in bare feet, jean Capris and an oversized Marine Corps boxing t-shirt. "Hey! Why'd you knock? We said to come in."

"I like to be polite when I haven't been to someone's house before."

"I have," Zach reminded her, gliding past Marianne with a curt "Hey," before dashing off to the backyard.

"He's so refined," Kara said with a groan. "Mr. Manners, for the win."

"He's ten. If he wasn't a little obnoxious, I'd worry." Her friend pulled her inside and gave her a side hug while closing the door. "But you know you're welcome to walk in. Graham said as much."

"Graham said as much," Kara muttered under her breath. "Am I overdressed?"

Marianne surveyed Kara's sun dress and wedge heels that had seemed like a good idea, and now appeared very out of place. "You're cute. It's a cute dress. Let's put that away. Zach's dessert?" she asked as she took the glass dish and walked it to the fridge.

"Says so on the label. He's got some chips he can eat, though there's plenty of that to share. Just have to—"

"Keep the utensils properly labeled for zero cross contamination. Graham's already on it. He went out and bought big plastic blue serving spoons, because that's Zach's favorite color, and has warned everyone that using them improperly is punishable by death."

Kara had to bite back the misty tears that threatened at the sentiment. "That's . . . a little extreme, but sweet."

"He's a sweet guy." Marianne popped the dessert in the

fridge and hooked an arm around hers, linking elbows. "When are you going to let him take you out? The man seriously has it bad for you. You know it. I know it. Everyone knows it."

"It's not a good idea, and you know exactly why." Feeling like an idiot because she couldn't fix what wasn't her problem to begin with, she shook her head. "I agreed to come over here because everyone else would be here and it's a get-together and I could bring Zach, not a one-on-one thing. If you think my being here is giving him the wrong impression, I'll grab Zach and we can go."

Marianne's teasing eyes softened at that. "Don't go. I'm kidding. Not about him wanting you, that's true. But you shouldn't feel bad about it. He won't make it uncomfortable."

That was a fact. Though he had hinted, and made her very aware of his presence and desire, Graham Sweeney had not once pushed the issue of asking her out. It was as if he sensed her invisible male-repelling force field she had erected around her life and Zach's, and respected it by standing just outside of it. Every so often, his toes might bump against the edge, but he remained outside the shield.

"Guess who's here!" Marianne walked out through the back door and announced them with a flourish. "Which isn't much of a guess, since Zach came out here five minutes ago."

Reagan, all five foot ten goddess inches of her, stood from the patio chair and came to give her a hug. "Yes! Now we're not outnumbered."

"Hardly," Graham said by the grill, hooking an arm around Zach's head. The boy put up a token protest and squirmed, but Kara saw him grinning. "Us men still have four, to your female three."

"Sorry, I wasn't counting those who couldn't drive yet." Reagan blew Zach a kiss, which caused him to blush and run for a soccer ball in the corner of the yard to practice dribbling.

"Nice." Kara settled down in a free chair and smoothed

the skirt of her dress down primly. "What are we talking about?"

"First match," Brad said. "Not for practice."

Gregory Higgs, upon whose lap Reagan was perched, groaned. "Man, we're here for fun. Don't bring work into it."

"But it's something we all have in common," Marianne pointed out. "We're all connected to boxing, or the Marine Corps team, in some way." She flushed as she looked at Reagan. "I mean, uh . . . okay sorry."

Reagan waved that off. "I got my job back. But it's not for me. Watching you guys box sort of made me queasy to my stomach. I'll be looking for a new job after this for sure."

"Then what else do we have to talk about?" Graham set a plate of burger patties on the table. "Hey, kid! Food!"

Kara bristled, then realized Zach liked the nickname and took no offense. He sprinted over to grab a burger, slap it on a bun and take off again.

"Guess he was hungry," Graham said with a smile.

"Are those—"

"They're from a peanut-free factory," Graham assured her.

He settled in a chair beside Kara, crowding into her space without even moving closer. The man was just . . . potent. That was the only word for it. Potent. It was as if he took over everywhere he was.

"He was. I didn't let him chow down on lunch like usual. Uh, the food," she began, but stopped short when he held up a hand.

"I made some potato salad without mayo or eggs. Extra relish and mustard so it's almost soupy, how he likes it. I double checked your blog to make sure the brands were the right kinds, without any of the cross-contamination stuff. And no tomatoes for the burgers."

She stopped, stunned. "Thank you."

"I like the kid." He shrugged and sat back with a beer. "I'd rather he didn't keel over in my backyard."

So many danced around her son's serious allergies, or

made them something sacred they had to talk about in hushed tones, or treated them like the most annoying inconvenience in the world. Graham simply made it normal, and didn't seem to shy away from using them as a good-natured joke.

So, tally time. The man looked like a Greek god, was smarter than anyone else she'd met, had the body of a serious athlete, and was contentious and sweet about her son's limiting allergy needs.

The man had to be stopped.

SHE was fire and light. Energy, amusement. Everything a man needed to survive. Kara was everything he wanted.

Zach, Graham thought as he watched the boy spend thirty futile seconds attempting to kick the soccer ball from its wedged position in the corner of his fence before resorting to his hands, was a brilliant bonus.

Kara leaned forward, animatedly talking to Marianne about something. He caught a glimpse of the tops of her breasts, with a few freckles dusting the creamy skin. The straps left her toned, muscular shoulders and arms bare. Yoga and Pilates had definitely done her body good. And the frilly hem of her dress fluttered around her calves, tanned and toned from summer sessions outdoors.

Her dress was the perfect showcase for what she was, class and femininity encased in a tough exterior that took no shit and managed to keep up with a tireless young boy by herself.

He'd been attracted from the moment they'd met. Her single mom status had given him a moment's pause—dating a woman with a child wasn't something he'd considered before—but he'd very quickly moved past that nonexistent hurdle. The fact that she was still single amazed him. Either the men in this town were morons, or she was very good at hiding herself away.

"Any new yoga stories?" Marianne asked, settling down

on the bench with her legs draped over Brad's thighs, a plate of the trifle-like dessert Kara had brought balanced on her knees. She brushed one hand over the back of his neck, as if she couldn't help herself. The Marine looked like he could slide into a puddle at her feet. Very different from how he'd been two months earlier . . . the stick-up-the-ass guy nobody wanted to hang out with because he was too intense for his own good.

"No new yoga stories." With a secret smile, Kara sipped her water and crossed her legs at the ankles. A delicate silver ankle bracelet winked in the fading evening sun. "I've been dealing with these guys too much. Well," she added, tapping a finger to the corner of her mouth. "There was that one . . ."

"Gimme!" Marianne leaned forward, upsetting the balance until Brad wrapped an arm around her waist and righted them again. "Spill. You know I live for these."

Her finger tapped once more, and he had the urge to press his lips against that corner. As if she knew tapping there would draw his attention. "I really shouldn't. Client privileged information."

"That's for lawyers and shrinks. Tell her, Sweeney," Greg prompted.

"That's for lawyers and shrinks," he repeated, deadpan, and they all laughed.

"Well, have I told you all about . . ." She looked up, scanned the backyard to see where Zach was, then ended on a whisper, "Shrink Wrap Man?"

Most shook their heads. Greg grinned and rubbed his hands together. "This is gonna be good."

"Okay. So you know how when you get hot dogs, they're all smushed together in a pack of eight? And the plastic is pulled tight over each of the hot dogs?"

Graham started to grin slowly.

Kara sat back and waved a hand as if she were telling a classy joke in a cocktail lounge. "His penis looks sort of like that in his skin tight leggings when he does Downward Dog."

Marianne burst out laughing, and Reagan gasped, eyes wide. "No!"

"Yes," Kara said solemnly, taking a sip of her water. "I wish not, but very true. I've actually considered having Marianne make one of her famous pamphlets about the importance of wearing clothes that breathe during yoga, so he stops wearing those pants."

"I'll do it," Marianne said with a gasp. "I'll do it, just for you."

"What's so funny, Mom?" Zach called out from the corner.

"Nothing!" she answered quickly, waving him off to keep him from coming closer. "You're doing great!"

Zach ignored that and ran closer to the group, scooping up a hot dog and taking a bite. Marianne burst out laughing, managed to squeeze out, "I'm gonna pee my pants!" and ran inside. The door slammed shut behind her.

"You should get a dog, you know," Zach told Graham around a mouthful.

"Zach, manners."

He shot his mother a chagrined look, swallowed, then said it again. "You should get a dog."

"Why's that? I've got you coming over here often enough to run around the back yard and eat my food. What do I need a dog for?"

Zach snorted and kicked the soccer ball into the back corner, sitting down beside him. Kara looked anxious, as if she didn't want her son to be a bother. To ease her mind, he slung an arm over Zach's chair.

"You need a dog 'cause you've got a back yard and you live alone. Why wouldn't you have one?"

"I'm gone a lot," Graham reminded him. "Especially with practice. Probably better if I wait on that."

"I'd come take care of him for you." Looking to his mother, Zach continued. "Couldn't I? I'm responsible."

Graham glanced at Kara, who had a stricken look on her face. "Bud, it's just not the time for a pet right now."

The toes of Zach's tennis shoes scuffed the concrete pad of the patio. "Yeah. Okay."

"Hey, Zach, could you run back out to the car and see if I left my sweater?" Kara rubbed her upper arms and shivered. "I'm getting a little cold."

"Sure." With a shrug, Zach held out his hands for the keys she dug from her purse and took off.

"I'm sorry," she said to him softly after her son let the door bang on his way in. "He's been asking for a dog since, I don't know . . . he could say the word 'dog.' I said we couldn't because we don't have a yard, and you do, so . . ." She lifted her hands in silent confusion.

"It's fine. Really. He's a boy, of course he wants a dog. I'm not offended." And if he thought for one minute Kara would let the boy claim ownership when he couldn't care for it, he'd go out to the pound tomorrow and pick up the ugliest son of a bitch mutt he could find. He loved dogs, too. But without someone around to care for the animal when he was gone, it wasn't fair.

"You didn't have a sweater in the car, Mom. But I found this sweatshirt on the table so, here." Zach thrust the oversized red and gold hoodie into Kara's lap. She stared at it, a little horrified. "You said you were cold. Put it on."

"Zach, you can't just take people's things without asking." She glanced between the three men. "I'm sorry, whoever he stole this from."

Graham bit the inside of his lip to keep from smiling. He knew for sure she'd sent Zach to the car just to get him out of earshot. Now he'd have some fun with it. "It's mine, and you can wear it."

"Oh, I couldn't." Her eyes narrowed, and her lips drew into a firm line. If she could have poked him with her fork, she would have. "Here."

"I insist. As my guest, it's my job to make sure you're comfortable. Let me." Torturing himself just a little, he stood and took the sweatshirt, holding it over her head. "Arms up."

His friends watched with amusement, and Reagan's eyes twinkled as Kara sighed with resignation and lifted her arms. He wiggled until the sleeves were in place, then stuck her head through it and let the material drift down. His fingertips skimmed the silky underside of her arms before dropping away.

Even that one touch would torment him for hours. God, she had the most beautiful skin.

And a missing head. Zach's giggles caused him to look back. The hood had flopped forward, and Kara's hands— covered by the too-long sleeves—were unable to push it back so her face could pop out. He helped maneuver the fabric until her head emerged. She gasped, as if coming up from a crashing wave. Her hair, once a smooth line of strawberry blonde silk, was fuzzy and a little mussed. For reasons that bewildered him, the flustered look on her face and the hair draped all over only made her more beautiful.

She met his eyes from upside down, and for a moment, the whole world faded away. His nose was an inch from hers. Her hair caught on her eyelashes, which were nearly as light as the strands. Those aqua blue irises were piercing. Was it his imagination, or did he hear her breath hitch a little, like his did . . .

"Mom, are they all coming to my Epi Pen party?"

Moment shattered, Graham jerked up and away.

"What'd I miss?" Marianne jumped back down from behind him out the back door.

"We were about to be invited to a party," Reagan said. To Zach, she asked, "What's an Epi Pen party?"

"My pens are expired, so I have to get new ones. Andplusalso, I'm getting bigger." To illustrate, he flexed and showed off a puny adolescent biceps muscle. "So I get new pens and I get to play with the old ones."

"First off," Kara said calmly, "andplusalso is not a word, as I've told you a dozen times."

"Mrs. Wrigby says it," he said defensively.

"Mrs. Wrigby has twenty-five ten year olds she has to garner the attention of. I'm sure if she thought it would work, she'd teach you geography while doing an Irish step dance. She says it to be funny. And secondly, they don't all need to come." She sighed and looked at Marianne. "I was going to ask if you wanted to come over and check out his new pens, since the new pens are different, and you might watch him from time to time."

"Because I'm a baby and can't stay home alone," Zach added, looking disgusted by the thought.

"Because you're ten, and I'm not comfortable with it yet," she shot back. "When he gets a new set of pens, I use the old ones for a quick brush up on training."

"Can I come?" Reagan sat forward. "I'm interested. I've read your blog a little, and I'm intrigued. I can bring a movie and popcorn, and we can make a night of it."

Graham waited for Kara to invite them all. After all, the guys had hung out with Zach on occasion, and Graham had taken the chance to hang out—not babysit, as he would never use the offending B word—with the kid to get to know him one on one. But Kara said nothing.

"Sounds good. Tomorrow night?"

Both other women nodded.

She sighed and rubbed a hand over her knees. "I think we'll head out then. Thank you," she added to Graham as she stood, "for the sweatshirt and the invitation."

He shook his head as she started to pull her arm out of one sleeve. "Keep it until you get to the car. You know how chilly it is now."

She glanced up at the sky, with the sun that still hadn't quite set yet, and the balmy seventy-three degree weather. "Right. Zach, head in and grab the dessert dish. We've got to go."

He looked like he wanted to argue, but one fulminating glare from his mother had him nodding and going in. But he ducked his head back out again and said, "Thank you for inviting us," before closing the door behind him.

"Mr. Manners," Kara murmured before standing herself. "Girls, I'll see you tomorrow. Gentlemen, Tuesday at the gym."

"I'll walk you out," Graham said before she could escape. "Not a problem."

She wanted to argue, but he sent her the same fulminating stare she'd given her son, and she simply stood and walked into the house. Zach was already heading through the front door to the car, so he had her in the house alone.

"Thanks again for coming."

She played with the strings of his hoodie. Though she was tall, the shirt swallowed her slender form. "You're really nice to keep asking us . . . I mean, including Zach and all. I know his allergies make stuff like this difficult." Her eyes, which had been wandering everywhere but at him, made contact with his. "I really appreciate that you made the effort."

He'd have done it even if he'd disliked the kid's mom. But the way she looked at him now, and the emotion in her voice for having made a simple potato salad . . . he'd keep a vat of the stuff in his fridge forever if she'd just keep looking at him that way. "It's seriously no problem."

"I've been doing this almost ten years. I know it's not 'no problem.'" She started toward the door, then, almost as a second thought, came back and kissed his cheek. "Thanks, Graham."

She took off before he could ask her to stay, or ask her to dinner, or ask her to marry him . . .

You know, the usual.

Probably best she made her escape now. He could tap dance around a closing argument in court, and couldn't manage to ask a woman to dinner. Or not that specific woman. He needed more time to prepare, and be ready to handle any argument she tossed at him for getting out of it.

He'd see her again soon. And he'd be ready.